This is what others have said about Claude's first book:
Afterworld - When Ghosts Disappear ISBN 0-9681387-0-5

Claude's book is great! A wonderful mix of Alice in Wonderland, Carlos Castenada, Jane Roberts and Robert Monroe ... It is one of those rare books that I could not put down ... the ending was very insightful ... mind expanding ... what more can I say.
- Mary-Anne Sutton The Eternal Moment Bookstore

This is the story of a man who dreams of his own death in a bleak, catastrophic future. Still aware, he explores the mystical realm of death, where he discovers the purpose of life is to gather enough spiritual energy to support consciousness until reincarnating back into an earthly body.

What makes this well-crafted story shine is Claude Limberger's original way of thinking. I feel we will enjoy other great books from him in this earth's future.
- *Lisa Snow* Magical Blend

Here is an adventure story that kept this reviewer riveted! *Afterworld* is about death, afterlife and consciousness. *Afterworld* is also about ascension, learning and enlightenment. Author and philosopher Claude Limberger has fashioned a can't-put-it-down page-turner that combines excitement with insight and illumination.

Grandfather Claude dies soon after the birth of his first great-grandchild. In his afterlife, Claude meets many different spirits and begins to learn spirituality and insight he never learned while alive ... knowledge that allowed him to ascend to wisdom and peace.

Afterworld is written beautifully on two levels. Level one is a superior action story that is alive with extraordinary events that are spellbinding as well as provocative. As good as level one is, though, this reviewer found level two even better! Level two, you see, teaches. And the message Claude Limberger imparts is "... that there is hope for all of us. Never give up hope. Life is a gift to be appreciated and not wasted. Use every moment as if it were your last."

Afterworld is imaginative and amazing! And yet, each chapter is a lesson in the affirmation of life. Even more, *Afterworld* is a voyage into mystical realms while, at the same time, to self-awareness and spiritual development! If I've given you the impression that *Afterworld* is really two books in one, you are right. Either one would be a truly good book on its own. Together, *Afterworld* is a great book ... one that improved my life on both levels.
- Richard Fuller Metaphysical Reviews

Pug Books by Claude Limberger

AFTERWORLD – WHEN GHOSTS DISAPPEAR
ISBN 0-9681387-0-5

TIMESTOPPER
ISBN 0-9681387-1-3

Pug Enterprises Inc. books are available at most book stores.
Or by calling 1-888-427-9777

TIMESTOPPER

BY
CLAUDE LIMBERGER

A book by Pug Enterprises Inc.

Timestopper ISBN 0-9681387-1-3

Published by Pug Enterprises Inc.
1060 Stacey Crt., Mississauga, Ontario Canada L4W 2X8

First Edition May 1998
Printed for Pug Enterprises Inc. by Transcontinental Printing Inc.
Cover Design by Frank Gal
Cover Illustration by Chris Stevenson
Author Photograph by Afsaneh Forghanian-Arani
Final Editing by Dawn Martin
Printed in Canada

Canadian Cataloging in Publication Data

Limberger, Claude, 1960–
        Timestopper

ISBN 0–9681387–1–3

        I. Title.

PS8573.I443T55 1998   C813'.54   C97–901032–2
PR9199.3.L53T55 1998

Triz 0123456

My thanks to Ron, Ray,
Noel, Charlie and Valerie
and to my best supporters ...
my wife, my son and my daughter.

0

Before

Have you ever had one of those days when you didn't feel like yourself?

1

Einu

"Einu! Wake up! Show more respect for the dead."

With a shock, I awoke.

The angry visage of my mother was almost at my nose. She had tried to keep her voice down, because we were at the funeral of my uncle.

"Just you wait until I get you home ..."

My mother broke off her angry words when she saw that everyone in the church was staring at us. Even the cleric had paused in his eulogy. She bowed her head, gave me a quick glare, then shut her eyes.

The cleric quickly resumed his words praising the deeds of my father's older brother. Everyone else in the small church kept looking at me. Their eyes were all on my back and I was sure they all thought that 'useless' was my middle name.

My mother was partly at fault for that. She constantly called me useless, and it didn't matter to her who heard it. I just bowed my head and tried to ignore it. At the age of fourteen, the other boys in the village would be called young men.

Yet they still called me a boy. It was an undeserved reputation.

True, I was somewhat clumsy but that was because of my huge size, my being almost five foot six. Even my uncle who had been considered tall was only five foot two.

My head slowly fell on the pew in front of me and my tears leaked out. It was not fair.

I loved my uncle. He was a hard teacher, but he was the only one who understood me. No one in this entire village knew what I was going through.

My mother's nudge caused me to sit up straight again. The cleric had been watching us. He was a kind old soul and had genuine tears of affection in his eyes. He must have been the only adult who was kind to me at all times. I came out of my own thoughts and paid attention to what he was saying.

"... and a kind soul was he. Jauru was a man that came to us as a stranger, but to all of us he never was a stranger. He took us into his heart, and showed us that he was a man of true heart. Why anyone would want to murder him is beyond our understanding. Do not dwell on deeds in the past. It is a time for healing. We are here today to pay homage to a great man, and to find love for those he leaves behind."

At those words Father Mahar look directly into my eyes. I averted them and stared at the floor.

At this moment someone's love was the last thing that I wanted. How could they understand? I had seen my uncle being killed but couldn't tell any of them about it.

Suddenly the room fell utterly quiet. I cursed silently to myself and knew what was happening but was powerless to do anything about it.

Time had stopped again.

It was hard to know if I could take it this time. My uncle was a powerful timestopper. He always told me to instantly freeze and hold my position no matter what was happening. But I couldn't bear to do this again, here and now.

Why was it happening again so soon?

Before my mother yelled at me for falling asleep, I had been holding my position for hours and was already tired, not to mention extremely bored.

I cautiously used my mind like my uncle had taught me then turned to look about the room. Everyone was caught inbetween the moment. They were perfectly frozen.

A tear had fallen from my neighbor Master Jaimi's eye and was just hanging in mid air.

TIMESTOPPER

I stared at the tear and relived yesterday in my mind.

2

Jauru

"Einu, pay attention to what you are doing."

Somehow while chopping wood my ax went awry, knocking the log off the chopping block. I sat on the ground beside our house to rub my leg and looked up at my uncle Jauru.

"Get up, get up. Don't lay about all day."

"My leg hurts, Uncle."

"Well you'd better get up, or else I'll give you some other body part to rub."

I jumped up immediately and saw him quickly hide a grin.

"Get back to your chopping, boy."

I had just set a log back on the block and raised my ax, when time stopped. With my uncle right beside me it was hard for me to hold my position. He would be angry with me if I moved but with the ax above and behind my head, the strain was too much for me. The ax fell. Just as it hit the ground I reeled from a blow to the side of my head.

"Why do you always forget what I tell you? Hold your position and if you can't then look slowly about to see if anyone is looking in your direction.

"Your life depends on it," my uncle said angrily.

While rubbing the side of my head, I said, "Is it safe?"

"Of course it's safe, or else I wouldn't be talking to you. Remember to be constantly aware at all times, while time is moving, and that way you'll know when it's safe to move when time stops."

My uncle looked quickly around then sat on a log.

"Come, sit with me," he said.

He sat long before saying anything again, then asked, "What are the rules for timestopping?"

I sat up stiffly and spoke as if in church. My uncle had me memorize his rules and always said my life depended on knowing them.

"Be alert at all times, even when asleep."

"Why?"

"So that when time stops, I know where everyone around me is at all times."

"Next."

"Remain motionless yet be totally relaxed."

"Why?"

"Remain motionless for two reasons. First, so that if time resumes suddenly no one around me notices anything unusual, and second, remain relaxed to conserve energy, because it's impossible to know how long the stop in time will last."

"Next."

"Never initiate a stop in time unless my life is in danger."

"Why?"

"For three reasons. First, I do not have the energy to initiate a stop in time and make it last. Second, to avoid the temptation to use my abilities for personal gain. And third, to avoid the attention of a rogue timestopper."

"And last."

"Keep my mind clear of all thoughts while time is stopped."

"Why?"

This was the part I never understood.

My uncle reacted to my silence by becoming angry.

"*Why?*"

"For two reasons. First, to prevent change from happening, and second, to prevent myself from going crazy."

"Good."

His anger subsided. I think my uncle thought that my

hesitation had meant I had forgotten his last rule. It was hard to understand how timestopping could change things or drive me crazy. If anything, it was extremely boring and tiring. I usually fell asleep after a long time stoppage. That was the main reason my mother called me useless and lazy.

My uncle was deep in thought with a sad air about him.

He turned quickly to me and said with urgency, "What have I told you about rogue timestoppers?"

The sudden change in his mood alarmed me. He was agitated. He had never been like this before.

"They're bad."

"Be more specific."

"They steal things."

He just looked at me. His silence suggested that he wanted me to say more.

"They use timestopping for their own gain."

"Is that all I ever told you?"

"That's all uncle."

I thought he was going to angry with me, but he kept calm and looked sad again.

"There is another type of rogue timestopper that I've never told you about."

My uncle told many interesting stories. But even interesting stories get boring if they are repeated over and over again as lessons. So whenever he had a new story, I listened intently.

"This type of timestopper is totally mad. He thinks that if he kills all other timestoppers the torment in his mind will stop. Some just attack madly, killing all suspected of being timestoppers … many innocent people die at his hand. Some attack using honor as a justification to kill others."

My uncle closed his eyes and raised his head to look at the sky. A tear rolled down his cheek.

"Boy, you must promise me, if anything happens to me, you must find a gnome, and have him teach you how to be a true timestopper."

"A gnome, uncle?"

"Yes. Promise me now!"

"I … I promise."

"And if a rogue timestopper ever comes around, I want you to hide if you can. But if he has seen you, then remember all your rules. *All of them!* Okay?"

"Okay uncle."

My uncle jumped up.

"Quick, grab the ax and rest it on the log as if you are getting ready to strike. Don't move and remember all I've told you. And don't forget your promise."

My uncle started to walk away from the house.

My heart nearly stopped when a strange voice broke the silence.

"Jauru, it's so good to see you again. Pity we don't have longer to catch up on old times."

Since time was still stopped, this had to be another timestopper. I tried very hard to stand motionless. A small dark-haired man in his mid thirties came into view.

"Caines. I can't say I'm glad to see you," my uncle said casually as he turned to talk to the stranger.

"It has taken me years to catch up to you. But here I am. I told you I would find you again. You couldn't remain hidden forever." He spat then said, "Where's your weapon?"

"I have no desire to fight you Caines."

"Well, that's just too bad. I'm going to fight you whether you like it or not. Now get your weapon. No one humiliates me and gets away with it."

"I didn't humiliate you. I just defeated you in combat," my uncle said calmly.

The stranger started shouting, "You get your weapon now or I'll start killing people!"

He walked towards me.

"All right, do not be hasty."

My uncle walked past Caines and entered the house.

Caines twitched as my uncle passed him. He watched him go into the house and then pulled out his sword. It was a long, slender single-edged blade. If we were in normal time, it would gleam in the sun because it was well oiled. But we were in stopped time. The sun gave no new light. I was only able to see him and his sword using the lessons my uncle had taught me.

In stopped time light does not shine on timestoppers. It takes a focusing of will to see during a time stoppage. When I was young, it was hard to see my uncle when he moved from his original time-stopped position. He taught me to use all of my will to see him as he moved.

Now Caines was rubbing his sword, and turning to look at me. As if he was looking for something to try his sword on.

Sweat poured down my face as Caines approached but my uncle emerged from the house before Caines got any closer.

"We don't have to do this," my uncle said.

"Oh, yes we do, old man," Caines replied.

My uncle pulled out a slender two-edged sword.

Caines laughed then closed the distance between them.

Both my uncle and Caines feigned a swing towards each other, then Caines suddenly moved by my uncle with lightning speed. Their swords clashed as they passed. My uncle moved forward and turned like a wild cat. Caines turned as well and there was a flurry of blows too quick to follow.

Both were trying to end the contest early.

My uncle jumped back, holding his sword in front of him.

Caines held his sword at the side of his head, keeping the point towards my uncle.

Both my uncle and Caines had sustained slight wounds when they had passed each other, and both had red stains growing on their shirts.

"What's the matter old man? Getting slower? Tiring more easily?"

My uncle didn't reply. He was trying to catch his breath.

Caines again closed in on my uncle. There was another series of quick strokes and then a noise that froze my heart. My uncle cried out. He jumped backwards. His left arm was hanging limply by his side. He sustained a large gash high up on his arm that bled profusely.

I didn't care about my uncle's rules anymore and gripped the ax tighter in preparation to aid my uncle, but found myself unable to move. I struggled against the force that held me, but I could only watch helplessly as events unfolded.

Caines laughed. He leapt forward again. My uncle tripped, falling backwards onto the ground. Caines swung down repeatedly but my uncle parried his blows with great skill.

He rolled and swung his legs at Caines, tripping him and trying to hit him while he was on the ground, but Caines rolled away and bounced to his feet. Jauru rolled away as well but he did not rise.

Caines lunged forward, plunging his sword through my uncle's thigh. My uncle attempted to get to his feet but fell in pain on his stomach as the blade pierced his body.

Caines pulled out his sword and my uncle weakly tried to defend himself but Caines disarmed him.

"Now old man, how does it feel being in opposite positions?"

"I can assure you Caines that I do not feel humiliated."

My uncle tried to sit up. Caines kicked him down again.

"No? No? Groveling in the dirt, with no chance of escape?"

Caines stooped down and grabbed my uncle's hair and pushed his face close to the ground.

I wanted to do something. This was torture, watching my uncle on the ground with a mad man over him. I would have done anything to help my uncle, but now more than ever his words burned in my ears. Relax. If I die, do not move. Your survival depends on it.

Caines let go of my uncle and stood over him.

He was weakening by the moment. Blood covered the ground in a growing pool.

"This is so sweet seeing you like this."

"Caines, this is no victory," Jauru said weakly.

"You're right. This is pay back time. I bet you wish you had killed me when you had the chance."

My uncle shook his head.

Caines placed his sword at my uncle's throat, plunged it in deep and twisted. He pulled out his sword and cleaned the blade on the convulsing body.

"Good-bye old man."

My heart shattered into thousands of pieces with those words. My uncle's body stopped moving and re-entered normal time as he died.

Caines returned his sword to his scabbard. He flinched at a cut on his side.

He looked around, then slowly walked towards me. Every step caused my heart to pound harder until it felt like it was going to jump from my chest.

I must have fainted, because when I returned to normal time I found myself falling to the ground.

When a timestopper loses consciousness, he becomes ordinary again, and he too stops in time.

I slowly came to and crawled to my uncle. I threw up and cried and cried. Others screamed and approached. The hunters gathered and vowed they would track down my uncle's killer.

They had not returned and it was three days since my uncle had died.

JAURU

Time resumed again. I was back in the church. My neighbor's tear hit the ground, and Father Mahar finished his words. The choir began to sing, then the ceremony ended, and I helped carry my uncle Jauru to his final resting place.

3

Janus and Maru

"Einu."

I turned to see who was calling my name. It was Janus. Of all the other boys in the village, only Janus chose to befriend me. Why, I didn't know. Janus was the most popular boy in the village, at least among the girls. I've heard more than one girl talking about him.

I had left the village after the funeral, under the excuse of needing to be alone. I was sitting on a large rock by a small stand of trees just outside our village. Janus must have followed me because it wasn't long after I sat down that he called my name.

"The hunters haven't come back yet."

Janus was trying to give me hope, even if that hope was of revenge. But he didn't know what I knew. The hunters would never find Caines. If they were lucky Caines would let them return alive. No, what my friend was mistaking for overwhelming grief was really fear. I was nearly paralyzed with it.

"It doesn't matter. They will never find my uncle's killer," I said calmly.

"How can you say that? Jocko is the best tracker in the

whole village, nothing gets away from him once he's on the trail."

Janus was most sincere, but how could I tell him what was going through my mind?

"It just doesn't matter to me, that's all."

Janus stood in front of me perplexed.

"Janus."

"Yes?"

"I …"

"What is it Einu?"

"I'm scared."

Janus misinterpreted what I was saying.

"Don't worry, you're safe in the village. I'm sure the hunters will find who killed your uncle. He won't be coming back."

I hadn't put much thought to Caines coming back. If he had wanted to kill me, he would have. No, my thoughts could not stray from the promise I made my uncle before he died.

"No. Caines will not be coming back."

"Caines? Who's he?"

"He killed my uncle."

"You know him?" Janus asked surprised.

"I saw him do it."

"What …"

Janus' voice trailed off.

"Promise me you won't tell anyone."

"I don't understand why you haven't told this to anyone, especially Father Mahar."

"Nobody would understand."

"I think we should go and talk to Father Mahar, right now."

Janus was obviously agitated. But I was in a much worse state of mind.

I burst out, "NO! I can't!"

Tears flowed freely from my eyes.

"I'm scared. My uncle made me promise before he died that I should go find a gnome and have him become my teacher."

Janus stood with a look of complete disbelief on his face.

"Why would your uncle do that?"

"I can't tell you."

"Why not? I'm your friend, aren't I?" Janus said angrily.

"I'm not normal. I have to leave the village."

"Leave? Why? I think you're going crazy. Your uncle's

death has affected your mind somehow. You ..."

I stopped time. I couldn't stand listening to Janus and knew that to show him would be faster. I moved behind him and started time again.

"... should ..."

Janus stopped in mid-sentence when he realized I was no longer sitting on the rock. He turned around frightened, and jumped when he saw me behind him. He took a step backwards and tripped over a rock and fell. He crawled a few more feet away and stammered, "How did you do that? Are you a sorcerer?"

"No. But I do have to leave. You understand don't you?"

"No. I don't understand a thing. How did you do that?" Janus said in a louder than usual voice.

"I can't tell you. My uncle made me promise not to tell anyone. It's too hard to explain anyway."

Our gazes locked. It looked as if he momentarily understood, then asked, "Why a gnome? Gnomes are dangerous."

Before I could say anything else, we were interrupted by someone shouting, "Janus! Einu!"

It was Maru. She always tried to stay as close to Janus as possible.

Maru came running up to us and said loudly, "Einu, your mother wants you home right now. She says you have work to do."

I groaned and really wasn't interested in doing my chores right now.

Maru came up to Janus, grabbed him by the arm and whispered something into his ear. Janus seemed distracted for a moment then annoyed. What ever she said to him, was not what he wanted to concentrate on at the moment.

I turned to leave. Janus stopped me by putting his hand on my shoulder. I refused to turn to look at him. He walked in front of me. Janus was weakly trying to make Maru let go of his arm.

"*Einu. Father Mahar.*"

I said rather loudly, "No" and walked around him and back towards my home.

Maru continued to pull on Janus' arm. They were heading towards the trees. He was putting up a passive resistance, allowing himself to be pulled, but not watching Maru or where he was going. Instead he never took his eyes off of me as I walked away.

I walked backwards down the cart path, watching Janus watch me. Maru stopped pulling Janus and glared at me. She knew that somehow I was responsible for the lack of attention that she was receiving from Janus.

He normally would be pulling Maru into the forest.

At that moment it was obvious to me that I would be leaving the village and wouldn't see Janus for a long time. I stopped walking. He looked sad. Maru looked at Janus and then to me. Her eyes met mine. It struck me as strange, but I didn't have the same feeling about not seeing Maru for a long time. A bond was being struck with her gaze that she was always going to be near me. She looked as if she felt something similar, but where my reaction was a mild surprise, hers was almost that of revulsion.

Maru broke the spell that we were all under, and yanked hard on Janus' arm, knocking him off balance. Maru kept pulling him towards the forest.

Janus looked back one more time before letting himself be surrounded by the trees. His look, even at the distance that was now between us, was quite discernible.

It was saying good-bye.

I stood for a moment on the well-worn cart path, staring at the trees, before turning slowly to go back to the village.

4

Mother

I entered my home and knew it was for the last time. There was no time to indulge in this feeling though. My mother was there.

"Einu, you no good lazy boy. Where have you been when there is so much work to do around here? Huh? Answer me, laggard. No answer, well get to the coup and feed the chickens, then milk the goats, or else there will be no supper for you tonight."

I turned and went back outside. My mother was angry. Angry at the loss of my uncle.

Without him, the amount of chores had more than doubled for us. My uncle had been an extremely industrious man and could easily do the work of two grown men.

She had resented the fact that my uncle had moved in with us in the first place and she got very irritated when he said he would be responsible for me.

Now she was furious at him for suddenly dying and leaving her with so much to do. She never acknowledged the work he had done for her.

MOTHER

I went to the coup and started to work, but stopped when I heard my uncle say, 'you promised me to find a gnome, and have him teach you how to be a timestopper.'

I looked about the coup, searching for the source of his voice, but saw no one. I thought I had heard my uncle's voice a few times since his death reminding me about my promise, but this time there was no mistaking his voice.

I decided not to delay my leaving any longer. It had to be now.

Uponing entering the house I searched for my mother.

"Mother?"

But there was no answer. So rather than go and find her I decided to go get ready for my upcoming journey.

I entered my uncle's room and got his travel pack. His sword was beside the pack. My mother must have put it there after the fight. I stared at it for a long time before deciding to take it. It made me think of Caines.

I took everything to my room. Inside the pack I found a map. It showed the countryside for miles around our village and the route to Finirton, the largest town near our village. It made sense to go there first. If anyone knew where to find a gnome that person would be there.

There were also some coins in a small pouch. My uncle had many coppers, some silvers and a pair of gold coins. This was a small fortune. Guilt overtook me and I quickly placed the coins back into the pouch then the pouch back into the pack followed by a change of clothes and a blanket.

In the larder I grabbed some dried goat meat, some dried apples, some fresh carrots and onions then placed them into the pack. I took one of my mother's pans and a knife from the kitchen and squeezed them in as well. I took a waterskin, filled it and tied it to the back of the pack.

The pack went on snugly and my uncle's sword fit inbetween the pack and my back. I was ready now to confront my mother.

She was behind the house plucking the feathers from a dead chicken. Her eyes were red. She must have been crying for a long while. She was muttering something to herself. It had something to do with my uncle.

"Mother," I said softly.

She jumped off her log and cursed, "By the saints, don't sneak up on me, you lump of a boy.

"You'll be the death of me yet."

She noticed the pack and sword on my back.

"Here, what do you think you're up to?"

"I'm leaving Mother."

"What do you mean leaving? You'll do no such thing. Get that gear off right now."

"I must."

She dropped the chicken and tried to pull the pack off of my back. I pushed her away.

She struck me across the mouth and said, "You will not defy me. You'll not leave me to look after your father's home by myself."

I slid the pack off my back. The sword fell down. I silently cursed myself to take better care of the sword.

My mother thought I was obeying her. She had a look of victory on her face.

What I had in mind was different though. I dug into the pack, searching for the money pouch.

"What are you doing now? Get back into the house," my mother shouted.

The pouch eventually emerged and I pulled out one of the gold coins and handed it to my mother. She looked at the coin in disbelief.

"Where did you get this?" my mother half shouted.

I didn't say anything, but got myself ready to go.

"Use the money to hire someone to help you."

"How dare you. This money was your uncle's wasn't it? It should be mine. You're telling me what to do with my own money. You useless clod."

She tried to strike me again. I deflected her blow.

Something snapped inside me. Her physical attack on me and the years of verbal abuse I had received rushed at me and raised my anger.

I struck her. She fell back from my blow and immediately started to cry.

I stood dumbfounded for a moment disbelieving what had just happened. All connection to her ended. I could leave and turned to go.

My mother screamed out at me, "Don't you dare leave. I am your mother. You have a duty to look after me."

I kept walking.

"Einu, you're useless, you know that?

"You were useless as a son, and you'll be useless out there. Where do you think you're going?"

I stopped. What was there to say? Nothing.

I should have just left, but had a nasty thought instead. It was irresistible. I walked back to my mother with a half a smirk on my face.

I started to say "Listen Mother ..." in my most serious voice, when I pretended to see something behind my mother and gasped, "... oh my God ..."

Then I stopped time just as she started to look over her shoulder.

I took off my pack and dug out the coin pouch again then took out a copper coin and put it in my mother's hand, taking back the gold coin.

Then I went behind the coup, restarted time and listened.

It did not take long before my mother shouted, "DEMONS!!!! Demons took my son. Demons took my son."

I stopped time again when others started to run to my home.

It was a mean trick. My mother was superstitious. Years ago she had told me how she feared that a demon would take me away when I was a baby and leave a copper coin in my place.

I gave her something to think about and walked out of the village. When I was no longer able to see the last home in the village there was a heart stopping sound.

It was the call of some wild beast, far away. But not far away enough for me. I had never before heard a wild call while time was stopped but I knew what the sound was. My uncle had described it to me many times. A Time Beast. He told me that they are not very big, and they usually don't bother timestoppers who are in their prime. But they prey on weak, young or old timestoppers. They're attracted to the source of time stoppages.

I started time immediately. I felt like the Beast could see me very clearly while walking in the open when time was stopped.

I held my sword tightly, and ran quickly down the path through the woods.

5

Leaving

"Einu!"

I nearly jumped out of my skin when my name echoed from the woods. I didn't want anyone seeing me leave the village. The episode with my mother and the howl of the Time Beast made me forget about my uncle's teachings to be aware of my surroundings. If I had just taken a moment to look around, I would have seen Jocko resting just inside the forest with two other hunters, Am and Jak.

As they approached, I could see that they all looked tired.

"Einu, what do you think you are doing?" Jocko asked.

Jocko was nearly as tall as me, but he had to be the only one in the village who was thinner than me.

"I'm leaving," I said, then tried to walk around him.

Jocko grabbed my arm, "You won't find him."

"What?"

"You won't find him. We got close a few times, but each time he sped up and got away."

"What are you talking about?"

"Your uncle's killer."

"Oh."

Jocko stood confused for a moment, before he asked, "Who did you think I meant?"

To be honest, I thought he meant a gnome, and was just wondering how he knew of my search for one.

I couldn't come up with an answer.

"Well?"

I changed the topic, "Tell me why couldn't you catch my uncle's killer."

Jocko let go of me and was eager to tell his tale.

"It was the strangest thing. We were following an easy trail. Obviously your uncle had wounded his killer, because we saw blood leading away from behind your home, and where he must have stopped and bandaged himself. We found a cloth with blood on it.

"Now that was the first puzzle. He didn't seem to be in a hurry, because he took his time. His tracks showed that he was only walking, not running.

"Yet, you said that it had just happened, and indeed we were there quickly. Your uncle's body was still bleeding even though he was dead. The biggest puzzle was the tracks leading away from the your home were all over the place and they were all extremely fresh. We thought we could catch him easily, but for miles the signs showed that he was gradually outpacing us, for his tracks were getting older as we went on. The confusing thing was that he was walking at a slow pace. Then just as we were beginning to despair, his tracks showed that we were now catching up to him. We ran to close the gap, knowing he always walked at the same slow pace.

"We caught up to him quickly. In fact we thought we could hear him just ahead of us, then we couldn't hear anything and the tracks again told us that he was moving quickly away, in spite of the fact that he had not increased his pace.

"And yet again, we came to a spot where we seemed to outpace him, but it was too late in the day to continue. So we made camp.

"The next day we caught up to your uncle's killer again, but we could not catch him. This happened over and over."

Jocko's style was to explain every single detail. He could talk all day about tracking. I wanted him to hurry his explanation because he would never let me leave until he finished saying what was on his mind.

It was apparent now why time had stopped so many times after my uncle was killed. Caines had stopped it to elude his pursuers. I couldn't explain to Jocko the oddity of the tracks, even though it was tempting. When time stopped, Caines would walk a certain distance before starting time again. The tracks would not age while time was stopped, but when he started time again they would age normally. But to the trackers, Caines seemed to be going faster than them until they got to the point where he started time again. Then they would start to catch up to him again.

"So what happened?" I said hoping the story would end soon.

"Well, something strange. We were resting when we suddenly noticed that our boots were missing. And what was worse was the fact that your uncle's murderer stole them. His tracks were absolutely fresh all around us. We followed them a short distance but again they showed that he was outpacing us.

"We decided that he must be some sort of sorcerer that could come up to us without being seen or heard and move like the wind to get away from us whenever he wanted. We knew then that we would never catch him.

"We made wraps for our feet and came home."

Jocko had wrapped some skins around his feet. The other two had done the same, but their feet had blood on them from missteps. They did not know how lucky they were. Caines could have killed them anytime he wanted. After watching his performance with my uncle, it was a miracle that he hadn't.

"Well, you should go back to the village and tell everybody. See you later, okay?"

"No, Einu you'll be coming with us, you can do nothing against a sorcerer. Besides who'll look after your mother if you go?"

My mother! How I wish now that Jocko had not seen me.

"Jocko, it is best that you do not try to stop me. Go back to the village and don't tell anyone you saw me, okay?"

Jocko grabbed me again and started to pull me back to the village.

I allowed him to pull me a short way without any protest, then I resisted with all my strength and quickly pulled away from his now relaxed grasp. Then I stopped time.

As soon as time stopped, the horrible sound of a beast again rang through the woods. It was much closer. I ran as fast as my legs could move me.

LEAVING

Running while time was stopped was somewhat dangerous. I had to rely on my ability to assess the upcoming terrain in my mind. My eyes were useless without any new light coming from the sun.

I started time as soon as I thought Jocko and the other trackers' keen ears wouldn't be able to hear me pounding through the woods.

As I tired, my pace slowed. Jocko wouldn't waste time trying to track me. I knew that he couldn't catch me in stopped time, but wanted to avoid it staying stopped, because of the Beast that seemed to be getting closer each time.

In the distance Jocko was calling my name. He could out run me easily and was in hot pursuit. Bushes cracked as the hunters followed my obvious trail. I stopped time again then heard the Beast. I ran. Fear crept over me as I faced an impossible problem. If I stopped time, the Beast would eventually find me and if I didn't, Jocko was sure to catch me.

I ran until my lungs were heaving. There was no sound of the Beast, but I could feel him getting closer. I started time again and had to rest.

But fate was not being kind to me. I had come to the forest stream. Janus had told me that he and Maru had a secret spot that they visited together, well away from the village.

Well, it was easy to find.

Maru was standing right in front of me and she didn't have on a stitch of clothes.

6

Maru

Maru screamed. To her it would seem that I had appeared right out of thin air.

I stood and stared at her not knowing what to do. In a moment Jocko would catch me and return me to my mother. Visions raced through my mind of some hideous beast tearing me apart. Standing in front of me was a beautiful girl, naked. Talk about confusing.

Maru quickly grabbed her clothing from a branch and ran behind a bush.

"What kind of a person are you, Einu? Spying on a girl taking her bath. Is that what you use your magic for?"

Magic? What was she talking about? What had Janus told her? Where was Janus?

"Well? Answer me!" she said coming from behind the bush.

She had all her clothes on. I was disappointed.

Maru was fearless. Faced with the unknown she would attack.

She had no fear of me.

"If I had known you were here, I would have avoided this spot."

"Are you saying that you had no intention of spying on me?!"

"That's exactly what I'm saying."

It was hard to understand her reaction. She turned red, not from embarrassment, but from anger.

"Are you saying that I'm not worth looking at?"

"No, no, you're very beautiful, I …"

"So, you were using your magic to spy on me!" she shouted, cutting me off in mid-sentence.

This was more confusing. I was tempted to just stop time again and flee, but my curiosity about what she had been told by Janus kept me there.

"I wasn't spying on you! It was an accident my being here."

"Sorcerers never do anything *by accident*."

"I am not a sorcerer!" I said angrily.

"Well, how did you just appear before me out of thin air, if it wasn't by magic?"

What could I say? Just saying that I was a sorcerer would be easier than trying to explain about stopping time. Sorcerers had a bad reputation. They were mostly evil men who used their magic for their own gain. It was insulting to be called a sorcerer.

"It has something to do with time," I said, hoping that that would explain it.

"Time? What has time got to do with it, or are you just trying to bewitch me?"

"No, I wouldn't try to bewitch you … even if I could."

My explanation had started forcibly, but it had ended weakly. My feelings for Maru had leaked out. I was jealous of the fact that she and Janus had something going on.

Maru seemed to catch my look because she smiled, moved very close to me, put her finger lightly under my chin, and said, "Besides, what would Janus think if he saw you here now?"

I was confused. My body was in turmoil. She was too close. Her mention of Janus' name, however, kept me from succumbing to the spell she was trying to place on me. Thinking of Janus made me think of Jocko, which brought back my fears that either Jocko or the Time Beast would find me. I stepped back, wondering how to leave gracefully, when we heard a noise coming from the woods. It was clearly the neighing of a horse, but there were no horses in our village. We used oxen for the farm work, and traveled by ox cart.

Then we heard shouting and someone running and the clear pounding of hooves heading our way.

We turned to see Jocko, Am and Jak running ahead of two horsemen. The horsemen were dressed for war. They were wearing chainmail armor and shields. One carried a flail and the other a long shafted ax.

The axman was closing on Jak. He swung the ax high above his head then down into Jak's back.

Am and Jocko split up. The horseman with the flail followed Am. The other horseman stopped because he could not get his ax out of Jak, so he let go and pulled out a sword when he spotted us. He wheeled around and charged at us.

We stood staring in disbelief. We'd never seen anything like this. The horseman came towards us with his sword held out like a spear pointed straight for my heart. This was not the time for pulling my own sword.

Instead I stopped time, freezing the horseman in his tracks just ten feet from us.

Immediately the Beast howled.

I picked up Maru, and threw her over my shoulder and ran.

The sound of branches breaking told me the Beast was not far behind.

It was obvious that carrying Maru was slowing me down considerably and the Beast would soon catch up to me. I could run no further. At first it had been easy to run with her over my shoulder but now my breathing was coming in heavy gasps.

I was about to stop and pull my sword before the Beast could catch me, when I looked up to see that I was approaching a single line of horsemen stretching across the width of the forest.

Running between the horseman, I looked back to see the creature almost upon us. It was a black blur.

I started time.

The Beast had thick wiry hair that stuck out wildly. The front of the Beast stopped quickly by digging in its front claws but its rear legs kept going. They came between its front legs. It managed to perform a twist in mid air and started running in the direction it came from, as soon as all of its legs were back on the ground.

The horses reared up, startled by the sudden appearance

of the strange creature. But soon the horseman had control of their mounts and were off in hot pursuit of it.

Maru screamed. Soldiers were running towards us.

There had been some men on foot following at intervals behind the horseman.

I put her down and shouted, "Run!"

If I stopped time to get away from them, then that would mean that the Beast would be able to get away from its pursuers and follow us again. I had to leave time flowing in order for us to put as much distance as possible between us and the Beast.

Maru found her legs. She ran like a scared rabbit. It was hard to keep up with her. I still had my pack on and was tired from so much running. Fortunately for us the foot soldiers were dressed for battle and not for running.

They were not gaining on us, but we were not losing them either.

Again we heard the sound of hooves.

We came to a small hill made up of loose gravel and scrambled up as best as we could.

The horsemen tried to get up the hill, but the horses fell and slid back. The foot soldiers tried to climb the hill, but their heavy armor made them slide back as well.

We made it to the top of the hill and though breathing heavily, Maru asked, "What's going on? Who are these strangers? How come I can't remember passing out? What are you going to do about it? What happens if they get to the village ...?"

I pointed towards the village. Black smoke was rising. Maru began to cry. I tried to come up with a plan while both comforting Maru and keeping my eye on the ground below. This hill had suffered from constant slides and there weren't many trees growing on it, so it was easy to see the activity down below.

The horsemen and foot soldiers were surrounding the hill.

There was nothing else to do but wait.

Maru noticed soldiers coming up the other side of the hill. She demanded, "Do something. Use your magic."

When she saw that I wasn't moving she said "Why aren't you doing anything? We can't stay here."

We were both too tired to run. Thoughts of stopping time and killing all these strangers while they were helpless passed through my mind, but I couldn't muster up the nerve. I just wasn't that ruthless.

I also thought of stopping time just before the foot soldiers got up here, but realized that meant carrying Maru down the hill.

"Maru we're going down the hill the way we came up."

"What? You're crazy."

Looking her straight in the eye I said, "Trust me. I know what I'm doing."

"What are you going to do? There are men on horses down there."

Maru wasn't moving, so I tried to pull her. She broke free of me and yelled, "What are you doing?"

I had no patience left to try and explain.

"Magic. I'm going to use magic before we get to the bottom."

"Aha, you *are* a sorcerer."

I resisted the urge to pinch her and started down the hill.

Maru sounded anxious when she asked me, "What are you going to do?"

"Believe me. You'll not notice anything until its over," I said sarcastically.

We were near the bottom when I stopped. Foot soldiers from above were stumbling down after us and there was a crowd of horsemen waiting a little further below.

"Are you going to do it now?" she asked.

Our eyes met.

"Yes."

I stopped time, picked her up and continued down the hill. It could only be hoped that enough time had passed for us to escape the Beast. It was many miles before we rested. Throughout the journey there were no signs of the Beast. I hoped that we had lost him.

I started time again and put Maru down. She gasped, then asked, "Did I pass out again? The last thing I remember was asking you whether you were going to do your magic, and the next thing, you're carrying me and we're on top of another hill. Oh, I recognize where we are."

Maru was looking at the smoke rising in the distance.

I handed my pack to Maru.

"Stay here. There's food and a blanket in here. I'll be back quickly." I smiled then said "Perhaps faster than you think."

Maru didn't get my joke and asked, "Are you going to use your magic to save the village?"

Looking out at the smoke I said, "I'll try my best," then I grabbed my uncle's sword and started back down the hill.

"Einu …"
I turned and saw a worried looking Maru.
"Yes, I'll try to find Janus first."
I stopped time and went down the hill.

7

Rescue

I could only hope that not much had happened at the village while time had been flowing. But what was I to do when I got to the village? I had no idea. How could I rescue everyone? By killing an entire army? I could hear my uncle Jauru telling me to stop thinking about it, and just do what had to be done.

My uncle had always stressed that a timestopper must master the state of non-thinking, especially when time was stopped.

He would sit beside me and watch. He always seemed to know if I was thinking when time was stopped and he punished me for failure.

My uncle had never let me stop time for very long. He told me it was too dangerous for someone so young to do it unsupervised. Personally, I never found anything ever to worry about until the Time Beast.

There was fear within me now. Fear of the Beast. Fear of the strange army and fear of what they would do to my village. But there was some other anxiety that I couldn't explain. It grew larger the longer that time was stopped. It was some sort of pressure that came from all around. The Beast must have had something to do with it.

A howl in the distance broke the absolute silence of stopped time.

I restarted time immediately upon hearing the howl and felt for certain that the creature could sense me while time was stopped.

The smoke over the village rose up higher and I ran.

I came to one of the outlying farms around the village. It belonged to Farmer Jonoh. The buildings were now burned almost to the ground. The farmer, his wife and his three daughters were lying on the ground dead but Farmer Jonoh's sons were missing. It could only be hoped that they had escaped.

I could just make out the forms of some soldiers on foot leading four young boys on their way towards the village. The fire and smoke from the burning farm obscured my view of them.

I crept with utmost caution using all the lessons in awareness that my uncle had taught me.

My uncle's sheathed sword was in my left hand, and I was ready to stop time in an instant if discovered.

I walked along the edge of the farmer's field among the low trees and bushes, until I reached the first house in the village. It belonged to the widow Hanu. Household items were being hurled out of the window forming a disordered pile.

I crept quietly back through the small orchard behind the widow's house, past two burning homes, until I reached my mother's house. It had just been set on fire, and two soldiers were walking away from it.

Quickly and quietly I ran to the chicken coup but stopped in horror when there, just in front of the coup, was my mother. Her face was buried in the dirt, but her head was cracked open and there was a pool of blood surrounding her body.

I stopped time as a defensive reflex, as if someone was just about to hit me.

However much my mother and I disagreed, she was still my mother. Why did I strike her before I left? My feeling of being so clever at my departure left me with an empty feeling.

The silence of stopped time weighed heavily on me and all the feelings that I experienced while growing up in my mother's home welled up inside me until I was ready to burst.

Revenge. That was all I wanted. I ran towards the two soldiers who had set fire to my home.

My sword came out on its own.

All I wanted to do was to kill them. They both wore chainmail armor and round helmets. I hacked at them but my sword was not a slashing weapon, it was a thin light weapon, designed for speed and I didn't do any damage. I lifted the chainmail on one of the soldiers. He had a thick padded leather shirt underneath. My sword could pierce the shirt but now, facing helpless enemies, I found it hard to put my sword to his body. I thought of my mother and raised my sword to his stomach. But my uncle's words came to me, 'never use your ability to stop time to impose your will on others.'

I let go of the soldier's chainmail in disgust, and put my sword back into its scabbard, unable to exact revenge. Something primal inside of me rose up but just as quickly fell back. I let go of my anger and resumed my search for Janus.

As I approached the center of the village, I noticed a blue aura, a blueness, a glow. I had never before experienced color in stopped time. The world had always been colored in shades of gray while I traveled through stopped time. Blue had never been part of my experience.

As I walked over to this strange glow, I passed by most of the boys in the village. They were sitting in a group, their legs tied with ropes and soldiers stood guard around them.

I arrived at the blue area, but could not see into it. It was a wall of shear color that blinded my ability to see what was on the other side. The blueness formed a half sphere around an area about thirty feet in diameter and fifteen feet high.

I wondered about entering it but was afraid. I decided instead to hide somewhere and restart time. I looked around and chose to hide under the porch at Jocko's house. It was solid wood, but there was a loose board which could be moved. I hid inside and restarted time.

Instantly there was a small man, wearing a robe, sitting cross-legged at the center of the area where the blue sphere had been. He looked around, stood up, brushed himself off and turned to watch a large man shouting at a boy. My curiosity kept my eyes fixed on this strange man but eventually the shouting drew me to the boy who was the object of the shouting.

It was Janus!

The large man pulled out a knife, grabbed Janus by the hair and slashed him across the face. Janus' nose fell to the ground and he screamed in pain, clutching his face.

His scream pierced my heart.

The robed man yelled at the large man, whose answer was to point at Janus with his knife.

This was too much. I stopped time.

But now where Janus and the two men had been standing, that strange blue half sphere had appeared again, having moved from the center of the village over to where Janus had been attacked.

I crawled out from under the porch, pulled my sword from its scabbard then headed over to the blue area. I knew that Janus was within the sphere somewhere, but a voice inside of me screamed for me not to go past that blue barrier.

Ignoring the warning, I tentatively poked a finger at the blue wall and it passed through. I pushed further and followed my finger into the blueness.

On the other side, the bluish light from the barrier gave an unnatural look to everything. Janus' back was towards me, hands at his face. The large and the small men stood on either side of him, turned slightly away from each other. I was sure that when I stopped time that they had been facing each other. No one moved. I knew instinctively that the space within this blue barrier was not in stopped time.

I bent down close to the ground and watched small insects move through the grass. One moved to the blue wall and passed through, so I poked my head out to the other side. The bug had stopped moving, it was caught in stopped time.

I approached the three still figures slowly and saw a red drop fall down in front of Janus. Blood. Blood from his face. His nose lay to one side.

I circled around, giving the large man a wide berth, so as to get in front of Janus. As soon as I came in front of him his eyes moved. He looked right at me, his eyes wide with fear.

I was confused. I wanted to run and grab him and pull him out of this unnatural place, but I stood frozen unable to decide what to do.

The shorter man yelled, "Now!!!"

The larger man ran as quick as lightning towards me. I was surprised, but had enough wits to swing my sword at the oncoming bulk of the man. He managed to duck below my swing and lunged at me. I quickly turned and stepped back to one side. But the large man's dagger grazed my left arm, causing me to drop my scabbard. I yelped in pain and ran.

The larger man finished his dive and rolled on the ground and came to his feet. He turned to pursue me.

It would have been easy to make it to the blue barrier, but the smaller man who had been just standing and murmuring to himself suddenly yelled, "Stop!!!" in a booming voice.

The effect on me was that my feet felt weighted down and it was as if an invisible wall of molasses surrounded me.

Time was somehow slowing for me. I looked over my shoulder to see the large man moving normally and realized that he would easily catch me.

My uncle's words about using my will to change things, came to me. I had not understood the concept, but now, I calmly willed my body to move, and ran.

"Don't let him get to the barrier!" the small man yelled.

The large man lunged, just as I made it to the barrier. He grabbed me but our momentum carried us totally outside the barrier. The large man was hanging in mid-air as he stopped in time on the other side of the barrier. I dislodged myself from his grip. I looked back at the barrier. It was moving very slowly in my direction. I ran out of the village, and exhausted fell to the ground. I checked all around me then restarted time.

I sat and thought, remembering all the details of what had happened, but a nagging pain in my left arm forced me to attend to it. I was bleeding. I wrapped some cloth from my under shirt around my cut.

Sadness overwhelmed me and I slowly headed back to Maru.

As I walked my thoughts became clearer and I could only conclude that the man in the robe was a sorcerer.

The cut to my arm made me feel vulnerable. I had always felt being a timestopper made me superior and invincible. But all the events of the past few days left me with a cold feeling. My mother's and my uncle's death, the Time Beast, an army destroying my village, and a sorcerer who was immune to my stopping time.

Now I knew all too well what my uncle had been saying to me, that the life of a timestopper is extremely dangerous. He always told me that timestoppers get caught up in events larger than themselves and only humility can see them through those events.

Well, I was feeling humble. All my energy was spent, I was tired, hungry, sore and had no more fight left in me.

RESCUE

There was one last thing to do before going back. When I came across some soldiers, I took a scabbard, and used it for my uncle's sword. It was a little too wide, but it was the perfect length.

Then I slowly made my way to Maru.

8

Beast

Time stopped.

It had nothing to do with me.

There was a howl in the distance.

For some reason the Beast could not find me. Still the sound of his howling caused me to pick up my pace a bit. I used up the rest of my energy climbing the hill where Maru was waiting.

She was curled up in the blanket. Her eyes were half open, looking in the direction of the smoke over the village. It looked as if she was forcing her eyes to remain open.

There was nothing to do but wait. I ate some dried meat from the pack that lay beside her and then took a small sip of water from the waterskin. It was almost empty. Maru must have been really thirsty.

I had been sitting in one spot for too long, because the air was getting hot and stale around me. One disadvantage of being a timestopper was that energy didn't dissipate away from the body as it did when time was flowing normally. And fresh air didn't flow freely toward the body either. So it was necessary to keep changing positions if time was stopped for a long period.

BEAST

My uncle told me the reason that we didn't overheat or just plain suffocate during stopped time was that timestoppers are able to influence the immediate environment around our bodies, so we can still breathe. And the air and whatever we are touching can absorb some heat, so we do not boil to death from the heat of our own bodies.

One of the first memories I had as a child was making objects hot by just touching them, and starting to choke by staying in one spot too long.

My uncle said that it was dangerous for a timestopper to day dream while time was stopped. He said something about infecting reality with my dreams. I never understood that.

My uncle explained that if I were to touch someone long enough while time was stopped that there was a possibility that they would notice me. I had never tried it because my uncle said that it was possible to drive that person crazy. In spite of the warning I thought of trying it on Maru. I longed to have someone else understand the loneliness of being a timestopper, now that my uncle was gone.

The Beast howled in the distance again.

I held on to my uncle's sword to try and comfort myself. It didn't sound far enough away for me. Though I couldn't really tell how far away it was, because my hearing him had nothing to do with my ears. I heard the Beast with that part of my mind that was sensitive to other creatures' thoughts.

Time started again. Some unknown Timestopper finished his task, or maybe Caines had found some other victim, but I was once again in normal time.

Maru was in front of me. She moved underneath the blanket. The blanket hugged her body in a very distracting way. My thoughts strayed from my current situation and back again to seeing Maru by the stream.

I sneezed.

Maru quickly rolled out of her blanket, jumped to her feet and stared at me in disbelief.

"How did you do that? Sneak up without me noticing? What happened? Where's Janus?" she said in a rush.

I waved my hands to ward off her barrage of questions. Maru was unstoppable when she was excited or curious, and right now she was both.

"Maru, Maru, please. I'm tired and I'm hurt. I'll get to what happened, just give me a moment, please."

"That's your own problem. Where's Janus?"

She asked her last question quite forcefully, emphasizing her anxiety by grabbing my shirt and tugging on it.

I grabbed her hands and slowly removed them from my shirt. The impact of what had happened hit me full force. Tears filled my eyes as I looked into Maru's. After a moment she too started to cry.

"What ... ?" Was all she could muster.

"They cut off his nose."

She gasped.

"I couldn't do anything to help him. They tried to catch me. I barely got away. A sorcerer has him."

She wiped her tears and became stern.

"What happened? Start from the beginning."

I took a deep breathe and started my story.

"Well, I stopped time then headed towards the village ..." I began to say, when Maru interrupted me.

"Wait a minute, what do you mean you stopped time? The last I saw, you were heading down the hill, then you suddenly disappeared. I thought that you were just doing some sorcery, and would be back in the blink of an eye with Janus. But you were gone so long, I got tired and lay down. It seemed like you were never going to come back, then you pop up behind me. Now you try to tell me some crazy story about stopping time."

"It's true, I can stop time. My uncle could do it and so could my father."

"You use your magic to stop time?" she asked slowly.

"No. I have no magic. All I can do is stop time."

"Show me."

Looking into Maru's eyes, I stopped time then walked behind her, and started time again.

She looked around, obviously surprised, then she turned and saw me.

Quickly she asked, "Can you teach me how to do that?"

"No. I don't think so. My uncle said that timestoppers were all born with the ability and are immune to time stoppages caused by other timestoppers. He also told me that he never knew of anyone who learned how to do it. Even though he did tell me of others that we had to watch out for. Sorcerers, gnomes and Time Beasts."

"I've heard a little about sorcerers and gnomes. What do they have to do with time?" she asked.

"Well, my uncle told me that timestoppers and sorcerers are natural enemies. Sorcerers have a way to negate the stopping of time. And until today I never knew what my uncle meant. That was how the sorcerer almost caught me. And gnomes as you know are immune to magic, but my uncle said that they are also immune to the stoppage of time. My uncle told me that gnomes are sometimes allies for timestoppers and I was leaving the village to find one."

"Why would you want to do that?"

"My uncle made me promise that I would if something ever happened to him. And something did. Another timestopper killed him."

"How do you know this?"

"It happened right in front of me."

"You had better tell me everything."

She listened to everything that had happened in the past few days, with all the time stoppages put into the right places. As I told the story, tears came unbidden to my eyes ... with the death of my uncle, leaving the village, escaping from Jocko, being thrust into saving Maru, then trying to help the villagers and finding my mother dead. Maru looked at me differently but I didn't know what it meant.

"Well, you certainly kept your wits about you, but what do you think happened to the Beast? And just what is the Beast anyway?"

"I don't know what happened to him, and as to what it is, all my uncle would tell me was to avoid Time Beasts at all costs."

"Good advice if you ask me, but what are we going to do now?"

The sky was red. It was near sunset.

"Well, I think we will have to sleep here ... and in the morning we should make our way to Finirton."

"Sleep? Out here? How will we do that? There is only one blanket."

"We'll take turns sleeping. Someone should stay on watch."

She looked around then said, "Nonsense. We could hear someone coming for miles up here. We'll share the blanket."

My heart jumped at the prospect. The weariness that I had felt earlier, left me.

She seemed to sense my change in mood and said, "We'll lie back to back, and we'll keep warm that way."

We lay down back to back, covered ourselves with the blanket and said good night.

I couldn't sleep, feeling the presence of Maru against my back and didn't want to move and spoil the sensation. I silently cursed myself for not having relieved myself before lying down, but the urge eventually went away.

Just as I was falling asleep, Maru, who I thought to be already asleep, turned and put her arm around me, which caused my heart to race for a while. In spite of her sometimes abrupt treatment of me, I really was beginning to think that she might like me. Eventually though I fell asleep quite content and had wonderful dreams, none of them involved any of the events of the past few days.

I had been asleep for many hours when there was a noise. My heart raced again but this time for a different reason. Reaching out from under the blanket and grabbing my sword gave me a sense of security. I held on to it tightly and listened, straining my ears for any other noise. I had the feeling something was lurking out there in the darkness. I listened for hours, until a light sleep overtook me. My dreams now took a darker turn with some unknown creature stalking me.

I fell into a pattern of a few minutes asleep, followed by a few moments of wakefulness.

This lasted until just before dawn when the distinct sound of footfalls came up the hill.

In the pre-dawn light, a black shape approached.

It shambled along on all fours, sometimes rearing up on its hind legs and walking upright for a few steps.

Maru awoke and clutched me.

There was nothing else to do but hold onto my sword and wait.

The Time Beast had found me again.

Maru tightened her grip on my arm until it became painful.

The Beast was now fifty feet away and it slowed its pace.

She resisted all my attempts to dislodge her grip from my arm.

"Let go," I whispered.

She didn't appear to hear me. Her grip didn't lessen.

I stopped time and pried Maru's fingers open.

The Beast leapt forward when time stopped and howled louder than it had ever howled before.

I jumped up and ran a short distance away from Maru then met the creature's charge.

In the state of stopped time, the Beast took on a more fearsome appearance. It was darker in my mind and its presence invoked a sense of panic in me.

I restarted time, for it would be harder to face it in that way.

It halted just in front of me and glared at me with red eyes. It stank and smelled of rotting flesh, probably from some festering wound. A wind carried its foul odor towards me.

Maru screamed. This distracted the Beast for a moment and I charged. Sword up high, I swung my blade down at the creature, but it leapt out of the way so quickly I didn't see which way it went. As I turned, I caught sight of it out of the corner of my eye. I didn't have a chance to get out of the way. Before it hit me I instinctively stopped time, but that didn't help. The creature hit me with its full weight and knocked me to the ground and landed on top of me. It pinned my arms and looked at me, its face inches from mine. Its breath was revolting, as the smell of its rotting teeth filled the air. Saliva dripped from its mouth and fell into my own.

Looking into its eyes, I saw my death.

I restarted time.

The Beast had the eyes of madness. It hovered over me and its presence in my mind grew. I began to lose my identity.

Then, as from a distance, the Beast screamed and loosened its grip on me. Maru stood over us with a large rock. She raised it and brought it down again. The Beast staggered away as best as it could. She had hit it on its head and blood was pouring down its matted hair.

She moved forward and tried to bring down her rock again, but the Beast moved too fast for her. She threw the rock, missing by only inches. It stopped, jerked its head up and stared at her.

It leapt at her with lightning speed.

I recovered and swung my sword at it, as it flew through the air past me. I meant to hit it on the side of its body, but it passed so fast, my swing hit it at its ankle, severing the foot from its leg. The Beast was already curling to clutch at its ankle as it hit her. She hit the ground with the creature howling on top of her. It quickly rolled off of her and tried to scramble away on three legs.

I got up and went to Maru, "Are you okay?"

She weakly nodded her head and pointed to the Beast. It was about twenty feet away and faltering in its attempt to get away.

I easily caught up to it and tried to stab it, but it anticipated my move and rolled to one side. My sword hit the ground.

The Beast made one last attempt to leap at me, but it instinctively tried to use both back legs. It screeched in pain and leapt wide of me going at least ten feet behind me, but I had swung my sword while it had passed and cut a long gash over the length of its body. It was in its death throws, when I approached it. It looked up at me and I stabbed it in the throat and twisted, just as Caines had done to my uncle.

I wiped my sword on the grass and walked back to Maru. She was crying.

I held her in my arms and we watched the sun rise. The sky was red, as if angry at what had just happened.

"It's over."

She just nodded, and I helped her back to our blanket.

She drank the last few drops of water, while I packed up our scant belongings, and then we walked away from where the Beast lay.

9

Finirton

As we left the body of the Beast behind us, I once again felt that the invincibility of being a timestopper was an illusion. The sorcerer, and now the Time Beast, revealed my vulnerabilities. But these realizations were secondary to what was overtaking me at the moment.

When the Beast had stared right into my face, its madness must have touched me. Images and faces danced across my inner vision. It was very chaotic and beyond any previous imaginations. The images would drive me mad if they didn't go away. I reached for my uncle's sword for comfort. It now felt a part of me and I claimed it as my own. I did feel more secure, but I still swayed a bit from the effect of having more than one image in front of me.

Maru must have noticed my distress because even though I was helping her to walk, she asked me if I was alright.

My perception was distorted for a moment and there before me was a shorter, older woman asking me the same question. I snapped back and replied, "Yeah, I'm okay. The Beast seems to have affected my eyes a bit. It'll soon pass."

I hoped.

"What was that thing anyway? It stank. And why didn't you just do what you do to get rid of it? You kept moving around so fast, it was hard to follow what was happening. Do you think we will run into another of those things ..?"

"Maru," I interrupted.

"Yes, Einu?"

"Haven't you noticed? It is hard enough answering *one* of your questions, but when you ask me so many in a row, it's nearly impossible. Could you please slow down and ask me only one thing at a time ... Please?"

Maru nodded and said, "As long as you try to answer me and don't hold back anything. I have to know what's going on. Okay?"

"Okay."

"Well?"

"Well what?"

"What was that thing?" Maru asked impatiently.

We had come to a stream running between two hills, and I helped Maru to sit on a rock. I filled the waterskin, so she drank from it, while I drank water from the stream.

"I'm not really sure. My uncle said to avoid Time Beasts, but he never really told me why. But there was something more than just confrontation."

"What?"

"I can't be sure, but it was as if the Beast was full of madness and that it wanted me to stop its madness."

Maru drank some more and watched the stream.

Eventually she said, "Do you think that we will meet another one?"

I put on a large grin and replied, "Not with you around."

"What is that supposed to mean?"

"Well, my uncle said that Time Beasts will only prey on weak, old or unprotected timestoppers. When my uncle was alive, I never heard a howl in stopped time before. And with you to protect me ..."

Maru whacked me on my arm.

"... it's true, no creature would dare come near me with you around ..."

I jumped away as Maru tried to hit me again.

"... your looks alone will keep them at bay ..."

This was too much for Maru, she came after me, trying to spray me with water from the waterskin.

She was still limping and I could easily keep out of her range.

"Einu, you're the only beast I have to watch out for."

When Maru stopped trying to get me, I came back to her. She splashed the last of the water from the skin into my face and laughed.

I took it from her and filled it again then took off my boots and washed my feet, when she splashed me from behind a rock. She laughed for she finally got her revenge.

When I had dried myself, I took out my uncle's map and studied it.

Maru found some berries to eat that were growing by the stream and watched me from a short distance.

"Well, where are we going?"

"I've already told you. We're going to Finirton."

"Do you think we have enough food to get there?"

"It would normally take about seven days to get to the market at Finirton by ox cart, going by the cart road. We should stay off of all paths until we are far from our village. We don't know much about what those soldiers were doing here.

"If you are not too badly injured then we should make it in about the same amount of time, about seven days."

Maru quickly retorted, "I'm okay. But I can't go without food. We should look for anything edible as we make our way along the stream."

She finished all the berries then continued, "We should try to catch some fish or crayfish."

"Do you want to eat them raw? I'll not light any fires until we're far from the village. So let's just eat sparingly and move as fast as we can."

I offered her my hand and helped her walk. She had to rely on me to help her over the rocky terrain, and so I got to stay close to her.

When we rested however, the memories of what happened started to haunt me.

The Beast and the body of my mother came clearly to my mind. Also, seeing Janus as a prisoner tore at my heart.

Janus. What will become of you?

What had happened to Father Mahar? Surely they wouldn't have harmed the old cleric.

And Jocko, did he get away?

My mind was torn.

I wanted to return and find out the fates of the others.

But fear of the sorcerer stopped me. I imagined all sort of horrible deaths at the hand of that evil man.

The sound of Maru crying roused me from my thoughts.

She looked up and then threw her arms around me and cried harder.

We held each other for a while.

"I miss him too," I said sadly.

She let go of me.

"When I left the village I thought that it would always be there. Who would have thought that it would be have been burned to the ground, and on the very day of my leaving. I'm beginning to think that I'm cursed."

"I hope not. It wouldn't be fun to have a cursed friend," she said while trying to compose herself.

The fact that Maru called me her friend made me feel happy. I smiled.

By the fifth evening after the attack on the village, we hadn't seen or heard any soldiers, so I decided to risk lighting a small fire. This brightened both our moods.

Maru and I curled up in the blanket close to the fire. She put her arms around me for warmth and we tried to stave off the chill of the night air.

I was calm about my fate and didn't worry about what had happened or what to do next.

This moment was pure peace and I wished to be able to recapture it at will. I fell asleep quite content.

The next day we decided to try and find the road into Finirton.

To my surprise the road was just over the hill of our last camp.

We made good time on the road. We didn't see a soul and were just thinking about finding a place for the night when we saw Finirton nestled in the distant hills.

It was a welcome sight.

"All's well. I think we should press on and walk in the dark until we get to the town. What do you say?"

"If it means I get to sleep on a bed instead of rocks, then I'm all for it," she replied.

It took us another two and a half hours to get to Finirton.

As we neared the town, we were able to observe the normal activities of the inhabitants.

I viewed these scenes knowing that the events at my village and what had happened there, could happen here. The people here probably would never imagine that anything like that could happen. I could only hope it didn't, especially not while we were in town.

We made our way to the inn.

Maru had worried about what we could do in Finirton to earn our supper.

I told her that we would be here only long enough to uncover where to find a gnome.

She was worried that I might abandon her. She felt better when I told her that was nonsense.

She was not very keen on looking for a gnome though and told me so. She was not so sure that it was a good idea.

We entered the inn and were greeted by a very burly character close to me in height but much wider.

"No weapons allowed," he said in a deep voice.

"We would just like to have a room for the night."

My voice sounded weak and very young to my ears. It didn't sound normal at all. I wondered why my voice should sound different than it did.

The rough man merely grunted and smirked at Maru.

He yelled out, "Barley! Two for the stables."

My pride was hurt so I took off my pack and brought out my money pouch. I poured the coins into my hand and made sure the large man saw the flash of gold as the coins went back into the pouch.

"No, we want a room in the inn. And make sure it has a bath."

I had put effort into sounding dangerous and added, "And you can carry my pack and sword to our room. We're hungry. What's for supper tonight?"

The man spit on the floor, then yelled, "Pitt!"

A young lad came running up, and said, "Yes, Master Darl."

Darl barked at the boy, "Take these two fops to the east room. Take this bag and the sword with you. Then show them to the common room. Make sure to ask them when they are ready for their bath. And get the six coppers for the room and supper."

Darl then walked briskly away.

The lad had to be only a few years younger than ourselves.

47

He smiled and said earnestly, "My name is Pitt. Do the young Master and Miss have any horses that need to be stabled?"

"No. Take us to our room."

We followed Pitt in silence to a cozy room that faced east with a view over a small garden.

Pitt put my pack and sword next to the bed and said, "Young Master, I'm afraid I will have to ask you for six coppers."

I pulled six coppers from my pouch and gave them to him.

Maru said, "I think a bath would be nice before eating. Pitt, do you think that you could do that for me, please?"

"Yes Miss, I'll send in a maid right away."

"Pitt, my name is Maru, and this is Einu. Pardon his rudeness. He forgets himself sometimes."

"Yes Miss Maru." Pitt said grinning.

Pitt started to leave, but Maru stopped him by saying, "And before you go Pitt, please show Einu to the common room. I'm sure he's hungry."

My plan was to somehow stay in the room to protect Maru, but she quashed that idea quickly and Pitt led me to the common room. Someone called Pitt's name and he disappeared through one of the doors to the kitchen, leaving me to find a seat.

I sat down in the smoke filled room and a young girl who looked just like Pitt put a bowl of stew, a large piece of bread and a small slab of butter in front of me. There was a large crowd and most stared at me during my meal.

Darl came in. He went over to the more boisterous patrons and I could hear the word fop again as they looked in my direction. The crowd burst out laughing.

A barmaid came over.

"Would you like some ale young master?"

"No thank you."

But before she could leave I asked, "What's a fop?"

She replied in a huffy voice, "That's not on here."

"What?"

She repeated, "That's not on here."

When she saw my puzzled look, she added, "This here's not that type of establishment. There's no fops here. You'll be wanting to go to the Wandering Goose. I hears that they allow them types there."

"No, no. You've misunderstood me. I'm not trying to find a fop. I'm just trying to find out what one is."

The barmaid looked at me with disbelief, then quickly said, "You're not 'aving me on, are you?"

I shook my head no.

She looked to the patrons on both sides of me, then moved closer and whispered in my ear, "A fop is a youg'un who does elderly men certain favors."

"Favors?" I said quietly back to her, "What kind of favors?"

"You know. Sexual favors."

She had to have been no more than a foot away from me as she spoke and she was looking me straight in the eye.

I blushed then looked away and stared into the empty bowl where my stew had once been.

Darl laughed again.

I flushed with anger, stood then walked over to where Darl and the noisy patrons were sitting.

I wanted to stop time. They all quieted and looked at me.

The silence was uncomfortable.

"Can anyone here tell me how to find a gnome?"

Their reaction surprised me. The entire table, and especially Darl, broke out into riotous laughter. Finally, when one of them gained enough composure, he said, "Now what would you want to be doing with a gnome, Master Fop?"

The table broke out into laughter again, with some holding their middles and others slapping the table.

When the laughter finally subsided, a cold rage enveloped me.

"I do not appreciate being made fun of. Now, if you can't answer my question, then don't let your mouth wag again. If you do then I'll have to shut it for you."

The others around the table all started to make 'eww' noises, and they watched for the response of the one who had answered me.

"Listen here young'un. You ought to respect your betters."

"I would if I saw any."

"Boy, I'm afraid I'll just have to teach you some manners."

He stood up and moved in front of me.

"Now, say you're sorry like a good little fop."

"I'm not a fop, but you're a pig," I said, deliberately trying to provoke him.

The man paused for a second then swung his fist.

I stopped time just before his fist connected with my jaw, moved slightly out of the way, and swung a punch of my own at his face. I started time just before hitting him.

The man was shocked. He had expected to hit me, but instead his fist flew harmlessly through the air, then he reeled back from my punch to his face.

All the others stopped laughing, some were rubbing their eyes and the rest of the common room became eerily quiet.

When he recovered he moved quickly towards me and tried to put me into a bear hug.

I stopped time again just before he grabbed me then went down to my knees and off to one side then swung a blow straight into the man's groin, and started time again, just before connecting.

The man went down instantly. I stood up as he rolled around on the ground in obvious discomfort.

Darl stepped forward, pulled a small well-worn club from under his apron and said straight to me, "Here there'll be none of that now, or I'll toss you out onto your ears."

Before Darl could get to me I stopped time and took the club from his hand then restarted time again.

I waved the club in front of Darl's nose. His eyes widened.

"I don't think you will Master Darl."

At that moment Maru came in from the hallway. She saw me from the doorway and put her arms on her hips. Her look said to me. 'So you can't be left alone for more than five minutes without getting into trouble.'

Someone in the room said, "Sorcery."

I tossed the club to the amazed Darl and said to him, "Bring us some more food to our room," turned then added, "and plenty of water."

Walking out I grabbed Maru's arm and turned her back down the hall.

"What was that all about?" she asked.

"Oh, nothing. Just man stuff."

"Man stuff, huh? You're right, it is nothing."

We went back to our room, where I tried to explain to her what happened, but she just got angrier with me. When the food came, Maru ate and I tried to take a bath, but was too self conscious to get out of my under garments. They got all wet.

FINIRTON

I got dressed again and was sitting quite uncomfortably when a knock came on our door.

10

Bartu

"Who is it?" I asked.

"My name is Bartu, and I might just be able to help you in your search for a gnome."

I went to the door and let in a man who was in his late thirties, his dark hair showing signs of gray. He had a noticeable scar on his right cheek.

"Einu, I presume?"

I nodded my head yes.

"And this must be Maru?" Bartu said smoothly.

Bartu had been in the common room. He had been watching me but there had to have been at least six others watching me just as intently. So I hadn't paid any extra attention to him.

"How did you know our names?"

"Pitt is a very friendly lad, and eager to tell all that he sees and hears."

Bartu sat in the chair by the fireplace. Maru and I exchanged glances wondering what was going to happen next.

"That was quite a show you put on out there."

"They had it coming."

"You know that the whole inn thinks you're a sorcerer."

My mouth tightened and I shrugged my shoulders, trying to hide the almost smug feeling that I had.

"But I have seen my share of sorcerers and can tell the difference between a sorcerer and a timestopper."

My eyes widened and my mouth dropped.

"How do you know about timestoppers?"

"I have been around and know the best way to kill a timestopper."

Fear crept over me and I asked, "How?"

Bartu stood up. Took a step towards me and said, "Like this ..."

Quick as lightning, he pulled a knife and threw it at the bed. It landed in the head board with a loud thud.

I saw the knife hit its target, then turned to see what Bartu was going to do next, but he had vanished.

Before I could turn to look behind me there was a knife at my throat.

I stopped time.

Bartu was frozen still. He wasn't a timestopper.

I took the knife from his hand, stood behind him and placed the knife at his throat.

I started time.

Bartu felt his own knife at his throat, but ignored it and said, "You have to distract a timestopper, then get behind them, being careful not to touch them, then you stab them quickly in a vital area."

"I guess you weren't quick enough," I said smugly.

"Lad, I could have killed you easily. I have got three timestoppers to my name already, and they were all much tougher and more experienced than yourself. Now if you please, can I have my knife back? I have already killed a timestopper because he took my knife."

I removed the knife from Bartu's throat and stepped back. He turned to face me.

"My knife?" was all he said.

I tossed the knife in the air, being afraid to get too close to him. Bartu grabbed the handle with lightning-like reflexes before the knife got half way to the ground.

Maru broke the silence, "Have you two finished playing your games? I'm getting sick of watching pointy objects being tossed around the room and pointed at people's throats.

"Now Bartu, I understand that you know something about gnomes that Einu might find useful. Not that I'm interested. But I would like to get this gnome thing over with."

Bartu laughed, "You do have a way of getting things said, do you not, lass. Well, Einu, if you agree to a truce between us. I will not try to kill you if you will not try to kill me. I just *might* be interested in taking you to someplace where there *might* be a gnome."

Maru said, "Just how *might* we be able to convince you?"

"I have only one weakness."

"Only one?" Maru quickly retorted.

"Yes. Gold."

I looked at him suspiciously.

He looked injured then said, "You do not believe me? Well, for the two gold pieces that you have in the bag, I will lead you to the genuine article. A real live, god-fearing gnome."

"How do you know about the gold pieces in my pouch?" I said, not trusting him.

"You will have to stop flashing that gold around boy, or you will attract more than the likes of me."

"Okay, I'll be more careful in the future about showing my money, but asking for my only two gold coins to find a gnome is a bit much, isn't it? I won't have enough left to buy food."

"Do not try and make me feel sorry for you boy. It can not be done. My price is my price. I will be back in the morning to hear your decision. If you do not make up your mind by then, I will be off to more exotic places than Finirton. Besides, I am sure that a resourceful timestopper like yourself has a way of *finding* some more gold."

Bartu went to the door, turned and said, "Tomorrow. Dawn. Bye-bye kiddies."

Maru went to the door and peeked outside. She closed the door and said, "I think I like him. He's a bit childish though, picking fights and calling us kids. But overall a likable guy."

"What are you talking about? He just wants my money. How can I trust him to lead us to a gnome? Don't you think he'll just get us out in the wilderness somewhere and kill us in our sleep?"

"Einu, you've been with me for too long. You're beginning to sound like me. Let's just get this out of the way and find your smelly old gnome."

"Why do think that gnomes are smelly?"

"Just a hunch. Anyway let's get some sleep. Why don't you curl up in front of the fireplace and I'll take the bed."

"But ..."

"No more talk. I'm tired. Besides we'll have to get up at dawn tomorrow and be fresh for our journey with Bartu. Goodnight."

She jumped into the bed, blew out the candles and rolled the blankets around her.

I took the blanket from my pack, used my pack as a pillow and curled up in front of the fire, being quite unhappy about my situation. I envisioned Bartu taking everything and leaving me naked in the forest somewhere. Also I didn't like the way Maru was starting to order me around and felt like I had no say about how to find a gnome. It began to feel like everything was being done according to some strange plan, in which I wasn't even consulted.

I fell asleep not very happy and awoke the next morning to Bartu's voice. He had entered our room without waking us.

"Wakey, wakey. Time for little kids to get moving, if they are inclined to do so."

My blanket had come off during the night, and because the fire went out, the cold air that came from the fireplace had chilled me.

Maru bounced out of bed, and said, "Come on Einu, let's get going. No time to waste. I'm sure that in two days we will miss this place, or I should say, the bath."

"Do we have time to eat breakfast before we go? And how about provisions for along the way. We should buy some food and at least get another blanket, if not two." I said very annoyed.

Bartu smiled, "We can eat on the road while we walk. And do not worry, I have enough food to last us long enough to get where we are going. And blankets. Oh, and lass, I am sure that you will not miss the baths here, once we get to where we are going."

Maru looked truly happy when she said, "Then let's get there already."

We quickly stuffed everything into my pack and I grabbed my sword and we made our way to the common room. All the shutters on the windows had been thrown open to let out the smoke and air the room. We heard horses and commanding voices outside, so we all peeked out the large window. There were eight horsemen in front of the inn. Darl was talking to them.

I held my breath and could easily spot the big man who had cut off Janus' nose. The man talking to Darl was the sorcerer who nearly caught me in my village.

The sorcerer was saying "... he's rather a tall lad, with dark hair."

Darl replied, "And was a girl with him?"

The sorcerer looked to the big man and he nodded, then the sorcerer said, "Yes, have you seen them?"

"Aye, I have, they're inside the inn now."

The sorcerer pulled a coin pouch from the folds in his robe and tossed it to Darl.

"Lead us to him," was all he said.

Darl smiled then headed for the door to the inn and waited for the men to get off their horses.

Bartu pulled me back quickly and quietly said, "Quick lad, take the girl out the back way through the kitchen, and get out of the town as fast as you can. Go to where you came into the village and stay hidden just off the road. And do not stop time no matter what, or else the robed guy will know you left and are on to him. Now go."

Maru and I raced out of the common room and through the kitchen. But just before we got out the back door, we bumped into Pitt, nearly knocking him over.

I cursed. I knew it wasn't wise to let anyone see us leaving, so I quickly pulled a silver coin from my pouch and handed it to Pitt, saying, "Don't tell anyone that we left this way, and if anyone asks, tell them we went to the market."

Pitt nodded, then we ran out the back, through a garden and down an alley leading to a lane with many shops. We walked quickly down the lane past the few early rising citizens, and ducked into an orchard when we saw that no one was watching us. We trespassed through the backs of some of the smaller houses of Finirton, and ran through farmers fields as we hit the edge of the town. A couple of dogs chased us and barked at us but we made our way around to the road where we had first entered Finirton.

We hid in a dense bush and had to wait an hour before we saw Bartu coming up the road, leading a heavily ladened horse.

I jumped up and waved. He took a quick look behind him, then waved for us to join him.

"Come on you two, we must travel far today. As I suspected, that group back there was not in town just to buy strawberries."

"Strawberries?" I asked.

"Long story lad. Here take this and follow me."

Bartu handed us each a chunk of bread and a strip of dried meat.

He left the road and led his horse up a steep bank. Maru and I looked at each other. Maru shrugged her shoulders, and then she followed Bartu up the bank. I hesitated on the road and said, "Strawberries?"

11

Ambush

Bartu had led us back into the hills that Maru and I had traveled through on our way to Finirton. Over the next few days we told Bartu all that had happened to us, from the time of the death of my uncle. He took in all we had to say silently.

We traveled quickly through the hills on a trail Bartu found. Maru and I had somehow missed it. Traveling it now, I found it hard to believe that it we could possibly have missed it. It was so obvious a feature of the landscape. I suspected that the trail had magically appeared after Maru and I left this area.

Eventually, we came to the part of the stream where I had washed my feet in the water. The trail was easily visible from here. I stopped and had to ask Bartu, "On our way to Finirton, Maru and I passed this very point, and traveled almost the very route we just came, yet we didn't see the trail we've been traveling on. How come?"

Bartu smiled and said, "I can not help it if you are blind lad."

Maru looked around and asked me, "Are you sure Einu? I don't remember this place."

"Sure you do," I said excitedly "See that rock?"

She nodded.

"Remember we were washing our feet there, and you kicked water in my face."

She looked hard then said, "I guess that could be the place. Rocks all look alike to me."

"It was."

Maru shrugged, and Bartu gave a laugh.

I looked to Bartu again and asked, "I'm not blind, so why didn't I see this trail?"

Bartu replied, "Lad, sometimes someone can not see the path they are on until they are actually on it."

"What?" I asked, not sure what he meant.

"Maybe you were so used to seeing just dense bush that the possibility there was a trail here escaped you. And since you were concentrating on getting somewhere, it made you blind to the easiest way there.

"And now that you are making your way to a different goal, traveling the same ground, the way is easier and more obvious."

"Huh?"

Bartu laughed again and said, "Forget it. You are probably just as blind as you are dumb."

"I'm not dumb," I said angrily.

Bartu gave a wide smile and said, "Einu, some people just do not know who they are. Look at yourself. A timestopper. You have a great gift and should have a better insight into the way the universe works, yet you do not even know who or what you really are. I bet that before your uncle died you had an inflated view of yourself, and since the death of your uncle you feel sorry for yourself, and believe that being a timestopper is now a burden."

It wasn't pleasant listening to Bartu voice my feelings.

"What makes you think that?" I asked suspiciously.

"Lad, you are an open book, available for anyone to read. You hide your feelings as well as a tree hides its leaves."

Maru laughed. She stood in front of me, looked me straight in the eye then kicked me in the shin.

"Come on let's get going, we've talked enough nonsense for one day."

Normally I would have stopped time and moved out of the way before coming to any harm, but Maru had caught me totally by surprise.

Bartu laughed and said, "Lad, you will have to have quicker wits than that if you are going to survive as a timestopper."

He continued to laugh as he walked down the trail. Maru followed. I rubbed my shin and sheepishly followed them.

Day followed day on the trail. The trail was never straight for very long. It slowly became obvious that the trail had evolved in four ways. The first was to take the path that was the most hidden from view. The second was to find the places that were the most scenic. And that we did. Waterfalls, sheer cliffs or ancient trees greeted us at every turn. The third was to always pass by water at frequent intervals. But the fourth was to take the easiest route as possible while fulfilling the first three conditions. This made for a longer journey but it was interesting and not that tiring.

Bartu didn't let us make a fire at night. Most of the food he brought was dried, why, was never fully explained. His standard reply was that it was the rule for this trail that no fires be lit on it.

After we had been on the trail for a week, Bartu would get up in the middle of the night and disappear back down the trail in the direction we had come from. He would be gone for a couple of hours, then return and roll himself up in his blanket and would be asleep again instantly.

Bartu never spoke of his night journeys. I was suspicious, and after the third night of his unknown activities, I had to ask, "Where have you been going at nights, Bartu?"

"Oh, so you have noticed me leaving? I thought that maybe you slept so soundly that nothing would wake you. But, lad, if I really wanted it so, you never would have noticed me coming or going.

"But as to where I was going, I was merely scouting."

"Scouting? At night? And wouldn't it be better to scout ahead, and not back where we have been?

"Good questions lad. Direct and to the point. I see that you might just have a brain in that head of yours after all."

Maru joined in the conversation, "You've been going somewhere at night?"

"Yes lass, as I have been saying to Einu here, I have been. Not that I expect you to have noticed. You sleep sounder than most bears and make more noise than one too."

Maru gave Bartu a deadly look.

I was glad not to be on the receiving end of that stare.

Bartu merely smiled and nodded his head yes, and this set Maru laughing. It was not the reaction I expected from her.

But before she could get too far into her merriment, Bartu said, "Shh, quiet lass, not so loud."

After a moment of silence in which we all listened to the sound of the wind and the animals in the trees, I quietly asked, "Why should Maru be quiet?"

"Not just her, but you as well, lad."

"Okay, why should we both be quiet?"

"Because we are being followed."

I looked around us and asked even quieter, "By whom?"

After a pause Bartu answered in an even quieter voice, "I do not know."

"Then how do you know we are being followed?"

"Listen," was all Bartu said.

We all stood and listened to the wind and the animals again.

"What are we listening for?"

"Can you not hear the complaints of the birds and the squirrels off to the rear and to the left of the trail?"

I heard only a vague rendition of what Bartu had described. Having grown up in a remote village set in the middle of a forest, I knew the sounds of complaints from the local animals. But I couldn't say this wasn't just normal animal noises.

"Not really. It hardly sounds like complaining."

"That is quite true, lad. But what you should be listening for is the sounds of the echoes of complaints."

"What?"

"It is quite simple, lad. When there is a disturbance in the forest, the animals close by the disturbance are usually dead quiet, but those that are at a safe enough distance are sending out warning signs to all the animals around. The animals that hear these warning sounds send out sounds of their own, but since they are far away from the disturbance they do not complain so urgently, nor do they signal as frequently. So they are in fact the echo of the warning sounds, and that is what you should be listening for."

I stood and listened, and in fact could hear calls that were a little more complaintive than those coming from animals in other directions. "How do you know that it's just not some big animal that's causing the disturbance?"

"Because that disturbance has been following us for the past few days, and has slowly been getting closer."

Fear gripped me.

"So for the past three days, I have been scouting back down the trail to find out who has been following us."

"Well, who is it?"

"I already told you lad, I do not know who it is."

"Well what have you found out then?"

"Plenty. More than I wanted to know. That is for sure."

I asked, "Like what?" to shake Bartu out of his silence. He was reluctant to divulge any more information.

"Well lad, whoever is following us is not using the trail," he said.

"So? Why is that such a big deal?"

"Well, let us just say that this trail *is* a bit special."

"So there *is* something about this trail that is different. Why didn't you tell me at the beginning?"

"I wanted you to figure it out for yourself, lad. This is a gnome trail."

He waved his hands up and down the trail for effect.

I thought I would see something different after Bartu's revelation, but it still looked like an ordinary trail.

"What's so special about it?" Maru asked.

"Ah, the beauty of a gnome trail, lass, is that the only way to find it is from one of the ends, it is virtually impossible to find from any other point. So we would appear to have disappeared off the face of the world, to anyone trying to find us, unless of course they were on the path as well. But of course they are not, so that leaves us with two possible pursuers."

"Who?" I asked anxiously.

"Either a gnome, or someone who is wise in the ways of magic."

"Which do you think it is?" Maru asked Bartu.

"Well, I doubt it is a gnome unless he was trying to scare us. I am sure he would try more direct methods than following us at a distance."

"Why couldn't it be a gnome?"

"Because lad, a gnome can walk through a forest without disturbing as much as an insect, let alone riling up a bunch of birds and squirrels. No, I suspect a sorcerer.

"Besides, I could not find a trace of a living creature following us.

"And only sorcery could hide the presence of a group as large as that following us."

"Group?" I said, even more nervous now. All I could think of was the sorcerer at my village and the army that was with him.

"Do not fret lad. If they have not found us by now, they probably will not find us before we get to where we are going."

It was hard not to be worried.

"And just where are we going anyway?" Maru asked.

"To find a gnome. Just where do you think a gnome trail leads to?"

"What should we do?" I asked.

"Just what we have been doing. Walk. But lad, if I were you, I would know the whereabouts of your sword."

Bartu put his finger to his nose then turned and walked on.

From that moment on I walked more cautiously, and was constantly turning to look behind us at the slightest noise. We were traveling as before. Bartu led the way. Maru was next leading the horse and I brought up the rear.

By that night I was more tired than at any time on the gnome trail, exhausted from worry.

I slept fitfully and woke regularly to listen. Bartu and Maru never woke once. It was near dawn when a deep sleep finally took me, but Bartu roused us earlier than usual and said, "We have to get to the gnome's cave before nightfall. We can make it if we go quickly and by taking turns riding the horse."

"What's the hurry?" I asked.

"Listen," was all he said.

I heard the usual pre-dawn racket from birds, but not too far in the distance I could hear the clamor of birds who were protesting the passing of unwanted visitors.

"They're coming," I said, looking at Bartu.

He nodded his head then quickly readied to leave.

I gathered my pack, and put it on the horse. Bartu ran in the lead. Next came Maru riding the horse and I jogged behind.

We kept up this pace until well after dawn. The sun was already high in the sky when Bartu called for a break. The horse was sweating and I was ready to fall over. Bartu must have heard me stumbling in the rear, because as soon as we stopped I threw myself onto the ground and closed my eyes.

Bartu threw some food on my chest to get my attention and then tossed me the water skin when I sat up.

"Eat. Drink. Then get on the horse, lad.

"We will have to go a little slower."

"I can run too," Maru said.

"I am sure you can lass. You have proved to be very hardy so far, but I was not thinking of you. I was thinking of the horse. He is already tired and Einu weighs a lot more than you do."

Maru smiled at Bartu, and he laughed back at her.

"Come on you two. That is long enough."

We continued on at a somewhat slower pace. Maru ran in front of the horse, which I rode at the rear. I was glad to be riding even though my horsemanship was not very good. The horse was keeping pace with Bartu without much prompting from me.

At noon we had another brief rest. This time Maru was glad to sit. Bartu, however, was unaffected by his morning run. He looked as fresh as ever.

After we ate and Bartu had checked the horse, we started out again. Bartu was in the lead, Maru led the horse, then I followed in the rear. And this time we walked. Bartu said it was to rest the horse.

We walked most of the afternoon without pausing. After a few hours Bartu climbed up onto the horse and quickened our pace. He stopped suddenly, dismounted, told us to stay put, and he went ahead a bit then came back.

"Get up on the horse lass. You will ride him for the rest of the day and if anything happens I want you to ride him as quick as you can and try to get to the top of the hills we are making for. They are called the bald hills. You can not miss them. And lad, we might have to run or fight, be ready for either. Just follow my lead."

I saw why Bartu had stopped. The forest came to an abrupt halt. The trail left the forest in a zig zag fashion, so as to be hidden to the casual observer, and then it virtually disappeared.

A grassland was in front of us and indeed was behind us as well. The forest we had just left was merely a point jutting off from a vast woodland that stretched out and away behind us.

There was a hint of a trail heading up to large hills in front of us. There was not much growing on them and steam rose up from various points among the hills.

We were now visible to anyone. The trail went through the deepest part of the grass, so that if we were just three feet tall, no one would have seen us. Maru sitting atop the horse, however, was very obvious.

AMBUSH

We followed Bartu toward the hills. The grass got shorter and shorter until it disappeared in places.

Pungent mists came and went, obscuring our vision and offending our noses.

We reached the hills. Bartu stopped and listened.

Rocks fell from the hill immediately in front of us. I looked up and there was a short strange man-like creature. He had large hands, a large head and a large nose. He was dressed in bright colors, green shirt and pants, a yellow vest, a red jacket and a pointed red hat.

He looked down and yelled, "You there, get out of my territory."

Without waiting for a reply he produced a long knife in his right hand and a club in his left hand, then ran towards us quicker than I thought those two small legs could carry him. He couldn't have been more than three feet tall.

I pulled out my sword, and readied to face the oncoming gnome.

Bartu turned and shouted to Maru, "Ride!!!" and hit the back of the horse. He pulled his own sword but turned his back toward the gnome.

Bartu had told me to follow his lead, but I couldn't bring myself to turn my back to the angry gnome.

I was just about to ignore Bartu and face the gnome alone, when Bartu moved into action. He ducked as he spun around and sliced his sword through the air where he had just been standing. I heard the sickening sound of a sword connecting solidly with flesh, and instantly there appeared a severed head and the body of a man in chainmail armor from whence it came. Head and body hit the ground, and Bartu spun around again alert for a sign of another unseen presence.

This was too much for me. I stopped time.

In the darkness of stopped time there were the lighter shapes of ten men who had been running towards us. They too were clad in chainmail. Some had swords, other axes.

Behind the soldiers the same blue dome-like wall that I had seen in the village was moving towards me, swallowing up the soldiers as it approached.

The gnome came up to my side and said, "Fighting them in stopped time won't help us boy. Start time again, and use your mind's eye to see them."

The gnome ran towards the dome and disappeared into it.

I started time again and saw the gnome dodging and diving around invisible foes. I saw him toss his club, and one of the soldiers appeared just before slumping to the ground.

Bartu was again swinging at an unseen opponent.

The gnome shouted at me, "Watch out."

I rolled to one side and jumped behind a large rock, while concentrating on the grass. I couldn't see anything, but in a flash I recalled a lesson from my uncle about using my mind's eye. Eyes can get in the way of seeing. I was to unfocus my eyes and try not to look at anything in particular, and a whole new world would open up to me.

I did just that, and could see the sword that was swinging for my neck. I lunged backwards and avoided the blow from the soldier who was trying to kill me.

I saw the rest of the soldiers and the sorcerer standing behind them. The soldiers were focused on killing Bartu and the gnome. Bartu was felling them one by one. The gnome made his way to the sorcerer and attacked him each time he made gestures in the air. The rest of the time the gnome was doing acrobatics to avoid the weapons of the other soldiers.

I couldn't watch Bartu or the gnome anymore because the soldier who had swung at me had come around the rock and was intent on slashing me with his sword.

I panicked and stopped time again. It didn't stop the soldier because we were both inside the blue dome. The sorcerer had run closer to me in his attempts to stay away from the gnome. Fortunately the edge of the dome was right behind me, and just as the soldier looked like he would hit me, I fell backwards through the blue barrier and he missed me. I scrambled the rest of the way out of the dome and was frustrated by not being able to see through the blue barrier. Just before I fell out Bartu was standing with his back to the dome wall. The barrier would be a hindrance to him, because if he passed through it he would stop in time, and possibly could be injured, by those within the dome who would still be in active time. I was torn as to what to do. It felt safer outside the dome ... the soldiers would not be able to harm me here ... yet Bartu was in danger. I wasn't a match for any of these soldiers yet there had to be a way to help him.

I knew deep down that if this sorcerer wasn't stopped now, then there wouldn't be a safe place for me anywhere. He would track me down eventually and catch me.

I felt a new resolve, that of a trapped animal.

It was me or him. I would have to become ruthless and devised a plan quickly.

I restarted time. The soldier was waiting for me. When he saw me he swung his sword and leapt at me. I raised my sword in defense and just as our swords met, I stopped time.

He was motionless. I had to kill him quickly and go help Bartu. But I hesitated. Killing a defenseless person stopped in time was something my uncle said was one of the worst sins a timestopper could commit.

I thought of my uncle and the village … the death that these soldiers brought … the sorcerer and his pursuit of me.

I acted.

The chainmail protecting the soldier's throat was easy to lift. I inserted my sword deep into his flesh, twisted the blade and withdrew it.

I moved back towards the barrier and started time, not wanting to see what happened to the soldier when time started again. I heard a gurgled noise of surprise then the loud thud as his body hit the ground.

I ran boldly up to one of the five remaining soldiers and slashed at him with my sword. My light weapon merely broke a few links on his armor and gave the soldier a shallow cut.

It surprised me how quick the soldier's reaction was. Only my own equally quick reaction saved me. I had tried to block his sword with my own and his sword hit the flat of my own, pushing it up against my chest and pushing me back.

By instinct I had stopped time. But since we were within the dome, nothing happened to the soldier.

The momentum of the soldier's blow carried me back into a backwards somersault. The soldier had carried through with his slash and cut through my shirt and left a minor gash on my side before I could fully get away.

It didn't slow me. I came to my feet again, ran towards the barrier and started time again. The barrier vanished and I ran to a point that had been beyond the barrier then turned to face the oncoming soldier. I had easily outrun him. He was in armor and my legs were longer than his.

My trap was to wait for him to pass through the barrier and then stop time again. It seemed to take him forever to get to me.

He raised both his hands above his head, sword gripped tightly, prepared to smite me with all the force he could muster.

I stopped time, but for some reason he kept coming. The barrier was behind me. The size of the dome had increased to envelope us both. The sorcerer smiled as he watched me.

The world went upside down for me, as it had after fighting the Time Beast. I saw myself in a different place. Strange images of a wife and children and a safe place to live passed by me. I wanted to be there, but dying would never let it happen.

With this place came a new knowledge and a new sense of determination.

I reacted by leaping forward and bringing the point of my sword to the soldier's chest. Our combined momentum caused my sword to pass deep into him.

But I didn't escape unscathed. The soldier's arms came down and the hilt of the sword hit me on the head. All I remember was the pain and the feeling of the soldier falling on top of me.

I passed out and felt nothing more.

12

Cliff

I awoke and with a sudden fear, quickly came to a sitting position. My head felt as if it had been split in two.

Maru pushed me gently back down onto a soft bed of quilted cushions.

My face was sticky with my own blood. Maru was washing it off. There was a plaster on the cut at my side.

"Stay still, Einu," Maru said angrily.

"Sorry. I thought we were still outside," I replied in my defense.

"Wanting to fight some more, right? Wanting to act like the hero, were you? What were you thinking? And of course it is up to the woman to bandage the brave hero after the battle isn't it? See to Einu is all they said after they carried you here. What if you had died, then where would I be? You didn't think of that did you? Did you?"

I lay back, taking the barrage of words that were coming from Maru. In a way I wished to be back outside fighting. It was much simpler than trying to come up with a response to Maru's angry words.

"No ... I didn't ... I didn't have time to think about anything. Actually I was trying to stay alive as best as I could."

Maru quietly fumed as she finished cleaning my wound and then wrapped my head with some linen that had been steeped in some herbal concoction.

I looked around. We were in a large room. The walls, floor and ceiling were all solid rock. The surfaces were all highly polished, and the multitude of colors in them was astonishing. It was well lit by a large fire burning in an immense fireplace and by many torches around the room. The fireplace had two small holes in the wall near the floor. I later discovered that these were air holes that led to the outside.

The furnishing were all very small, except for two large chairs and one tall narrow table.

The room was full of scents. Fresh herbs were hanging on racks to one side of the fireplace. The cushions I was on gave off a floral scent. And in the fire place was a wood that burned with multiple colors and gave off a smell like some deep forgotten forest.

I kept my gaze to the ceiling because Maru got upset at me for moving my head too much.

Even the ceiling was amazing. It was perfectly smooth but shaped into a perfect dome. The different rocks that made up the ceiling made strange patterns. Smoke from the fireplace and the torches made its way up to the dome. Staring at smoke and stone made me uneasy. That strange tug came again, calling me to some other place.

Shrugging it off, I broke the silence. It was apparent that Maru was going to stay quiet. "I don't remember what happened. Is Bartu okay? And the gnome?"

"They're okay," she said when she was finished ministering to me. She got up and went over to a pot hanging by a small iron bar in the fireplace. She removed the lid and ladled some of the contents into two small bowls and brought them back to where I lay. She helped me sit up and said, "Eat, it'll help you get your strength back."

I ate and became stronger with each mouthful of this wonderful stew. It was hard to identify anything in it, but it more than satisfied my hunger.

"What happened after the soldier hit me on the head?"

Maru stopped eating and said, "You're lucky to be alive, you know that don't you?"

I nodded my head, stopping when it complained about being moved.

"Well, after Bartu shouted 'ride,' it took me a little while to get control of the horse because of the slap he gave it. I eventually stopped and watched what was going on. But up until you were knocked unconscious I had a hard time following what was happening. Everytime I blinked the scene changed completely. I didn't see you being knocked out, but did see you run, then turn and face the soldier that was chasing you. The next thing you're lying on the ground underneath him. I thought you were dead.

"Well, at that moment the sorcerer ran to where you were lying. The gnome followed closely behind him, and two soldiers followed the gnome.

"Bartu was left to fight the two remaining soldiers.

"The sorcerer got to you first and pulled out an amulet from his pocket. He obviously wanted to put it on you but the gnome jumped at the sorcerer and hit him with his feet and knocked him away from you. Then the soldiers tried to hit the gnome. One had an ax and one had a sword. But he dodged them like nothing I had ever seen before. They swung their weapons but always just missed by a whisker's width.

"Meanwhile the sorcerer had recovered and was just about to put the amulet on you when the gnome did a flip through the air and swung his sword and caught the loop of the chain with his sword and ripped it from the sorcerer's grasp. He then flung the amulet high into the air, away from the sorcerer.

"When the amulet landed there was a loud noise, smoke and a bright flash of light. The sorcerer screamed. He pulled a rod out from his robes and he vanished in a bright flash of light that streaked away across the sky, faster than I could follow.

"The remaining soldiers weren't as keen to fight after that. The gnome had cut one of them on the leg as he had rolled past, and had slit the same soldier's throat in another slash of his sword, when he jumped back past him again.

"The other one started to run but the gnome threw his sword and it lodged in the soldier's back and he fell, screaming.

"When the amulet landed with such a loud noise, the two soldiers fighting Bartu turned to see what had happened.

"But Bartu ignored the noise and killed both of them on the same stroke. I came back and Bartu carried you here. The gnome told me to care for you, and gave me bandages, cloth and a bowl for water. So that's what happened, are you satisfied now?"

I had listened with great interest to Maru's story. But more amazing to me than the story was how quickly she had spoken in telling the tale. She can talk without the need for taking many breaths. Hearing her speak quickly without hearing her take in any new air left me feeling the need to inhale for her.

Before there was a chance to reply to Maru or ask her anything else, Bartu and the gnome came through an ornate door that was designed to look like part of the wall. It was made of wood but it was painted to continue the patterns in the wall around it.

Bartu came in and sat by the fire.

"Good to see you well, lad," he said as he smiled at me.

I smiled back at him. He appeared to be much like his old self, although more tired.

The gnome went to the pot then got some stew for himself and Bartu.

"That was a good workout," Bartu said as he relaxed on a cushion by the fire and ate some of the stew.

"You're getting old. You took way too long to kill the hired help."

"Hired? They were professional soldiers, not untrained whelps, I tell you."

"Ah, you're just looking for an excuse, they were all just puppies, I say to you."

"Excuse me," I said.

"You can excuse yourself if you want," the gnome replied, "the door is right over there."

He pointed to the door by which he and Bartu had entered.

"That's not what I meant."

"Well what did you mean?" the gnome said with a sharp tone.

I was unsure what to make of this strange character.

"I ... uh ..."

It wasn't easy to think clearly under the scrutiny of the gnome.

"Speak up. Speak up. I don't want to guess at what you might want to say. Just say what you mean and mean what you say, as my granddad always said."

"I just wanted to get your attention," I said after a moment of silence.

"Well, I would say you have it lad," Bartu said.

72

The gnome was glaring at me so hard that he looked like he was about to strike me.

I meekly said, "Well, I was just wondering what happened to the sorcerer?"

The gnome burst into laughter. Bartu broke into a large smile as he looked at me then the gnome.

When the gnome quieted down somewhat I asked, "I just want to know, what the strange light was when he disappeared?"

The gnome looked like he was going to burst his buttons on his vest as his small pot belly was moving up and down at a furious pace.

When he had finished laughing I said, "What's so funny then?"

"Einu, if that had been a sorcerer, you would not be sitting here talking to me right now," the gnome said, the wide grin still on his face.

"He was a sorcerer, I saw him doing magic at my village. He even cast a spell on me, and I couldn't move properly."

"That was but an apprentice to the sorcerer Malux. A whelp barely worth bothering with. So don't be trying to scare me with stories of sorcerers when there were none about. I've killed my share of sorcerers in my day. Why even your father and I killed the sorcerer who trained Malux in the ways of magic. It took me years to recover from that one, so don't try to tell me what's what," the gnome said.

The gnome laughed a bit when he saw my astonished look, then continued, "But as to what happened to him. He had a device which cast a spell of return. He went home by magical means."

I digested that bit of information for a few seconds then blurted out, "You knew my father? How come I never heard about this? Why didn't my uncle say anything?"

The gnome scrutinized me for a moment.

"Who are you?" I added.

"Quite right. Quite right. I will tell you everything you need to know, but first, we haven't been formally introduced this time. The name is Cliff."

"Cliff?? That's an odd name."

"Not among gnomes lad," Bartu added, "They commonly give names that have something to do with rocks."

"That's right. My mum gave me that name when she stopped my dad from throwing me off a cliff after I was born."

"What? Why would he want to do that?" Maru said with obvious disbelief.

"Well, my dad said he had too many children, and he didn't need another one, and since I was the sixth child by his sixth wife, he was totally justified."

"I can't believe you're saying this," Maru said with vigor, "Why was he justified in killing his son, even if it was his thirty-sixth child?"

"Well under gnome laws, he was bound to have to start a new clan, and that was a very expensive and huge undertaking. It involved moving the entire family to a new place to live, where no gnome has lived before. He had to build a gnome's home, and that could take many many years to finish. My dad was already pushing three hundred years old at my birth, and it would probably would have taken the rest of his natural existence to finish the home. That was why he was anxious to get rid of me."

"But obviously he didn't kill you. So what happened."

"Oh what a bright lad," the gnome said sarcastically, "Well, my mother managed to stop him. It was quite a fight. She had to break both his arms before he would stop trying, and actually stop to listen to her. Then she convinced him to let me live among some of my mother's cousins. They told me while growing up that I was an orphan. It wasn't until later when I started to court one of my half-sisters that the ugly truth came out. I caused quite the scandal and had to leave my home and I became a wanderer. I teamed up with a few timestoppers just for something to do. Your father was one of the best. Relentless he was, but stubborn too, that's what got him in the end. Your uncle was more practical, he led a quiet life, and took it on himself to train you, after your father died. But your uncle was better than your father ever was. He understood what it meant to be a timestopper, whereas your father only thought he knew. It was strange how your father always managed to do the right thing, even though he didn't understand why. In the end he guessed wrong and was killed by Malux. He thought he could kill the apprentice by himself, after we had killed his master. But Malux was a tricky one, and now it has come to you to kill him. He is one of the last truly powerful sorcerers and with his death, the world can finally be free of magical overlords."

"Me? Why do I have to kill him?"

"Well, if revenge is not good enough for you then you will have to search your soul to find the reason why."

"How can I be expected to kill a sorcerer? When I couldn't even kill his apprentice or his apprentice's soldiers for that matter."

Cliff answered through a wild smile, "That's where Bartu and I come in. Don't worry Einu, we will train you. Oh yes, we will train you."

The way he said that was ominous.

"Just what do you think your name means anyway?"

"No one has ever told me."

"Einu, it means 'the one' in the old tongue. Your father named you not knowing what it meant either, but he always did the right thing."

I stared at the fire in the fireplace and felt trapped. Trapped by a fate that was beyond my understanding. It felt unavoidable, but instead of accepting the words that Cliff had been saying, rebellion grew in my heart.

"What if I don't want to kill anybody. Surely my uncle didn't want me to find a gnome so that he could train me to kill a sorcerer," I said defiantly.

"Well firstly, you didn't find just any gnome. You found me, Cliff, friend of your father. Of all the gnomes, I know the most about timestoppers and sorcerers. I have traveled much among you tall ones, and understand your quirky ways. So I am the best possible gnome that you could have found.

"But if you are not interested in fulfilling your destiny, I will wait for the next one to come along to take your place. So you're free to go anytime you want."

Freedom came with those words. I no longer had any destiny and didn't have to do anything if I didn't want to.

"But of course there is no telling how long it will take before another timestopper will come along who is willing to finally rid this world of evil sorcerers," Cliff said.

Cliff looked as innocent as a newborn child as he spoke.

"My mother always tried to make me feel guilty, so that argument will not work on me. I was unable to exact revenge on my mother's killers, so how do you expect me to avenge the death of a man that I barely knew? My father was gone most of my life, he died before I had a chance to get to know him."

"Well, boy, from what you have told me, there really is no good reason to get Malux. But fate is a funny thing. One rarely knows what one's fate is, but when someone does find out, then that person usually tries to avoid it at all costs, just to prove that they have free will. It's a waste of energy really. Take a deep look at yourself, and ask yourself if you believe that you have free will. And if you find that the answer is yes, then ask yourself if you should go ahead and rid the world of Malux. Why waste a window of opportunity that has arisen? The circumstances that led to your birth will never be repeated. You and you alone are the right person to kill Malux.

"On the other hand, if you exercise your free will and chose not to kill him, then he will probably die a natural death. But before he dies, he will have the opportunity to train many apprentices like the one that almost got you. They will become like Malux, and your choice will make it harder for future generations to rid the world of the evil that is on this world.

"The window that is open for you is showing you that evil is at the weakest it has been for a millennia. Why give it an opportunity to grow? Act now. Make your choice. It is yours to make."

He looked hard at me before continuing, "But if you do make a choice, be clear about it, because the clearer you are about a choice before you make it, the easier it is for you. But if you waver and are unsure about what is you want to do, before you do it, the harder it will be for you."

Cliff's words washed over me like the tide. The choice was mine to make. The memory of a wife with children came to me again. It seemed that this would never be unless I went through with the task ahead of me. Staring at Maru I wondered if it was she who was the woman in my vision. She smiled at me, and I resolved to do it. It didn't require any more thought. There was no doubt about accomplishing my goal. It would take some time to prepare, but in the end it would be quite easy.

"Good boy, Einu. You are a quick learner. You can do it as long as you keep this feeling in mind," Cliff said.

"How did you know what I was thinking?" I asked, taken aback.

"You're an open book boy. Besides I've seen that look of conviction and confidence hundreds of times before," Cliff added.

"And I will look forward to teaching you how to finally use that pig sticker that you call a sword, and make it something that is dangerous in your hands," Bartu said with a laugh.

"Well, it looks like we're going to be here for a while, so where can a girl take a bath? I thought that you mentioned something about that on our way here, Bartu, did you not?"

Bartu and Cliff broke out in roar of laughter. Cliff walked to a back wall and opened another hidden door, and said, "This way young one, there is a hot spring down this passageway that I think you'll find to your liking."

Maru grabbed a small blanket and followed Cliff through the door.

Bartu looked at my bandages and said, "She does good work."

He looked at the rest of my body as if trying to see what I was capable of.

"Well, as soon as you are healed, you will be made into a fighter. Cliff will probably talk your ear off, so take the opportunity to rest now. You will not have much in the future.

"Oh, and by the way, you owe me two gold pieces."

Bartu smiled, got up, grabbed his sword and went back through the first door, leaving me to wonder at all that had happened. I never really said what my intentions were, and yet everyone acted as if all had been said out loud.

Right at this moment I wanted to be comforted and told that everything would be all right.

But since there was no one to do this for me, I curled up in a blanket … and went to sleep.

13

Training

Everyone left me on my own to heal and it was not long before I was. They kept busy during this time but wouldn't let me go anywhere or do anything. Maru took to the habit of having long baths, being gone for a minimum of two hours each day at the hot spring. She did the cooking but wouldn't talk to me while she was preparing the food. We did eat our meals together however, but that was the only time we were all together. No one ever stayed for long. Maru got Cliff to show her how to play with crystal bowls that he had made. Bartu went outside a lot to practice something and Cliff always had something to do. I was going crazy doing nothing.

So one day after Maru had gone to take a bath, I decided to take a walk outside. Cliff's home was underground, and it was driving me crazy to not see the sun for so long.

The door to the outside opened inward and led to a smooth, straight corridor to a dead end. There was a very small hole in the left wall which offered the only source of light. There was a torch holder but it was empty. I entered the corridor, but I worried about the door.

It was built to close naturally if left unattended. I thought it wise to leave it ajar because I couldn't figure out how to open it from the other side, but Cliff would complain if something was left in the doorway to keep it open.

The door closed behind me and it was dark going to the other end of the corridor.

The corridor ended at a flat wall, but my finger found a small circular indent. I pressed my fingers down and this caused a door to slowly swing towards me.

It was even darker on the other side of the door for it was a natural cave. The opening to the outside world was in the distance. The light coming into the cave barely illuminated the doorway.

The cave had a different smell to it than Cliff's home, which was always that of a fresh herbs. This cave smelled moldy and the air was damp and cold.

The door closed behind me. A primal fear gripped me. Something was watching me here and it was enormous. I wanted to get outside. So I made my way forward towards the light.

I stopped, and my heart nearly with me, when a large stone fell and cracked as it hit the cave floor. It was hard to tell where it fell. The sound echoed throughout the cave, and took some time to die out. High pitched squeaking noises started all around me. It had to be bats, I tried to assure myself.

That thought did nothing to stave off panic. If it were not for the light, I'd be sure to be screaming and running around frightened.

As if right on cue, the light faded to almost nothing. The sun must have gone behind a big black cloud to make such a drastic difference.

Then another rock fell, sending echoes dancing all around me. The squeaks were louder.

I stopped time, figuring that whatever was in this cave would be frozen, and my escape would be easy.

Instead, voices echoed. Some seemed close, some seemed far, but all were whispering. There were too many to distinguish what was being said. The sound was eerie, and an uncontrollable urge to run came over me.

I started time again, and managed to take a step. Then another and another. I sped up and quickly stumbled through the dark towards the dim light in the distance then stubbed my toe and fell. I scrambled on all fours before getting up and running.

It was now easier to see. The entrance was in sight.

But just before getting there, something dark jumped out at me from some hidden cranny.

I screamed in fear and instantly thought of a Time Beast.

Cursing for having forgotten my sword, I tried to run past the creature. But it stopped and said, "You make enough noise to stir my ancestors' bones, you do."

It was Cliff.

"And it certainly took you enough time to leave my home and come out to play."

I had stopped running the moment Cliff spoke then turned and snapped at him, "Are you trying to scare me to death? What were you trying to do anyway?"

"I've just been waiting for you."

"What do you mean?"

"To begin your training. Or have you forgotten already?"

"No. I have to admit that my thoughts lately are of nothing else. When are we going to start?"

"You started the moment you passed through my door. We couldn't begin until you were ready."

"How did you know if I was ready?"

"You wouldn't have ventured outside unless you were feeling better. So unless you have some better questions, let's go outside and find Bartu, so you can improve your swordmanship."

"Tell me first, what were you doing to me in the cave?"

"Me? Nothing. Why?" Cliff said innocently.

"While time was stopped, I heard voices …"

"Voices, was it?" Cliff interrupted me, "What kind of voices?"

"Well, it sounded like many different voices. They were all whispering something I couldn't make out."

"Ah, so you finally heard the voices. I was beginning to wonder if you were ever going to hear them. Bartu and I were beginning to think that there was something the matter with you."

"Why?"

"Because most timestoppers start to hear the voices when they are a lot younger than you. I don't know of any timestopper that went fourteen winters before hearing the voices. Didn't your uncle ever mention them?"

"Not really … but he did ask me about voices when I was really young. Yes, he asked me if I heard anyone talking when time stopped. I said no, and he just shrugged and said something like, 'I'm sure that you'll tell me when you start to hear them.' But that's about it."

I stood in thought for a moment before continuing, "So just what are these voices?"

"It's your collective species consciousness talking between the moments. It's how you know things about how to be human, and its also how your species discusses the rules of your collective reality agreement." Cliff said with a look of total seriousness.

"*What*???"

"Yes, you're right, it's a little early for you to understand that concept. Instead of trying to understand what they are, you should just try to listen to the voices for a while. But before you do, make sure that your mind is quiet, or else you will just interfere with your attempts at listening."

"Now you sound like my uncle."

Cliff smiled at me then said, "But enough … enough chit chat, boy. Outside with you and I'll get your sword. Bartu's been waiting to get you under his *patient hand* for the past week. So … go … GO!"

I moved slowly out of the cave entrance and felt a sharp sting on my rear. Cliff had flicked a small piece of leather to make me move faster. He took a step forward and I ran from the cave.

The sun came out from behind the cloud, and the world turned brighter instantly. It was a wonderful late spring day. The promise of a hot summer was in the air. Most of the trees had their leaves. The flowers sent a delicious smell of life through the air. I took a deep breath and forgot all about Cliff's home. Everything out here was alive. In the gnome's home the same smells were present but it was more just a memory of all that was alive.

There were steams rising all around the hills and occasionally a waft of moist air drifted by. Cliff had explained that he lived near some hot springs. He said places where earth, water, fire and air met were magical places, and everyone should spend some serious time living near them to hear the music that was produced. The location of the springs were not readily apparent. My attention was focused on finding them when a sharp point jabbed me in the back. I stopped time and turned. It was Bartu. He had put his sword against my back.

I started time.

"Lad, you should not be looking at the clouds until you know you are in a safe place. I could have put my sword half way through you before you knew what was happening."

"Isn't this a safe place?" I laughed at him.

"I am serious, lad. You have to realize that there might not be any safe places on this world any more, now that Malux knows about you."

It was hard to become worried on such a marvelous day. It was something about being outdoors after being underground for such a long time that made me lose some of my previous sensibilities. Nothing could make me worry. I was alive, enjoying being so, and nothing could stop me from being that way.

But at that moment another dark cloud moved in front of the sun, and the world looked duller. Bartu looked somewhat sad. But he quickly perked up to his usual self again and said, "Where is your sword, lad? We have much to learn today. I want to give you at the very least, the basics about holding a sword, so that you can look like you know what you are doing when you are fighting."

"Cliff said he was going to get it and bring it out for me."

Bartu laughed.

The cause of his laughter was not obvious until he said, "Well I would check your sword carefully before you use it, lad. Gnomes are notorious tricksters."

"Nonsense. That's merely a falsehood that you humans tell in order for others to mistrust gnomes," Cliff said as he appeared beside me.

"Nonsense yourself. What about those snakes that you put in my bed roll?" Bartu answered back.

"I was merely testing your awareness, my friend."

"And the generous portion of salt in my porridge?"

"Merely an attempt to broaden you sensory perception," Cliff snapped back.

"And the grubs in my cap?"

"I explained that one to you in great detail. There wasn't anything to put them in, so I used your hat only as a temporary container, until a better one could be found."

Bartu laughed again, then turned to me and said, "And be careful what you ask a gnome as well. They have answers for every questions that you could possibly think of ..."

"And more than you can think of," Cliff interrupted.

" ... but the answers you get rarely make sense," Bartu continued.

"Of course they wouldn't make sense to a thick thinker like yourself."

"Well, sometimes thick thinking can get you through some situations better than being too quick with your thoughts."

"You always manage to bring your conversations back to your wives, don't you? And you always have to remind me of my failure to marry the only female that would tolerate me."

I stood confused at the conversation. At first I had followed it, but eventually lost where it was going.

Cliff noticed this and said, "Bartu has a strange way of dealing with women. He pretends that he's dumb and gets them to do everything for him. He thinks that very clever. He was so good at it and he liked it so much that he married more than one woman and left them in different towns. But of course they found him out and their relatives banded together and tried to kill him. He managed to escape intact but he can't show his face in either town any longer. That's where thick thinking gets you."

Bartu then said, "But at least I can hold my tongue. Our famous gnome here, as you know, was going to marry one of his half-sisters, when he figures out his true heritage. What does he do? Instead of keeping quiet, he tries to force his father to acknowledge him. His father, of course, denied his heritage and tried to kill him again. Cliff evaded his father then tried to escape with his half-sister so they could marry anyway. But he was caught, and the rest of his family tarred and feathered him, before they ran him out of their home. Very quick thinking that was."

"Bartu, you just do not understand us. If I had pulled it off, I would have gained much prestige among gnomes, but alas, that is all spilled water under my bridge now."

"I think the two of you are ridiculous," Maru said.

She was standing ten feet away. I had not noticed her join us. First Bartu, then Cliff, now Maru, they all had somehow approached without me noticing.

"How can a women understand what a man is going through when a women is involved?" Bartu said with a serious face.

"What kind of nonsense is that? Men were all born dense. None of you make any sense, and sometimes I feel that there is no way to breach that fence that divides us," Maru said emphasized with a serious look.

Cliff said, "Not bad. I'll have to teach you some more subtle usage of your words, my dear. But we've wasted enough time bantering. Come, let us leave these two to do some serious fighting."

Cliff placed my sword on the ground by a bush. Maru smiled and then walked away with the gnome.

Bartu was smiling as well, as he watched the two of them leaving.

I picked up my sword warily, remembering Bartu's earlier warning. The scabbard had slightly crushed a small strawberry plant. I picked a few strawberries off the plant and offered one to Bartu.

He laughed and said, "Going to take up sorcery as well, lad?"

"I don't understand."

"Sorcerers use strawberries in their spell casting, lad. They use them to create a space around them that timestoppers can not affect."

"Oh."

After finishing the strawberries I asked, "So just how does magic work?"

"I do not pay as much attention to detail as does Cliff. You should really ask him that question, but if you want my opinion ... magic works because the sorcerer wants it to."

"What kind of an answer is that."

"It was only my opinion, but if you want to find out more, either ask Cliff, or ask a sorcerer."

"I'll ask *Cliff*."

"But not right now. What I want you to do now is hold your sword up and defend yourself."

I pulled my sword out of the scabbard and to my surprise the blade was red.

Bartu laughed as I examined my sword closer. It smelled of strawberries. Cliff must have smeared some on the blade, and from the smile that Maru gave before she left, she must have known about it as well.

When Bartu had stopped laughing and after wiping it on the grass, I held my sword in front of me at an angle relative to the ground, with the point slightly raised to the sky. Bartu took two steps away from me, turned and lunged with his sword towards me, slightly twisting his blade. It slid along mine and curled around it. My sword flew from my hand and the tip of his blade stopped within a hair's length of my throat.

I stopped time. In a real fight my death would have been certain. I stepped back, picked up my sword then went behind Bartu and put it on his shoulder, before restarting time.

Bartu immediately said, "Okay let us try that again. Only this time I will tell you how to hold your sword first. Stand straight and hold your sword out."

He stood beside me and straightened my arm out.

"Hold the sword level to the ground, and make sure that your elbow is pointing straight down to the ground."

I did this, but he still wasn't happy.

"Make sure your palm faces up. Hold the sword so that it points out straight from your body. Again make sure that it stays level to the ground. Okay now hold that position."

He moved in front of me.

"Now always keep the point of your sword pointing at the center of my body. This time I will lunge at you again, but much slower. Keep your sword perfectly level while you turn your wrist until your palm faces down. Remember to keep your elbow always facing down towards the ground. Now let us try it."

Bartu slowly moved his sword forward, sliding it along mine. As his sword moved forward. I turned my wrist. His sword deflected down and off to my right.

I was amazed at how easy it was.

"That was simple."

"It is easy once you know what you are doing, but if I suspected that you knew something about sword fighting, and seeing you hold your sword just like you did would be a good hint, then I would not aim for your throat. Instead I would aim for your hand. If you can not hold onto your sword, you can not defend yourself."

Bartu smiled, "You let your elbow move too much when you twisted your wrist. Keep it towards the ground."

I repeated the movement while he talked.

"That is better. Practise this until sundown. Hold your sword out and turn your wrist back and forth. Good. I will be back later."

He walked away leaving me to practise this simple move, but after a while my arm started to hurt and it was getting hard to turn it.

The sun had hardly moved in the sky, and already it was hard to continue on.

I lay down to watch the clouds then lost myself completely in the intricacy of the clouds' movements.

They pulled at me and I saw them with a deep clarity of vision.

I was no longer a single entity and felt a complete duality of being rush over me. I was no longer just Einu lying here watching these clouds but I was someone else at the same time watching clouds in a different place and in a different sky.

I could almost be that other person. But a sudden fear of losing myself came over me. A voice said, "Watching clouds is dangerous boy."

It was Cliff.

"They can take you to distant places if you let them. I don't think you're ready for that ... yet," he said with all seriousness.

He stood over me for a moment. I sat up and then Cliff laughed.

"What's so funny?"

"I was just imagining what Bartu would do to you if he found you lazing about. When he sets a task for someone and they don't do it, he can get quite upset. If you think your uncle was a hard task master, just wait until you run afoul of Bartu. He already feels that you wasted enough time just lying around my home. He wanted to start your training the day after the fight, but I convinced him that you were not mentally ready for his training. He never would have accepted the excuse that you were not physically ready, wounds or no wounds.

"So boy, you have me to thank for the holiday that you just had, but now is the time to bear down and finish the task ahead of you. So up with you and get back to waving your sword around through the air."

I got slowly up and began to repeat the movements that Bartu had taught me.

Cliff stood and watched me for a while before he said, "It's okay to talk if you want. In fact it would probably enhance your ability if you performed your sword movements without thinking about them, while we discussed other matters. Do you have anything that you want to ask me?"

It was my turn to laugh. Thousands of questions went through my mind.

"Yes, but I do not know what I should ask first."

"The person who can not ask a question when he has the chance, is lost, my boy."

I remembered my earlier conversation with Bartu about strawberries and magic.

But what came out of my mouth was, "What is magic?"

"Magic is the extension of the sorcerer's will, using the energy from the environment to sustain that will."

"Huh?"

"It's very simple. But let me use terms and situations that you are familiar with to explain it to you."

He smiled then asked me, "How do you stop time?"

"I don't know. I just do."

"Well I'll answer you. But don't stop your sword movements."

I had paused to better concentrate on what Cliff was about to say, but continued when he reminded me not to stop.

"Well you stop time because you will it to stop. You use your own energy to maintain your will. That is why you get tired if time is stopped for a long time and as you have noticed, it is more tiring if you initiated the stoppage in time than if another timestopper had initiated it."

"Okay."

"But now imagine if you could use the energy of an object to stop time instead of using your own energy. You wouldn't get tired and the object you had chosen would be used up. And when the object was totally used, then time would start again."

"So why don't timestoppers use objects to stop time?"

"Because they are not sorcerers and can not do magic."

"Okay then, why don't sorcerers stop time?"

"Because they would use up most of the matter in the universe casting such a spell. The energy requirements to cast a spell to stop all other things in the universe except the sorcerer are incalculable."

"I don't understand. If sorcerers and timestoppers both do what they do by will, but sorcerers use the energy of objects and timestoppers use their own energy, how come timestoppers can stop time? Why don't they run out of energy. Or are we so powerful?"

Cliff looked at me with all seriousness and said, "You are that powerful. Don't you know the source of your energy?"

"No."

"When you stop time, you tap into a natural ability of all intelligent beings. The ability to tap into a higher state of being. With timestoppers though, all the natural barriers of going into such a state are almost non-existent. When you are in such a state you can tap into the energy of thought. Not just your thoughts but that of all beings, especially that of your own species. So the source of your energy comes from the thoughts of all other humans. That is indeed an awesome source of power. This power is contained within yourself. Do not get a big head on those shoulders though. This power is within everyone. You just have no barriers in being able to tap into it."

"Oh."

I moved my sword back and forth for a while, letting what Cliff had said sink in then asked, "But explain to me what the strange blue dome of the sorcerer's apprentice was and what it has to do with strawberries?"

"Well sorcerers could never be able to duplicate the ability of a timestopper by using magic the way they understand it, but neither could they let themselves be vulnerable to any timestopper that wanted to get rid of them, so they developed spells that protect themselves from the effects of time stoppages. They developed spells that affect their local environment, and are triggered by the stoppage of time.

"If time stops, their spell kicks in and they are encased in a shell that is not affected by the time stoppage. It just so happens that one of the main components to power this spell is strawberries."

"Why strawberries?"

"It doesn't have to be strawberries. It could be anything but sorcerers are so scared to try new combinations once they find a working one. It just happened that the first sorcerer to find the 'local time doesn't stop' spell, used strawberries. So sorcerers have been using them ever since."

This explanation satisfied me.

Cliff smiled at me while my sword moved through the air. His smile invited me to ask more questions.

My mind wandered back to earlier in the day and to the voices.

"Cliff, I know you told me not to think about it, but I can't help myself. Can't you tell me more about the voices that I heard when time was stopped?"

"I already did."

"What? I don't understand."

Cliff grinned then said, "I just told you that timestoppers have no barriers to joining to a higher state, and because of that you have access to the thoughts of all the others in your species. These thoughts will sound like independent voices to you."

"Oh … OH! I understand."

"Do you? You really haven't heard them long enough to really understand. Listen for a while and then you will truly understand. But be careful. Some timestoppers are driven crazy by the voices. You've already met a timestopper that was driven crazy."

I thought of Caines.

"No it wasn't Caines. He's not quite insane. He just wants to stop the voices by killing every other timestopper. No, I'm talking about the Time Beast. He only appeared to be a beast in the mind of all others. He was really just a human who couldn't handle hearing the voices of every other human and just wanted them to stop. He was seeking another timestopper to place his consciousness into at the same time it is in his own body, to act as a shield from the voices. The voices stop when one lives a duality."

I remembered when the Time Beast towered over me, and now knew what had been happening to me. I shuddered, for the madness of the Beast could have become my own.

My sword now moved back and forth almost as if on its own. I stared off into the distance and looked at my existence differently now. It was an amazing day. So much had happened. I had a notion that days like this would become normal and the simple days of my youth would never return.

My enthusiasm from earlier in the day was now completely gone. My armed burned with fatigue. I turned to ask Cliff if I was finished, but he was gone.

As if in answer to my question, Maru approached.

When she was close enough she said, "Well, are you coming in or not?"

My sword dropped to my side.

The sun went down behind a distant hill and we were plunged into shadow. It was strange to feel time move so fast. I could have sworn only a few moments had passed since Cliff started to talk to me.

I smiled at Maru, and said, "Yes."

14

Eighteen

Time did indeed go by fast. Four years had passed since my arrival at Cliff's home. In that time many strange creatures and people that called Cliff friend came to visit. There were some regulars, who came once a month. Some younger gnome cousins came with food supplies and plenty of fresh herbs that Cliff waited for anxiously.

There were some that came once a year. Forest sprites brought strange roots and plants that Cliff quickly hid in one of the many cellars that he had. In exchange for these roots and plants, Cliff gave the sprites bowls that he made from crushed crystals, that when touched correctly with smoothed sticks made a wondrous sound. It sounded like the bowls actually sang. Cliff called these sounds the voices of the earth. Maru had become very proficient at playing these bowls and occasionally played for all of us.

The most interesting of all were those who came only once. There were many humans who would normally be dismissed as either rogues or beggars. There were those who looked like wildmen, and at the opposite end of the spectrum were two fully armed knights with their squires. All of these proved to be interesting to talk to. Their stories were amazing.

There were also those who were frightening to look upon. Beasts that talked some strange language. Some had huge horns, and some large teeth. In spite of their differences they all looked related in some way.

All of them though eventually talked about Malux.

Apparently, Malux had been sending out raiding parties for years. He took all the young boys back as prisoners to be trained as soldiers in his ever growing armies.

Finirton had been burned to the ground in my first year with Cliff because of this search for new recruits.

That too was why my village had been razed, and all but the young boys killed. Malux had declared war on all his neighbors and was raising armies to crush them.

Cliff said he had a burning desire to conquer the entire world, to make it safe for himself and his apprentices. He uses his magic and huge armies to defeat anyone in his path. No one had been able to stand up to him. All the neighboring kingdoms, and even the barbarians to the south, had fallen to Malux's armies.

Listening to this news made me anxious.

Cliff said that Malux sent spies out to try and find his cave and us with it, but we weren't to worry because the earth was protecting us.

Even with his assurances there were times when he wouldn't let either myself or Maru outdoors. He said that it was too dangerous.

Maru was always upset during those periods. She hated missing her bath outdoors. She just loved the huge mud pools and heated spring-fed pools that were just a short distance from Cliff's home.

It was at these times that Bartu would give me some of my hardest tasks to perform.

He would blindfold me and sneak up on me. It was my task to defend myself from Bartu's inevitable attack.

On this day he had given me a staff to use. Bartu had trained me in the use of several different weapons. He always said, 'you never know what you might have to use as a weapon someday' and everyday handed me something new, such diverse objects as chairs and spoons, and expected me to fight with them.

I held the staff loosely in my hands, prepared for anything. In all my previous attempts there was nothing to feel or hear. Bartu could be absolutely quiet in his movements.

But this time was different. The feeling of being in more than one place came upon me again. The effect was the same as if time had stopped. Yet time was flowing normally. With my mind's eye I was able to see Bartu moving silently towards me. On all other occasions when he made me do this exercise with him, I had failed miserably. Bartu usually gave me a hard whack to some tender part of my body to emphasize my failure. But now his approach was crystal clear in my mind. He moved extremely slowly, placing one foot ever so delicately down after the other, not making a sound.

He paused for a moment and studied me. It appeared that he sensed that I sensed him. He tested that theory by leaping into the air and he swung his staff over his head and brought it down in an arc aimed at my head.

My staff went into the air to block. The staves made a sharp noise as they met. Instantly I moved to the side and swung my staff around to hit Bartu on his back, but he had put his staff behind him after his strike and blocked my blow.

We then went into a dance of movement, striking at each other in a rapid series of blows. Each skillfully blocked. I reacted as if I had the use of my eyes. We had performed this exact series of moves many times before, when I was not blindfolded.

We moved apart and each waited for the other one to make a move.

Instead Bartu relaxed and said, "Take off your blindfold, lad."

I took it off and saw the broad grin on his face.

"The lesson is over. As I told you when we started doing this almost a year ago, the eyes are wonderful tools, but if you suddenly lose your sight, for whatever reason, that is no excuse for you to become helpless. Now that you know what to do, I expect you to practise your new found ability."

When Bartu says that he expects me to practise I better practise. He doesn't tolerate any procrastination. I immediately closed my eyes and tried to see the room again with my mind's eye.

Bartu laughed.

My eyes opened and he said, "No, you do not have to practise right away, lad. You deserve a rest. No more lessons or work today. You are eighteen today, and you are now a man. It is time that you start to make decisions for yourself and no longer have others tell you what to do."

EIGHTEEN

"You should discuss these matters with me Bartu, before you go and make such weighty decisions," Cliff said as he appeared from a dark corner of the main room.

I had not seen him, nor noticed him with my mind's eye, while fighting with Bartu. There was only stone in the spot where Cliff had been hiding.

"Ah, you worry too much. The lad is ready I tell you. This fight proves it."

"I think you are becoming unobservant in your old age Bartu. The lad is not as good as you think he is."

"What do you mean, friend? This lad has the best skill that I have seen in anyone besides myself."

To prove it he threw his staff at my head. I easily caught it in one hand and twirled it under my arm.

"Ah, you can't say he's ready just because he can catch a stick. If that was the case, then I wouldn't have waited for him, and would have just found a large hound and gone with it to Malux's castle."

"But the lad finally sees," Bartu protested.

"You trust that. He does it once and you're ready to go to fight Malux?"

"He is a timestopper. He has been seeing with his mind all his life."

"Only when time has been stopped. Not when he is in his normal state. He still hasn't dealt with his dual nature yet."

"Ah, I still say that you worry too much." Bartu ended.

I did feel that I was physically ready, but was curious as to what they were really arguing about. In four short years Bartu had trained me to be almost as good as he in a fight. But Cliff always said that I hadn't paid enough attention to my inner nature yet, whatever that meant.

"Excuse me, but can I ask something?"

Cliff gave me a 'don't bother us now because we are discussing something important' look, laughed and said, "Ask away my boy."

"How did I manage to use my mind's eye just now when time was not stopped? My uncle, you and Bartu tried to teach me how to do that. Up until now it had never happened. So how did I?"

"You touched upon your dual nature," Cliff replied.

"You keep telling me to listen to the voices to help me understand my true nature, but to be honest, I hate listening to the voices. I just want them to stop and don't want to listen to them anymore."

Cliff shook his head in disapproval.

"That is exactly what I would expect to hear from a timestopper that is either on his way to becoming another Caines or a Time Beast. The problem is, my boy, that you want to control whether or not you can hear the voices. You wish to go back to the innocence of your youth. Well, get this through your head. You can't go back there, so stop fighting the voices, and for God's sake stop trying to control them. They just are. The only way to temporarily stop them would be to kill all other timestoppers, and to do that you would have to become like Caines. And even that would be only a temporary measure. As you approached old age you would begin to hear them while time was not stopped. You would hear them all the time, and the only way to stop them then would be to kill all other humans. You would have to be the only one left, and then you would have to listen to yourself, all by yourself, which I can assure you would be much worse.

"*So stop fighting them!*" he added.

Cliff had said this so many times in the past few years that I was tired of listening to him. Cliff always urged me to stop time to further my experience with the voices but I refused and noticed that time stopped less frequently from other timestoppers. Cliff thought that Malux was hunting them down for some reason. So I had given up stopping time, partly out of fear that Malux could somehow find me as well, but mostly to avoid listening to the voices that were driving me mad. They were never-ceasing and totally incomprehensible. I could rarely make out what was being said, and when I did, it was very weird things, like 'time moves forward,' 'our thoughts are private' and 'we ignore those consciousnesses that leave their bodies.' These sentences haunted me. They repeat themselves endlessly and randomly.

I shook my head and refused to think of them, and instead asked, "Well, voices aside, it would be nice to understand how I could see Bartu with my mind's eye in normal time."

Cliff laughed.

"Boy, whether you like it or not, there is a connection."

Ignoring him I said, "Before I could use my mind's eye in stopped time and there were no voices. It was so simple to 'see' things then. Now the voices tend to distract me and I do not see as well in stopped time. Just now there weren't any voices. I was in normal time and could see clearly with my mind's eye. Why?"

EIGHTEEN

Cliff looked deep into my eyes and said, "Boy, what you have just described is what all timestoppers experience. When you are born and are just a babe you realize that you have the ability to stop time, but you are blind. You have not yet learned to 'see' yet while time is stopped. You do not do it often because it is tiring. Mothers love timestopper babies, because they sleep so much. Eventually you learn to 'see' while in stopped time. It is natural for you. When you join to your higher species consciousness you just 'know' that you can 'see' while time is stopped."

"What do you mean by joining to my higher species consciousness?"

"Just what do you think you are doing when you stop time? Haven't you been listening to me? Just what do you think the voices are?"

Cliff waited for an answer, then continued, "Anyway, as you get older, you start to 'hear' voices when time has stopped. Again this is natural. First you 'see' then you 'hear.' And again you just know how to do this, because of your being in a higher conscious state. I should clarify that not all timestoppers 'see' then 'hear.' Some 'hear' then 'see.' But that is not something that you should worry about at the moment, because you are still having a problem with the voices.

"But that is not all that happens to timestoppers. Eventually your association with your higher consciousness allows you to 'see' in what you call normal time. As I said, eventually you will 'hear' the voices in normal time as well. It is all natural. Do not fight your own nature. It is a fight that you will never win."

Just at that moment Maru came into the room singing a slow happy tune.

And while on the subject of fighting my own nature, in the past four years, the relationship that Maru and I had had changed.

As I got older, I felt these very strong urges towards her. She had rebuffed all my uneasy advances. I felt itchy whenever she was near and found myself unable to stop the itch.

I even spied on her a couple of times when she went to take her bath, but was caught and punished. Maru got to pick the punishment ... very ordinary food for a whole month, and twice the usual number of drills by Bartu during the same period. Needless to say that discouraged me, but it was hard not to look at her as she left for her bath each day.

Another thing that I disliked was when she and Bartu flirted with each other. Sometimes they must have done it just to bother me. But I was still compelled to spy on them whenever they were alone just to make sure that they were not doing anything else.

Bartu had noticed me and asked what I was doing. I told him, and he laughed harder than ever before. When he finished, he said that I had nothing to worry about, that he liked his women slightly older and much less complicated than Maru.

Once in a while I had my doubts, and when Bartu caught me in that mood, he had a good laugh.

"What's going on in here now?" Maru asked when she finished her tune.

"Oh, we are just talking about the voices again."

Maru looked at Cliff disgustedly, then turned to me and shouted, "You know Einu, the problem you have has nothing to do with thinking."

Maru grabbed her blanket and promptly marched straight to one of the caverns which led to a small, hot pool within the labyrinth of caverns in which Cliff calls his 'home.'

When she was gone, Bartu said to me, "Way too complicated that one. I would have thought the opposite. I would have said that the problem you have has everything to do with thinking."

"You're both wrong. His problem has everything *and* nothing to do with thinking," Cliff said to Bartu.

"Boy, look, it's not as hard as you're making it out to be. The voices that you hear are the sum of all the thoughts that are human. The higher state of that collective exists to be tapped into by all within that collective. Your problem is that you are trying to understand it in parts, when it can only be understood as a whole. I mean, with an act of will you could pick out a voice that is familiar to you. You could find Bartu's or Maru's or anyone else's that you want to hear …"

At that moment I thought of Janus.

"… It is not hard. I am quite sure that you could do it if you wanted …"

The image of Janus became crystal clear to me. It was almost as if he were right beside me.

Cliff's voice faded into the distance.

"… But when you listen to an individual voice, there is a danger …"

EIGHTEEN

I could see Janus back at my village. He looked agitated.

"... You could lose yourself ..."

Instinctively I knew that to 'hear' what Janus was thinking I had to stop time. Cliff was now just a voice coming from a distant place. His voice could barely be heard.

I stopped time.

"... Einu! No! Don't! ..."

Janus' thoughts became clear to me. My inner voice joined with Janus' inner voice, and my inner sight joined with Janus' sight.

There before me was the village as seen through his eyes.

A man stood staring at me.

There were armed soldiers all about me and the other boys of the village.

The man gave me an unusual look, then came up and started shouting at me.

I recognized him. He was the companion to the sorcerer's apprentice. To my horror, there was the sorcerer's apprentice sitting in the center of the village.

I knew what was happening and looked under the porch of Jocko's house. There was movement. That was me under there, watching the man shout at Janus.

But I was now Janus. The man continued to shout at me. He was getting angrier by the moment because I wasn't paying attention to him. When he pulled out his knife I instantly remembered what happened next, but instead of reacting to the threat, I froze.

It couldn't be real! It couldn't be happening!

The man grabbed my hair, and just before he sliced with his knife he whispered to me, "You'll thank me for this later boy."

He moved his knife with lightning quickness and with total accuracy. I thought about moving much too late.

Pain hit me. I watched in horror as my nose flew off in front of me and hit the ground. The pain spread like fire through my head and liquid quickly covered my mouth and chin.

I screamed and fell to the ground while clutching my face.

I wanted to disappear, to go back to Cliff's home, but nothing happened.

The sorcerer's apprentice got up, came over and started yelling at the man with the knife.

I tried to stop time, but to my utter horror, nothing happened.

Now I screamed louder, not because of the pain, but because of my present situation. Why hadn't I listened closer to what Cliff had been saying?

15

Janus?

"Why did you do that?" the sorcerer's apprentice demanded.

"He was being disrespectful," the man with the knife said calmly.

"He was the best looking one in the whole village. The Master will not be pleased with this, General."

The General calmly waved the knife at me and said, "You had not yet claimed him. Besides I am within my rights to do anything with any prisoner, unless of course you claim him, then I can do nothing. Sorry, Apprentice Drux, if you want him then you can have him."

The General turned towards me and calmly said, "Get up boy."

The pain was never ending and the blood still flowed from between my fingers, but I got up.

"He's no good to me now. Master Malux would find some horrible spell to try on me if I brought this boy into his presence. No, turn him around. I do not want to look at him any more."

The General smiled as if greatly pleased, then playfully spun his knife. Just at that moment a blue sphere and a blue light appeared all around us. I knew instantly that the younger version of myself, the one in my own body, had stopped time.

The General looked at Drux and said, "What is it?"

"The timestopper is near. Very near. This one is not very strong. My guess is that he is still young. Perhaps we can trick him."

Drux stood in thought for a moment then said, "Hold the boy."

The General turned me around and held me firm.

Drux said a few words, and I became paralyzed but I could still breathe and move my eyes, yet that was all. I tried to fight it, then relaxed. Fighting was not the way to overcome the spell. I willed my body to move, but felt a different kind of resistance. A mental resistance. I had never experienced this before and instinctively knew that this resistance was the same resistance that didn't allow me to stop time. It slowly dawned on me that maybe, while in Janus' body I could not use my natural abilities of will and timestopping.

Drux said to the General, "Now hold perfectly still. He just might come in here. You watch that way, and I will watch this way."

Then there was nothing but silence. Eventually the footfalls of my younger self approaching broke the silence. I remembered in great clarity the scene my younger self was now seeing, and the overwhelming emotions ... especially the fear.

There was some movement to one side then my younger self came into view. The other me seemed huge from the perspective I now had. My eyes widened in fear. Not because of what would happen, but because the sight of seeing myself standing in front of me made my mind jump to the thought that maybe I would never be able to go back to my own body. This frightened me out of my wits. I felt the loss greatly and stared wildly at myself, longing to go back to my own body. Then the thought that maybe *I was Janus* came to my mind, and maybe I was now back where I belonged. It was confusing and tears mixed with the blood on my cheeks. I now watched as if from a distance.

Drux shouted, "Now!"

The General lunged at the young Einu and missed. The young Einu winced, dropped his scabbard, and ran out of my field of vision.

It didn't matter. I remembered what happened.

Drux shouted, "Stop!" in such a commanding voice that my heart skipped a beat.

He then shouted, "Don't let him get to the barrier."

There was the sound of running and some grunts then everything went silent. Then I could hear slow footfalls and caught sight of the blue sphere slowly moving towards me.

Drux said, "Get up, he got away. We'll have to track him. Now that I know what he looks like it should be easy ..."

The barrier had continued to move while Drux was talking, and now it was right up to my face. Before Drux finished what he was going to say, the barrier passed by me.

Suddenly it was gone and normal time resumed. Now this was unusual, because I remember not restarting time until after leaving the village, and not enough time had gone by before normal time resumed ... unless of course I had been caught in the time stoppage and had been unable to stay aware of it when the blue sphere passed. That thought left me feeling cold. I missed my ability to stop time more than my nose or Janus' nose.

I was still confused and stood there unable to move as more and more blood streamed down my face. A soldier came up to me. He roughly tore away my arms from my face with one hand, then raised up a red hot piece of metal in his other. A scream tried to leave my throat but no sound came out. He placed the metal on my nose. The pain was so intense that all I remember was the scream inside my head, and then passing out.

16

General

I awoke on the ground, choking on water that had been thrown on me and had gone down my throat.

The General was standing over me.

Bandages covered my face.

"Get up, we're leaving this place and returning to the fortress."

My movements were slow, as the pain from my face coursed through my entire body.

"What is your name boy?" he demanded to know.

No reply left my lips. The General misunderstood this silence.

"It's best that you learn now not to be so insolent. Answer when you are asked a question and matters will be easier for you. There are many parts of the body besides the nose which can find their way to the ground."

I took the meaning of his threat immediately and wanted to say 'Einu' but remembered who I now was. The other boys from the village would know that to be untrue.

"Janus," I said softly.

"Speak up," he said sternly.

"Janus," I said louder but not more convincingly.

"Well Janus, we shall get to know each other better. You see, I have chosen you, so you are safe from the clutches of all of Master Malux' apprentices, not that they would probably want you any more, now that you are missing that pretty nose of yours. Do not worry, you are in good hands with me. I have chosen you, but *not* in the same way that they would have chosen you. No, I have a special purpose in mind for you."

The General turned and shouted at some soldiers to brings horses.

"Can you ride?"

"Yes."

Bartu had trained me to ride and to fight while riding, but it might be different being in Janus' body.

A soldier brought up two horses. One horse was huge. It was bard in leather armor and could easily hold anyone dressed in heavy armor with ease. The General mounted it and turned to watch me.

I wanted to jump up and quickly master the smaller horse. She appeared young and flighty, but part of me shied away from being too bold.

So I cautiously climbed up, making sure to keep my balance, and took my place in the saddle. The horse immediately took two steps backward before she knew who was in control. My mind knew what to do, but my body did not react naturally to my knowledge of horsemanship. It was as if I had to think about what I wanted to do, then my body interpreted how to do it.

The General watched me closely. He shook his head with approval, then turned to the other soldiers and began to shout orders. He turned back to me and said, "You seem to know what you are doing. You look like you just need some more experience and you'll be a fine horseman. Now follow me and keep close."

He turned his horse and went to what was now the front of the line consisting of soldiers, young boys, wagons and many animals … beasts of burden and livestock.

He shouted the order and everyone began to move.

Other soldiers on horses rode past us and down the ox-road ahead of us.

I followed behind wondering what would happen and was just adjusting the bandage on my face when Drux rode up beside the General.

"Where are we off to, General?" Drux demanded.

"Well, according to the reports, the only place left around here is Finirton. If your timestopper is heading anywhere, it must be there."

"Are we taking the town when we get there?"

"No, I'm afraid not. Our Master gave us explicit instructions to gather two thousand new recruits and be back before the summer solstice. And you know what would happen to us if we didn't make it back in time."

Drux shuddered and said, "Yes, but a timestopper would be a good trophy to bring back. Master Malux would be most pleased."

The General paused in thought for a moment then said, "Don't worry, I'll spare enough men to protect us while we search the town. In the meanwhile I'll send scouts out to watch out for our young timestopper."

Drux spat then said, "Sending scouts out will be useless, they could never catch a timestopper if he has any wits about him at all."

I secretly smiled at what Drux had just said. 'If he had any wits at all.' I wanted to laugh but held my tongue.

"No, I will find some spell to help track him. If anyone can find him it is I, just you remember that General," Drux said with a slight twinge of anger in his voice.

He then rode back to one of the wagons, got off his horse and climbed inside. A young boy dressed in a white robe immediately grabbed Drux' horse and walked beside the wagon.

The General watched him go, and he muttered to himself, "And take all the credit for yourself, no doubt."

He then turned to me and said, "How do you like the Apprentice, Janus?"

I said nothing, fearing to speak my mind, and not being capable of saying anything complementary.

The General laughed quietly and said, "My thoughts exactly."

He stared at me a short while longer then said, "Come ride beside me awhile. I'm sure that you'll be better company than the Apprentice."

I rode up beside this rough man. I had never really looked at him for any length of time up until now. My curiosity was aroused and part of me almost liked him. I'm sure under any other circumstances, having your nose cut off by someone would instantly set up a lifelong hatred for that person, but something about this man ...

The General noticed he was under scrutiny.

"Looking at my good looks I see."

He pointed to a large scar that ran from his mouth up to above his left eye. It was quite an obvious feature of his face and only the most unobservant could have missed it. But it appeared just as he pointed it out to me.

He laughed at my surprise.

"No, you are not crazy my lad. It is just a minor glamour spell that our Master has given me for being an obedient servant. I got this scar in his service before becoming a General, and since our Master does so hate the sight of anything ugly, he gave me this spell so he doesn't have to look at my imperfection.

"And now he will not want to look at you either. The better for the both of us I say."

He chuckled and for some reason I smiled then winced because of the pain in my face.

He noticed and said, "In good spirits already? You must have a good disposition. That's good. You'll need it where we are going. The fortress of our Master is not so pleasant, even though to an outsider it appears so. You'll find out soon enough.

"But enough of me doing all the talking. Is there anything you would like to say ... or ask?"

He earnestly appeared to want to start a conversation with me.

My curiosity took over, "How did you get that scar and how did you become Malux' general?"

I wasn't as curious about the scar as about how he became a general.

He laughed for a moment.

When he finished he said, "You're a bold lad. I'm sure I made a good choice in slicing off that pretty nose of yours, but enough of that. I will tell you what you want to know. Because both events happened on the same day, there is only one story to tell. First I must warn you, however, that from now on you must address me as Master or General Harauld, especially when someone else is around. But more important, never, never, say the name of Malux without saying Master in front of it. Better to say The Master or our Master. If anyone hears you not following that rule, you, my dear lad are in deep trouble. I have seen some have the flesh flayed from their backs for not saying Master.

"So learn that one very quickly, or else not even I will be able to save you."

The realization that I was just a piece of property now came to me and all the earlier warmth I had felt for this man left me.

Looking him straight in the eye, I said with venom on my tongue, *"Yes, Master."*

He knew instantly what I meant and said, "Good. You are a quick learner, but do not give me your hatred. You should save that for someone else."

He winked then smiled.

My hatred dissolved.

He laughed quietly and said, "Now I will tell you my story and perhaps you will have a greater understanding of my situation."

General Harauld paused for one moment. He looked back at Drux' wagon, then started his story.

"I was just like you. I was captured by one of the sorcerer's armies out getting new recruits on one of the Master Malux' first raids. It was just over twenty years ago when I was a lad of seventeen and my village was burned to the ground. Fortunately for me, even without this scar, I was no beauty. So I was placed in the common ranks of the soldiery."

Harauld raised my curiosity again, "Why is beauty so important to Master Malux?"

Harauld looked at me with a serious eye and said, "Male beauty my lad ... especially young males ... you'll find out soon enough. In fact I'd rather you find out for yourself, for it is not a pleasant topic. Our Master has many habits not worth discussing.

"Anyway I learned quickly as a soldier, and soon it was found out that I had fast feet and a good memory, and soon became a messenger. Being a messenger had its advantages. Sometimes you learned secrets that otherwise would not be known among the common soldiers, and your face became known among the officers. Believe me it is always good to have friends when your life is always in a precarious situation.

"So it wasn't very long before I made it to the position of head messenger and was in charge of making sure that all messages were sent and received for the general himself. Truk was his name. He was the general before me. Truk was very unimaginative, and he always relied too heavily on Master Malux' magic to bail him out of trouble.

"Well, unfortunately for us Master Malux decided that he had enough of Truk and planned to get rid of him. Our Master has this nasty habit of killing his officers if they ever fail in the task that he sets for them. The bad news was that he sometimes killed all the officers in a lost battle and sometimes the messengers as well ... if he was in a particularly unhappy mood. This keeps the officers on their toes and rarely do they retreat, because it is better to die in battle than to be put to death by our Master. He has some extremely nasty ways of killing people."

The General had a pained look on his face when he said that to me. He paused, closed his eyes for a moment then continued, "It was during Truk's last battle, over ten years ago, that my status changed. Truk was sent out to defend our border against an incursion by an army led by a prince of what was then a neighboring kingdom. Master Malux had no ability as a diplomat and the neighboring king decided to invade our lands and get to our Master before he got to him. It was a good plan because the majority of our master's armies were busy on a new campaign over fifty leagues away.

"Our Master, seeing the danger, naturally blamed Truk for not leaving enough troops for the defense of our borders. So he magically summoned Truk back to the fortress and sent us out to defeat the army with nothing but the garrisons of the border keeps. Unfortunately for me, Truk asked for his officers and messengers to be at his side, and I found myself with the others riding out with a small contingent of horsemen from the fortress garrison that Truk begged to have along, because there were no horsemen at the border keeps.

"Needless to say, these troops were not our best, nor were they sufficient in number to match the army against us. But Truk, confident that our Master would send fire from the sky or make the ground swallow up our enemies, boldly gathered up his army and went to face the prince on the field of battle."

General Harauld paused again, then gave out a wild laugh. He appeared for a moment to be quite mad. He laughed harder when he saw that I was looking at him strangely.

"Do not be afraid of me, Janus," he finally said after he stopped laughing, "You only saw the battle lust that gets upon me when I am in a fight, or remembering one.

"General Truk had sent the main body of his army against the enemies.' Like I said, no imagination. Our forces were not doing very well and the general was just beginning to wonder when Master Malux would do something, when we were surprised by a raid of horsemen and horse-archers sent by the prince against our command position. General Truk was among the first killed. He was struck by an arrow in the chest. I carried him away from the field and realized that he was dead. No one had seen us leave, so no one found him until after the battle.

"Now I really feared for my life, because if we did not win this battle, there was a good chance that we all might find ourselves roasting slowly over hot coals while Master Malux watched. So I quickly devised a plan to pretend that the general was still alive and would say that he was wounded, but that he was still capable of giving orders. I found some of the other messengers and sent them with the general's 'new orders.' I ordered the main army to disengage the enemy and retreat to the small hill where the general had his command position, and used the archers to cover their retreat. I then sent the reserve infantry into the battle. Half attacking the right flank and the other half attacking the left flank.

"Then I went up to the captain of our horsemen who had just finished defeating the raiding party. Krue was the best field commander that the general had, so I said that the general had ordered him to go down to the field of battle and take command of the retreat. He was to set up the best defense he could on this hill and hold at all costs.

"There was hesitation in his eyes. He asked me who would take charge of the horsemen. They were by far the best troops that we had. They were seasoned hardened veterans, well trained.

"I told him without wavering that I was to take command of the horsemen and was to lead a raid against the prince's command position. Krue looked at me in disbelief and all he said was 'You!' I almost yelled at him, 'Those are the general's orders. Must I remind you sir of what would happen to you if our Master found out that you questioned the general's orders?'

"That was too much for Krue. He rode off. But I could not have pulled it off with a strange officer. Krue was used to me delivering important messages from the general, and it didn't hurt that everyone has a fear of Master Malux, and what he might do to them if he hears unfavorable reports about them.

"Remember that, it may come in handy some day."

The General gave me a big smile and looked deep into my eyes again.

"Anyway, I felt different once I found an ax and a shield, I jumped up onto one of the horses who had lost its previous rider, and gave the order to ride. There is an exhilaration of leading others into battle, and having the power of making life and death decisions for those who followed.

"I led the horsemen off the battlefield and through a small wood that stretched behind the enemy. We rode hard through the forest, not giving the scouts of the enemy much of a chance to warn the prince of his peril. Then we burst out of the trees and straight into his camp. We didn't really surprise him, but we attacked so fiercely that we broke through his defenses on our first charge.

"There were only one hundred of us as I led the charge, versus his three hundreds defending. Most of our losses were from the prince's archers, but his infantry and cavalry were no match for us.

"It was during the initial charge that I received my scar. My opponent struck over my shield with his sword, hitting me in the face. I had on only a light cap, not a battle helmet, otherwise the wound would not have been so severe. He lost his arm from my ax, for doing that to me.

"After being wounded, I lost my composure and yelled at the top of my voice, pulled out my sword and charged straight at the prince's colors. The others followed and we struck down all that opposed us. I came face to face with the prince and hewed him down in one stroke.

"It was really a lucky blow, but sometimes fate is kind to you.

"I jumped from my horse and quickly separated the prince's head from his shoulders then dropped my shield and grabbed a pike and put his head on it, got back on my horse and started yelling 'the prince is dead.'

"There were less than forty of us left, and out on the battlefield I saw our forces being pushed back on all sides. Krue was keeping the troops together, but they would not last much longer so I ordered the rest of the horsemen to follow me once again. We charged down the hill, across the valley, and up the other hill.

"Our horses were now stumbling with fatigue. I kept urging the rest on, fearing that we might come too late. Only thirty or so of us made it from the attack on the camp. The enemy was not too worried about us as we approached.

"I held up the head of the prince and that only enraged them even more. They were on the verge of victory and they knew it.

"But what do you think happened at that moment?"

I shook my head, waiting to hear the conclusion of the General's story.

"No guess. Well, I'll tell you."

He smiled a big broad grin and said, "It turns out that Master Malux had been watching all the events on the battlefield with his magic. His interest picked up the moment that old Truk died and he saw what I was doing. He was fascinated that someone had enough cheek to try and pull off the impossible ... snatch victory from the jaws of defeat without the use of magic.

"Master Malux decided to help me in a small way. He cast an illusion to aid me. When we charged up the hill, it appeared that we had burst into flame, and a wall of flame was now coming up the hill instead of horsemen. They could no longer see us. They saw only fire and the head of the prince floating above the flames.

"The enemy now fled in front of us. If we caught up to anyone, we would hew them down and to the others on the field it would appear that they were overcome by the fire.

"The enemy wavered, then fled. Krue, seeing that they were running, held his men together and killed as many as he could during the route.

"We had won. I was so happy and knew that we would be spared from our Master's wrath. I thought of a good story, that the general had died from his wounds and that it would be easy to resume my duties as a messenger. Little did I know of the extent of our Master's magic. Even though he could not hear what was said. He saw that the general had died before I carried him off, and that messages had been sent after to the captains, and the results of those actions. And of course, he could just ask them what I had said.

"So it wasn't long before I found myself in front of Master Malux to give an accounting of what had happened at the battle. He, of course, let me prattle on about carrying out the dying general's orders, before he revealed that he knew all.

"At that point I had visions of stakes being slowly pushed into my body, but our Master totally surprised me and made me the new general. He said I impressed him with my tactics and bravery.

"It was so hard not to burst out laughing at that moment. But I managed it and I've been the general now for twelve years."

The general now lowered his voice and said with his teeth clenched, "But I have never forgotten how I entered into the service of Malux."

He hadn't used the word 'master.' I looked deep into his eyes as he continued.

"And neither should you. Those who were close to you are now either burning or rotting back at your village, just as was the case at my village, all at the bidding of one man. A man I'm sure that you will come to hate as much as I."

An image of my mother lying dead outside our chicken coup came to me. As Einu I long ago had to come to deal with the fact of my mother's murder. For a year after leaving my village I had nightmares of my mother calling my name as she died and I always got there too late to save her or even hear her dying words. Cliff had helped me deal with my feelings. Now something different was happening to me. My thoughts strayed to Janus' father, mother and three sisters. Twitches ran through my body.

There had been constant wetness in my eyes since the loss of the nose on Janus' body, but now tears were flowing down into my bandages. Also, up until now the pain from my nose had somehow not felt as real as pain had in my own body. It had felt somewhat removed or distant. Now it was more real than any pain I could remember. Before it was like a numbness, but now someone had woken up the pain by sticking a pin into it.

Sickness overtook me. My gut began to tighten. I had trouble breathing and threw up on the horse. I leaned to the side and finished emptying my stomach.

Tears flowed nonstop, soaking my bandages. My only thoughts were of the loss of the village, my home, Janus' home and all who lived there. I was reliving everything that happened but from a different view point. It hurt just as much as the first time. No. The hurt was worse, because I now found memories that I never had before. Memories of Janus playing with his family, the love he had for them, and so much more.

As much as I was fascinated with these new memories, bringing them to the surface made me hurt even more. My body sobbed uncontrollably. I held myself, swaying back and forth in the saddle, and knew that these new memories were from a life that could never be again. Life was irrevocably changed.

And it was all due to one man.

My horse slowed and turned off the path.

The General had stopped and ordered that I be taken to one of the wagons, to be cleaned, have my bandages changed, and given a space to sleep.

This was done. I felt all life had been crushed out of me.

I slept long and woke periodically from my illness, not being able to keep track of anything.

The fever that swept through me weakened not only my body, but also my will to live.

The General said that he was going to Finirton and would rejoin me soon.

The rest of the journey was a blur. But one day I awoke and found myself among sacks and barrels. I sat up and looked outside the wagon. There was a large city ahead. But what had caught me eye were the huge walls of what appeared to be a giant's castle inside the city walls.

17

Fortress

The first thing I noticed about the city was the fact that all within it were men. There were no women or children. There were some groups of younger men, all of whom carried swords ... none that could be mistaken for children however. The majority of the men in the city were past their prime and graying. None looked happy and all looked busy.

As the wagon rode deeper into this place, the next thing I noticed was the smell. It must have been very powerful indeed for me to notice it. Having lost some of my olfactory ability and having a large bandage on my face, it was really more of a bad taste in my mouth. No one else seemed to notice it, but it threatened to make me ill all over again. Apart from the obvious smells of human waste and garbage, there were intermixed some very distinct odors which were beyond my experience.

The wagon was making its way down a twisting road towards the great walls at the center of the city. It was a slow journey because of the mass of men crowding the road in front of us.

Eventually the wagon arrived at the huge wall.

A small man poked his head into the wagon and said, "Good, you're up. I was getting tired of having to wipe your butt. So get out and I'll tell you your duties."

The man disappeared from view. As I got up, my new body complained at any large movements. I was naked, but couldn't find my clothes. Men came into the wagon and started to unload it.

The small man reappeared and said with an annoyed voice, "What's taking you so long? I said get out here."

"I can't find my clothes."

"You won't find them. They've been burned. Put this on."

He threw me a white robe and a red scarf.

"I don't have the right robe for you yet, so just put this one on for now and make sure you wear the scarf."

I hastily put on the robe and the scarf and stepped shakily out of the wagon. The wall beside me was impressive. It was at least forty feet tall and was one solid piece of a light gray colored rock.

"Stop gawking, get inside."

Someone shoved me from behind towards the enormous doors of the fortress.

The wagon had finished being unloaded and an old weather-worn man drove it back towards the city gate.

Following along with the others who were carrying items from the wagon, it felt like I was part of the baggage and was glad that no one except the short man was paying any attention to me.

We passed through the open doors and walked under the arched entrance, then through a second set of doors and into the immense courtyard of the fortress.

The space inside the walls was larger than I could imagine. The entire town of Finirton would have fit inside here.

Around the walls were many buildings. Some were obviously stables. Young soldiers were going in and out of others and some had all sorts of men and boys coming and going.

All of the boys were dressed in robes, the majority of which were plain white. Some had red trim around their wrists and only a very few had red trim around their collars.

The men were usually older and wore plain brown tunics.

What was most striking of all was the white castle at the center of the fortress. It had four towers, each with a silver roof, and it was as if the fortress walls was made of one solid rock.

Our group made its way straight towards this magnificent structure. I was in awe as to how it could possibly have been built. Surely it could not have been made in any ordinary fashion. Magic of the highest order must have been used.

For the first time I now began to doubt Cliff's assertion that it would be easy to just walk right up to Malux and kill him. How could he be so confident that it could be done?

Malux must yield great power just to have created this place, let alone control it.

Weakness overtook me again giving me some trouble walking. I was an insignificant being here, in the very center of power on the whole planet. Without the ability to stop time, I was nothing but one more boy among the thousands. Powerless to influence even the smallest event that occurred here daily.

I was staggering towards the castle by now and was not able to keep up with the baggage carriers.

The short man came up beside me and said, "Steady on, lad."

He put my arm around his shoulder and helped me the rest of the way.

"Forgive me for my weakness," I said, happy for his help.

"Get over it. Weakness is something that is not tolerated here."

He pointed over to the east end of the fortress. There were corpses of men who had been killed by having stakes driven through them. They had been tied upside down, by their legs, to poles before the stakes were driven into them.

I tried to summon some strength and looked hard at the dead men and resolved not to be one of them.

"My name is Ei... er, um, ... Janus. What's yours?"

The short man looked at me with one eye closed and said, "I know your name. As for mine, you'll have to show more respect for my position before I'll just blurt it out to you, even if you are General Harauld's chosen one. I'll not lick your feet, even if you can get me killed."

I didn't know what he was talking about.

"I'm sorry and didn't mean to show any disrespect. This is all just very new to me. So would you please tell me your name, master?"

He chuckled and slapped me lightly on the back, seeing that I was steady enough to walk on my own, he said, "I am not your master. In fact it might be said that you just usurped my position, and that I may be forced to call *you* master.

"My name is Brun. I look after the General's house and servants. It was surprising to hear that the General had finally chose a favorite. It seemed that he never would, having been afforded special status from Master Malux. Politics being what they are, I guess he was finally forced to chose one. But it certainly is a strange way to choose one, by first cutting off his nose."

He examined my bandage as we walked.

"I was summoned by Master Harauld to tend to you on the way back to the fortress. He didn't trust anyone else to do the job.

"You will have to be trained in the ways of looking after the household. It's traditional that the chosen one has that duty."

"Excuse me Brun, but just what is a chosen one?"

Brun laughed. He found what I said so funny he had trouble keeping on his feet.

"You don't know?"

"No."

"Well, it is not my place to spoil the Master's fun. You'll not here from my lips what your other duties will be. No doubt Master Harauld is saving that information for his bed chamber."

There wasn't too much time to think about it, because we were now at the castle.

We quickly entered through doors of finely polished silver.

The inside was even more magnificent than the outside. There was polished marble all over the place. Rich embroidered tapestries adorned the walls and the polished metal that was everywhere glinted from the light coming through stained glass windows. The inner courtyard we had entered had a odd roof. It was as if cloth had been made rigid and formed into a dome. I noted that stained glass windows above the door that we had just entered were not visible from the outside. There were no signs of windows, just plain white walls.

Stranger still were the activities that were going on in here. There were dozens of totally naked young boys standing in a line. At the end of the line older boys were closely inspecting the younger boys and then rubbing them down with oils.

The older boys paid particularly close attention to the genitals of the younger boys.

Brun noticed what I was looking at and said, "Checking for flaws."

The boys that had been finished being oiled down were then herded into the center of the room and made to face towards a large throne. These boys were all fair of face and *were* without flaws.

This was what the General had saved me from. Janus' body would have ended up there, it was nearly flawless. He was very handsome before his nose had been removed.

My own body would have been spared as I would not have made it to the group of flawless boys.

Now I knew what was going on here, and what a chosen one meant. I was nothing more than a fop. A plaything for those who have power over those who do not. Anger filled me. My strength returned, and I vowed to find a way to bring down the house of Malux.

Just as my new strength returned, the room was instantly quiet. All movement stopped.

Brun grabbed my arm and whispered in my ear, "Be still and be as insignificant as possible."

Brun bowed his head and stood motionless.

A group of lavishly robed figures entered the room. In the lead was an old balding man with a long, thin white beard. The way everyone was acting around him made me believe that he was Malux. When I saw Drux walking behind him I was sure of it.

Malux walked up to the group of boys and said to his followers, "When I have chosen, the rest are yours to fight over."

Malux quickly walked along the line, choosing about a dozen, then walked to the throne and sat down to watch the others 'fight' over the rest of the boys. There was a small amount of bickering, but there was also an obvious pecking order. Drux appeared to be number two in that order. When the time came for the last one in robes to chose, there was only one boy left.

Malux now gazed about the room and he saw me watching the events taking place in his hall.

Our gazes met momentarily, and I quickly looked at the floor. I was certain that his gaze was still on me. Images of a painful death flashed before me when Malux said, "Clear the room. I want to try out my latest spoils."

Brun said to me, "Quick, let's leave this area."

Malux went to the center of the room and was disrobed by two servants.

Others placed large cushions on the floor and Malux lay down on them.

Just as I exited the room the older boys were leading the chosen boys towards him, and I saw that none who remained in that room had clothes on.

18

Retraining

We walked through the castle until we came to one of the towers. It was about forty feet in diameter and rose to over one hundred feet in height.

Brun explained that this tower housed Malux's important staff. The lower levels were for the administrators, the middle levels were for the advisors and the top two floors were for General Harauld.

The lower of these two floors held the General's servants. Brun had a small room beside the kitchen.

We didn't stop on this floor. Brun took me right up to the top floor, straight into the General's bed chamber. There were only three other rooms on this floor. The largest of these rooms held trophies from the General's past battles. It also had a large table where the General ate and met with important visitors. Best of all, there were two sleek, black hunting hounds. We immediately became friends as they jumped up and licked me in greeting. Their names were Stir and Vex.

The other rooms were smaller than the bed chamber. One was a small library and the other was a large privy.

Upon entering the bed chamber I saw what power can buy. All the furniture, including the bed was made of ornately carved oak. Sheets of the finest silk covered the feather stuffed mattress. Maru would have said that the best feature of all was a large bathtub made of copper. It looked brand new because it was completely untarnished.

Brun entered behind me and said, "Get in the bath and I will bring you the proper clothes that you will be wearing from now on."

I walked over to the bath and looked in it. It was empty.

"But there's no water."

Brun quickly looked in and said, "That clod, Dux. He was to make sure that the bath was full for you when you got here. I'll give him what for."

After muttering this to himself, he turned to me and said, "My apologies."

He then turned to the tub and said, "Hot water!"

The tub was instantly full of steaming water. A strange tingle went up and down my spine to see the water appear like that.

"Now get in."

"How did you do that?"

"It's a magic tub. A gift from Master Malux to our Master. Being a general has its privileges."

The water was almost scalding.

"It's too hot," I protested.

"Now don't complain. I'm pretty sure that our Master didn't chose you because you were a wissy. There must be some good qualities that he sees in you, because he has had the choice of thousands of others before he chose you. So hurry up, and in with you. Take off your bandages. I'd stay and bathe you, but there are other duties to attend to. If you'll excuse me."

Brun didn't wait for a response from me. I was glad he wasn't going to hang around to bathe me.

There were steps up the side of the tub which made it easy to get into. I felt like a turtle going into his soup pot, but slid in. Brun finished unpacking a bag of the General's, then said "Now scrub yourself. Hot water helps get the dirt off. If you want the water to be cooler just say cooler."

He left the room. I said 'cooler' to the tub. The water temperature lowered. I silently cursed Brun for not telling me earlier. Hot water was not one of my favorite things.

After bathing, I grabbed a towel from the table beside the bath, dried myself, then used another towel to wrap myself in. I walked around the room and stopped to look out the window. The shutters were carefully tied to either side.

There were many examples of fortress life to be seen. There was a great amount of coming and going. A constant line of men carrying barrels, sacks and buckets, going to different places throughout the fortress.

No one smiled, no one laughed. Most of the men were glum, sad. None looked happy.

Brun entered the room again.

"Finished already I see. Here is something for you to wear."

He took a white robe from the top of a pile of heavy clothes he had carried in and handed it to me.

The robe, except for the bright red collar, looked no different than the white robes that all the other boys in the fortress wore.

"What is the significance of the red collar?"

"You certainly use big words for a young lad," Brun said as he scrutinized me closely.

"But to answer your question. The red shows what body part someone would lose if that someone forced himself upon you without your Master's permission."

It took me a second to understand what Brun just said. But I understood and again realized that I was just property. Something that could be given away to gain favor for his master. A fop to be used if the master so desired.

Outside there were few boys with red on their robes, but most of those had the red around their wrists.

I spotted one man walking by without a hand, and wondered what he had done to lose it.

"Don't worry lad. That collar makes it safe for you to walk the fortress without fear. Most other boys are not so lucky," he said in a serious tone.

"There is only one in the fortress who could ignore your collar. But I do not think Master Malux would even like to look at you ... thanks to the knife work of our Master."

Brun chuckled while he unfolded the other clothes that he brought in. There was some light leather armor, complete with a stiff pair of riding breeches. The leather shirt had a red collar.

It was my turn to laugh.

121

The General must have had other plans for me and he wanted to keep me safe. Making me his chosen one was the only way to accomplish it.

After I donned the robe he said, "We should not laugh so loud. People get suspicious around here when they hear laughter."

Brun's face turned serious as we now looked out the window together.

He pointed towards the gate and said "Our Master's coming. You should wait here, but I better go and make sure that those slouches in the kitchen have everything ready. I'll never understand how our master chooses his servants. He certainly didn't chose the cooks because they could cook."

Brun left and I watched the General approach the castle. Everyone moved out of his way.

The General rode up to the front of the castle, but he didn't enter. Two soldiers stepped up and said something to him. He then rode around the far side of the castle and disappeared from view.

It was a long time before the General came into the room. He looked tired but he smiled when he saw me.

"It's good to see you up and well. I heard that you were ill the entire way here but see that your face is healing well."

My face was still sensitive to the touch. I wondered what it looked like. The General didn't have any looking glasses in his house. The closest I came to seeing myself was while taking a bath, but it was too hard to get a good look at my reflection in the bath water.

One strange thing was the fact that there was no more obstruction while looking to either side. My nose no longer was there to block my vision.

"I'll have to get you something that you can wear over your face when you go out. It won't do us any good if our Master has you banished, or something much worse. Needless to say I think you should keep as low a profile as possible. I have waited for you a long time and don't want to lose you now."

My curiosity prompted me to speak.

"Why?"

He looked deep into my eyes and said, "You are the one … I see it in your eyes and know it in my heart. But I didn't expect someone as young as yourself. Have no fear though, I will train you."

"For what?"

The General became slightly agitated and said, "The time is not right for you to know, besides the walls have ears. Let's begin your training instead."

General Harauld grabbed a sword that hung on the wall. He had weapons of all descriptions hanging on his walls. The sword he threw me was not unlike my uncle's.

I held it like Bartu had taught me. My hand was not as steady as it had been in my own body, but I kept it pointing straight at the General's chest as he went to get another sword.

"Who taught you about swordplay?" General Harauld asked with surprise in his voice.

The truth wouldn't serve me here, but it was hard to come up with a plausible story.

"A traveler who came to our village."

"And did this traveler have a name?"

I wanted to say another name but Bartu came to my lips almost unbidden.

"Bartu."

"Bartu?" He said with even more surprise in his voice.

At that moment he lunged at me. I twisted my wrist and parried the General's attempt at skewering me. I didn't do it cleanly but my movement had been effective.

"Just how long was he your teacher?"

"I don't know."

The General swung his sword and I ducked. He had deliberately left himself open with his exaggerated swing. I used the opening he created to leap forward, holding my sword at my side, keeping the hilt of my sword toward the General. The flat of my sword hit him on his belly and slid along his side as my momentum took me past him.

I had not been careful to keep my sword flat. Part of the edge cut open his tunic and opened a small wound on his belly. I leapt away from the General and turned again to face him. The General had tried to get out of my way, but had been too slow.

He now just looked at me in amazement and said, "Truly you speak the truth. I never would have expected such a move from such a young lad as yourself. Bartu must surely have been your teacher. If you had used the edge of your sword, my guts would have been at my feet."

At that moment Brun knocked on the open door.

"Enter," was all the General said.

Brun came in and saw the blood on the General.

He almost shrieked, "Ah, what happened here. I leave you for five minutes and a boy almost kills you. Do you want me to have him whipped?"

"No. There would be no point in that."

The General smiled at me before saying to Brun, "No, it was my mistake. I underestimated the abilities of our fine young lad here. It won't happen again. From now on, everyone should treat him as an expert swordsman."

Brun examined the General's wound.

"Should I call the surgeons?"

"No, they will ask too many questions. You bind it."

Brun left the room in a hurry. The General grabbed a cloth and held it against his belly.

"So you know Bartu. That rascal. I tried to recruit him in the past, but lost too many men trying. He just laughs now whenever I ask him to join up with me."

"So you know him?"

"Let's just say I've run across him a few times. We respect each other. He is a great fighter. You only run across his kind once in a lifetime. I could probably last longer against him than most, but have doubts about being able to defeat him in single combat."

It had always been obvious to me that Bartu was an expert fighter, but hearing the praise of the General made me see Bartu in a new light.

"So Bartu must have been teaching you recently. Is that correct?"

"Yes," I said, not wanting to continue this conversation.

"So, that's why I ran into him in Finirton."

This news was a surprise. Bartu had never mentioned anything about meeting the General. He must have met him in that hour while Maru and I were waiting outside of town.

"We both asked what the other was doing in that town, but neither of us gave more than a cryptic answer. He seemed to know what I was doing there, but he played dumb. It was plain that he knew about that young, tall timestopper."

I began to feel very uncomfortable.

"Bartu left the town shortly after our conversation, but the story gets more interesting from here. Apparently he teamed up with the timestopper and a girl and they made their way to a gnome. Drux caught up with them, then lost all the men that I sent with him before he fled using magic that Master Malux gave him."

There was another knock at the door.

"Enter," the General said again.

Brun rushed in and quickly tended to General Harauld. The General didn't say anything while Brun worked.

I left them and walked over to a small war ax that hung on the wall. I placed the sword the General gave me on a table then took the ax off of the hook that held it on the wall. Bartu's lessons about using an ax returned to me. My new body was unfamiliar with the movements I was trying to execute. I tentatively began to twirl the ax in my right hand over and over again. As moments passed, the movement became smoother and smoother. I transferred the ax to my left hand and did the same thing. Eventually I kept the movement going while transferring the ax from hand to hand.

Bartu always told me that if you looked impressive with a weapon, that that could give you an edge over a nervous enemy. Sometimes you might not even have to fight if you could so impress your enemy that they turned and ran.

Bartu had made me practise such impressive movements for many hours at a time. It was fun doing them here. Janus' body had an excellent dexterity to it and could move it so much more easily than my own large body. The process of having to think about what I wanted to do with it was becoming easier.

I was now tossing the ax into the air and catching it, all the while keeping it turning. This was so engrossing that I didn't notice Brun or the General. When I finally stopped, I saw Brun sitting with his mouth open, staring at me. The General too, was watching me. Brun had not yet finished putting the bandage on the General ... he was still holding it.

"I was going to ask you Master if punishment for the lad was in order for touching one of your weapons without permission, but I will wait from now on for you to tell me what to do about him. I now understand why you made this lad your chosen one and will never doubt your judgment again. After seeing this, I now expect our cooks to become master chefs in no time at all," Brun said.

The General laughed, "He is amazing, is he not? Did you see how clumsy he was when he started and how he improved moment by moment until he now looks like an expert axman? He's a natural. He learns in moments, what it takes others years to master. If I had known Bartu's students were so good, I would have tried harder to press him into my service."

Brun finished bandaging the General and asked, "Is there anything else that you require Master?"

"No, you may go."

"Your meal will be ready within the hour."

"Good."

Brun left and the General asked, "I still find it curious as to how and when Bartu trained you, and more importantly why? What interest could he have had with you?"

I just shrugged my shoulders.

"There were secrets in your village to be sure ... there was a murder in your village just days before we arrived ... I doubt much that Bartu had anything to do with that ... then there was the tall timestopper ... Einu, I believe his name was. Did you know him very well?"

"No," I lied.

"Are you sure?"

"Yes. Einu kept pretty much to himself."

"Why do you lie to me?"

"What do you mean?" I asked as innocently as possible.

"I had lengthy talks with the other boys in your village and found out that the tall one and yourself were great friends. In fact the timestopper had no other friends except yourself. So why do you lie to me?"

I kept silent.

"Listen Janus, there can be no secrets between the two of us. We must trust each other."

Suddenly I was left feeling empty and wanted to trust the General more than anything, but how could he believe that I was Einu without thinking me mad? No, I couldn't tell him. I came to the conviction that my life as Einu must be left behind. I was Janus and would act totally like him. I was determined that no one would know my secret and I would just have to look at everything from Janus' point of view and ignore my own.

Then Cliff's voice came to my mind, 'a good defense was sometimes found in an unexpected attack.' I knew the General wanted an explanation, but instead asked him, "If we are to have no secrets, then tell me what you have chosen me to do."

The General was taken aback. He paused for a moment before saying, "Sometimes you seem much older than you look. But you are right. If I want you to tell all, then I must also."

The General sighed as he looked at me. It was as if all his hopes lay in his next statement.

"You have been chosen for a very serious purpose."

The General paused again before continuing in a hushed tone, "To become the best fighter that you possibly can ... to become *my champion*."

He wasn't telling me all that was on his mind. There was a deeper secret that he was keeping back.

"I see," I said then slowly nodded my head.

The General's face lost its grimness then he laughed and slapped me on the back.

"You make me feel young again Janus."

He then rubbed his belly and said, "I have a pain in my belly that I got from somewhere. The only cure for it is food. Let's find out if Brun has our food ready."

The General walked out of the bed chamber and into the large room with the table. I followed but saw no food on it. There was a servant waiting by the stairs. He had the largest eyes of anyone I had ever seen.

"Dux, go tell Brun that he should hurry with the food."

Dux ran down the stairs and out of sight.

"Sit and we shall wait for our dinner."

The General sat at one end of the table and I at least fifteen feet away from him at the other end.

The General continued, "Tell me Janus, when I started to talk about timestoppers, you didn't even flinch. It was as if you knew all about them. For certain, knowledge about them is not very common. I know about them only from being in service to our master. And in fact, I had never encountered one until coming to your village. So it can be assumed that your friend Einu told you some of the secrets that the society of timestoppers hold?"

I smiled. Again it was hard to keep from laughing.

"I can tell you no secrets about them," I lied, "because Einu only just told me about his ability to stop time on the very day of your attack on our village. I did not believe him at first, for he was very distraught over the murder of his uncle, and when he told me he was going to leave the village to find a gnome, I was sure that he had cracked. So he made himself disappear, and then reappear behind me. I had to believe him then. I hardly had time to understand what he had said to me, when the next thing I knew a soldier caught me returning to the village from the forest and put me with the rest of the boys in the village.

"A strange coincidence that. Einu choosing to leave the village on the same day that you attacked."

I was proud of myself and had said everything with conviction. It was easy to do because I put myself truly in Janus' shoes. Even though I was not too sure about the details of Janus' capture.

The General paused in thought then said, "I no longer believe in coincidence. If I did, you would not be sitting here with me talking to me right now.

"Before we met, I had a dream about an important task, and that I had the help of a man with more than one face. A strange dream ... but what drew me to you was the fact that when I first laid my eyes on you, I saw you as having two faces."

An eerie feeling crept over me. The time that the General first saw me was the time when I had become Janus.

"When I was convinced that you were the champion in my dream, I acted quickly. You were much too pretty to be left alone. So I went to you with the intent of pretending that you were disrespectful and would punish you by disfiguring you. I was somewhat surprised when it seemed like you were playing along with me. You kept looking around me at something. You were distracted and didn't care that I had your life in my hands. Then you cooperated completely with me in letting me cut off your nose. I have to admit I find it somewhat puzzling, but one should never question what one has to do in life. Just do it and get it over with I say. But you'll have to tell me, what was so important that day that you ignored me?"

I was at a loss for a moment, then I realized that the truth as seen from Janus' eyes would be a sufficient explanation.

"I saw Einu hiding under one of the porches just behind you and was wondering what he was going to do. To be honest I thought he could rescue me."

The General laughed.

"That tall lad certainly has luck about him. It is not often that someone escapes one of Drux' spells and me in the same day. But if it were not for Drux, I'm sure that he could have rescued the entire village if he wanted."

At that moment we heard a lot of noise coming from the stairway. Through the open archway to the dining room came Brun, Dux and two others carrying platters full of food. They placed the food on the table and quickly brought some plates and knives from a nearby cupboard.

When six places were set the General said, "Everyone sit and eat."

He turned to me and said, "This is Bree and Anu, our cooks for tonight's meal."

We bowed our heads to each other. They looked at me closely for the first time, sizing me up.

The General said for all to hear, "For the short time that we sit here, all are equal. Partake of the food and have no fears. We eat now in silence in respect for our creator, and when we are finished our meal and have paid our thanks, then we will sit a small while and talk. Now let us bow our heads then eat."

We did this and after a short while, as if a silent signal was sent, everyone reached for their food and ate.

The fair was modest. Half a pig, some greens and bread with butter.

I have to admit that the food tasted very bland. It didn't taste bad, but nothing would have inspired anyone to have multiple portions even if there had been enough for any. Bree and Anu just had to be introduced to the herbs that Cliff had introduced me to.

Before we finished eating, we heard someone running up the stairs. We all turned to see a man in a green tunic, puffing heavily.

"Excuse me Master, I did not know you were eating."

"What is it Goryl?"

"Master Malux has sent me to give you notice that you will join him at tomorrow's mid-day meal to discuss the future campaigns."

"Is that all?"

"No, he was also very specific in saying that he expects your chosen one to accompany you tomorrow."

The General's face looked worried.

"Take a place at the table and we will discuss this at the end of our meal."

Goryl got a plate and knife then sat and had the remaining scraps of food.

The General sat deep in thought, periodically taking a mouthful of food.

When all had finished eating, the General said, "Goryl why do you think that Master Malux is interested in Janus here?"

"He has had many discussions with Apprentice Drux about your last gathering mission."

The General's face showed anger.

"Again Drux. I can't believe he is serious about trying to replace me. He will do anything to try to make me look smaller in the eyes of our Master. He convinced Master Malux to let him come with me, just so he could find something I did wrong to tell our Master about. And there would have been nothing to tell if I had not found Janus here."

All at the table turned to look at me. I felt very self conscious.

"What is so special about him?" Bree said with a sneer.

"He is the answer to one of my problems. There is more to him than meets the eye."

They all looked at me again. The General's words made me as uncomfortable as the bandages about my face.

"Just ask Brun," the General continued.

"Ay, if I had not seen it for myself, I wouldn't have believed it. Just give him a new weapon and he masters it in just a few moments. And not only that, this lad here gave our Master a wound across his belly. How many of you could claim to have done as such to our Master? And he is only a lad of barely fifteen summers. So do not question the choices of our Master. We have all been chosen for our own special talents." Brun said with much enthusiasm.

"Not only that, but the lad showed skill in not spilling my guts on the floor by using the blunt of his weapon instead of the edge. I know for a fact that Janus here has had one of the best teachers, and combined with his natural abilities, he may just become the best fighter that ever lived," the General said forcefully.

All I wanted to do right now was sink down in my chair and become invisible. Bartu had pushed me every day to become better and better. He said each day that it may be the last day of training I may ever get. So I was to pretend that it was so and to give everything that I had. Who knew what tomorrow would bring.

Bartu would defeat me everyday. I tried harder and harder to best him, but never could. I didn't feel deserved of the praise of Brun and General Harauld. It had seemed a long four years. But now I realized that I might have the opportunity to kill Malux tomorrow. Was I ready? It certainly didn't feel like it. I wished silently for another four years in which to train for the event. The stares of all in the room and the silence that accompanied them weighed upon me. It was almost too much to bear.

The General said, "Perhaps this is not the time to discuss these matters," as he looked at me, "Let us all go to our beds and perhaps the new day will look much better."

The others got up and cleaned the table, gave the bones to Vex and Stir to finish off and took the plates downstairs with them. I was left alone with General Harauld. He looked at me then said, "Come you must sleep in my bed as my chosen one."

We got up and went to the bed chamber.

"Tonight we will discuss no more. I see that you are weary. You have only just recovered from your illness."

He was right. My legs could barely hold me.

"Get in the bed. But you must sleep naked. It is a condition of being a chosen one. Do not worry, I will not make you fulfill the other requirements of that position, but we may have to fake it. You see, sorcerers have a way of seeing what is going on far away. Fortunately for us they can not hear what is being said when they use their magic, and one can usually tell when they are watching. One gets the feeling that something is walking up one's neck or perhaps the feeling that something is pulling on the inside of one's belly. In either case, it is a surety that magic is involved.

"Now get in the bed and I will be right back."

I took my clothes off and got under the blanket.

He left the room and called for Brun. There was a sound from the stairway of low voices before the General re-entered the room.

When the General saw me watching him, he said, "I merely ordered Brun to make sure that you have a patch for your nose for tomorrow. He will have something that will make you look prettier than you are now."

At that moment I felt both a tingle on my neck and the feeling like something was being pulled from my stomach.

The General came over to me and said with hardly moving his lips, "Do not worry. I know what to do and will not hurt you. I am a good actor, but after we are finished make sure that you cry. It is very important."

He pulled the blanket off of me, turned me onto my stomach and got some scented oil from the table beside the bed. He rubbed it onto my behind, then took his own clothes off and rubbed some oil on himself before getting into the bed and pulling the blanket back over us. I was laying on my side when the General slid up to me under the blanket and started to rub up against me.

It was obvious that he was not interested in me and was merely acting as he said he would, but it was still an unpleasant feeling.

He thrashed around for a few moments, groaned then rolled over and quickly fell asleep and started to snore.

I felt ill and used in spite of the fact that it was only an act. It did not take much in order for me to cry. I merely thought of my situation and wished it were different, and that somehow I could go back to being me.

I wished now that Malux had never been born.

Tears ran down my cheeks. I cried like a small child and held my pillow close to my chest and curled around it.

The feeling of someone pulling on my stomach disappeared as did the tingle on my neck, and I cried myself into a sound sleep.

19

Malux

The next morning it was hard to remember who I was and where this bed had come from.

I had dreamed, and remembered seeing myself in a strange, yet somehow familiar place. The same woman and children I'd dreamed of before reappeared. She was my wife and they were our children and we were happy and content being together. In some ways she resembled Maru, yet in other ways she looked different.

The dream was not set in a place known to me. I couldn't understand the marvelous devices that inhabited the place, but the woman was the most important aspect of my being there. She was the focus of all that I saw. Just to be with her made me ignore the wonders. The dream had felt so real that my waking felt like the unreal part. It took me a while to orient myself. I absent-mindedly rubbed my mouth and accidentally touched the spot where my nose had once been. It was still very sensitive and the pain brought the room fully to my consciousness.

At that moment the General entered and said, "Time to get up and break our fast."

He threw me my robe and smiled.

"I see that you are a good actor too. It was easy to believe those sobs I heard over my fake snores were real."

My pride prevented me from saying anything. I was too tired and didn't have the strength to fight against my circumstances.

The General looked at me and said, "Are you all right? You haven't said much since dinner last night."

What he had said was true. I had turned completely inwards and had just let events wash over me instead of being part of them. That would have to be remedied.

"Yes, I am fine. I've just been thinking, that's all. You'll have to admit that things have come at me pretty fast, and as everyone has pointed out, I am but a lad."

I smiled. That cheered the General up.

"Good. Because you are about to go into the presence of our Master. One wrong word, look or action, can get some other body part chopped off. Maybe something that you are unable to do without, namely your head. So be careful. It would be best for you to stay absolutely silent, and let me do all the talking, but if you are forced to speak, do not forget to say 'Master.' I've been lax at not insisting you say that when you've been addressing me up until now. So practise."

"Yes, Master."

"Good. But we have no idea what will really happen when we get to the dining hall. Keep your wits about you, and do all that is asked of you without hesitation, even if it is unpleasant, or you could get us both killed."

There was a knock at the door.

"Enter."

Brun came in holding a piece of black cloth.

"Ah, Brun. What have you brought for the lad?"

"Well, Master. I thought hard and long what would serve the lad best. It could not be colorful, because that could make the apprentices jealous, yet it had to look worthy of someone of the lad's status, so I made it from black felt cloth. It also had to have some sort of shape to give him a more normal looking appearance, and the three strings will make it look fashionable and will hold it firmly in place as well. The cloth also has a hollow space inside and has two small hidden holes in the bottom so the lad can breathe."

"Good work Brun."

The General held it up and examined my new 'nose' then handed it to me. Brun then took it to put on my face and tied it in place.

The nose was well padded, so it was comfortable to wear. It was hollow as Brun said and air did flow though it. It had the general shape of a nose, having small pieces of wood in it to help it keep its shape and the three strings held it snugly on my face. Two running under my ears, and one running up over my forehead.

After I put it on, Brun and the General both started to laugh.

"There now, don't he look just like a dandy, Master?"

"I think you made him look too good, Brun. But what else could I expect? You are the best at what you do."

"Let us eat quickly now. There is much to do before we meet with Master Malux," the General said.

We went to the table and the meal and the gathering and proceedings were almost identical to yesterday, except that the pork was smoked and we had raw eggs to go with it.

The table was cleared as before and everyone left me alone, except for the dogs. They paid close attention to me, but there wasn't much play within me today. I just sat on the floor with them, petting them and thinking. I worried about my meeting with Malux and whether it was the time to try and kill him.

It wasn't too long before Brun came in and said to me, "Now we must make our way to the main dining chamber. We will meet General Harauld outside and you will stand behind him and follow him wherever he goes. Do not look at anyone. It's best if you look at your feet. Speak only if spoken to, and mind your manners. Is that clear?"

"Yes."

"Remember your place. You are the property of the General. You have no voice of your own. Everything that you are is devoted to the General. Got that?"

"Yes."

Brun winked and smiled.

"I know it is a lot of dung, but thinking that will keep you alive. Now let's hurry."

We went down the stairs and out of the tower to the interior of the castle. We passed through the great hall. There were many servants cleaning the room. It was already spotless. I wondered what they were trying to clean. The cleanliness?

We went through a large set of double doors on the far side of the hall and into a lavish dining area. It was enormous. It could easily hold over three hundred and still feel roomy. There were many tables arranged around the room but in the center there was a huge semi-circular table. And at the head of the curve was a large chair. All of the furniture was made of the finest oak, edged lavishly with silver. There were large stained glass windows all around the room. They all had scenes on them, and I was shocked as to what was depicted on them. There were many scenes of young boys and men in various positions, and others held scenes of torture of the vilest kind. But the common theme was that all the subjects were naked males in various stages of arousal.

The room itself was full of garishly attired older men standing, talking to each other, and with servants busily preparing the table for a meal.

Brun saw me looking around and gave me a sharp slap to my mid section and discreetly pointed to the floor. I bowed my head and Brun led me to where the General was standing. Brun had me stand behind the General who introduced me to the two men he was talking to.

"Ah, Krue, Frar this is my chosen one, Janus. I found him recently on one of my gathering expeditions."

He turned to me and said, "Say hello to Master Krue and Master Frar."

"Greetings Master Frar. Greetings Master Krue."

"Frar here is one of Master Malux' chief advisors and Krue is the best captain in the entire army. If anything ever happened to me, I've already recommended him to be my replacement."

Krue looked somewhat embarrassed by this statement, but he quickly said, "The day something happens to you, will be the day I know that something really serious is afoot."

Frar looked somewhat annoyed then said, "Now if we can get back to the requisition for supplies you made General ..."

Frar stopped talking and the whole room went silent with him. From one of the small doors at the other end of the room, Malux entered.

He looked about the room at everyone present. He even paused a second to look at me. I remembered to look down and quickly lowered my head.

The whole room started to move toward the large semi-circular table. The General went to one of the ends with Krue.

He motioned for me to sit on a hard stool beside his comfortable-looking chair.

I dared a peek around the table. All the apprentices were there, and beside each of them sat a young lad dressed in a red collared white robe like mine. There were other boys sitting at the table but they had red only at their wrists.

When we were all seated Malux said, "Food!"

The room was so quiet that it was easy to hear him. After his one word, there were sounds everywhere. White robed boys came in with many platters of exotic foods. There were shouts from all around the table, for wine, ale and other beverages. Some were calling for obvious favorite dishes, ranging from oysters to quail eggs.

Some of the adults stopped some of the boys after they had put their food platters down and they commanded them to go under the table. The men would stop talking and some even rolled their eyes to the top of their heads. After a while the boys would emerge from under the table and run quickly out one of the doors.

It was obvious why the boys ran, when one boy who banged a knee getting out from under the table, screamed and fell with a knife in his back, thrown by the very one who had commanded him to go under the table in the first place.

When the boy fell, there was a round of cheers from those next to the man. One even slapped his back as they laughed and ignored the fallen boy.

Other boys came quickly up to the fallen one and dragged him out as fast as they could.

The rest of the servant boys appeared to be agitated after the incident.

It was hard trying to eat after witnessing the fall of the boy.

Malux just ate on. He watched all that happened and smiled at every wicked act. He also watched those who watched, and he soon caught my eye. He looked at me for a while before I really noticed him watching me. I quickly looked at my plate, but the damage had already been done.

The room went silent again, then Malux said, "General, I see that you have finally agreed to join the rest of us."

There were a few chuckles from around the table.

"I am always with you Master," the General half shouted.

We were far enough away from Malux that normal conversation was awkward.

"Yes, yes, but tell us about your latest addition to your house."

The General stood then grabbed me by my arm and half lifted me off of my stool.

"This is my chosen one, Janus. I found him in a small village on our way back from our gathering mission."

"Bring him closer. I would look at this *boy*," Malux said ominously, emphasizing the word boy.

The General led me up to Malux, not taking his arm from mine.

"Here he is Master."

"I understand that you cut off his nose. Why?"

The General shifted his weight then said, "He was being disrespectful, Master."

"Then why not kill him outright? I understand that he was a very handsome lad before you removed his delicate little nose. It couldn't be that you were trying to deny me a new pleasure were you General?"

"I would never think of ever denying you anything, Master. Take the boy if you wish," the General said sincerely.

Malux responded by shouting angrily, "Do you take me for a fool, General. I will take the boy and kill him on the spot unless you can show me how he can be of any use to me."

I looked up at these words then to the side and saw Drux with a large wicked grin on his face. The General started to sweat.

After a brief delay the General said, "The lad is already an excellent fighter, Master. He will become a fighter of great renown under my tutelage and will bring glory unto yourself as one of the fiercest in the your personal guard."

Malux smiled and said, "A wild boast, General. Are you so fond of this lad, that you would stake your reputation on such a claim? How did you discover this fact, by merely looking at him?"

"I will stake my reputation on this claim, for I have personally seen the boy in action, Master."

"Then prove it."

"Captain Krue, fetch a hand ax for the boy," the General said in a stern voice.

Krue got up and went to the large doors and took from one of the guards a hand ax that he carried in his belt. Krue came back quickly and handed the ax to me.

For a brief moment the thought of throwing it at Malux crossed my mind, but I felt it would be a wasted effort.

The General looked at me and said, "Show our Master what you can do."

The ax began to twirl like the day before, only this time I was more sure of my abilities. I got the ax up to a good speed then started to transfer it back and forth between my hands. When I had transferred the ax back and forth over a dozen times I started to throw it into the air and catch it. Sweat poured down my face, as one mistake here could probably cost me my life.

After tossing the ax up four times in front of me, I tossed it up behind me and turned to catch it. I did this twice and then twirled it a few times between my hands and stopped suddenly.

There was some applause from around the table, then Malux said, "This proves that he is a good juggler and entertainer, not a good fighter. Since you can't prove he is a fighter then perhaps I can."

Malux suddenly shouted, "Bring out Heru."

There was silence and a pause, before a young man of perhaps eighteen or nineteen years of age came out. He was dressed in a loin cloth and his muscular body was covered in oil.

"Heru. Kill this boy. What weapon would you use?"

"Sword and shield, Master," he replied.

His voice was much higher than would be expected from his appearance.

"Can my chosen one pick another weapon, Master?"

"It seems that one has been chosen for him already," Malux replied.

"Then can he at least have a shield, Master?"

"Do not gainsay me General, or I will kill him on the spot myself."

The General bowed to Malux then stepped towards me.

"Take your robe off, Janus, it will only hinder you. Then wrap it around your free arm. It will serve as a poor man's shield."

I reluctantly took off my robe and stood there naked. Fighting this way wouldn't feel any better than being hindered by my robe, but I obeyed and wrapped the robe around my arm.

Drux said, "That won't save him, General."

The others around the table started to make rude remarks, noises of approval and whispers of 'death, death.'

After Heru got a sword and shield, we moved in front of the table, directly in front of Malux.

Malux said, "Only one is to remain standing. Fight!"

We squared off. I tried to remember all that Bartu had told me of fighting in this situation. He said to try and turn the disadvantages into advantages.

I had a short weapon, with a short arm length. My opponent had a long weapon with a longer arm. That meant I either fought far away or really close, never in between.

Heru didn't hold his sword level. He held the hilt of his sword lower than the point. These were the things to try and somehow use to my full advantage.

Heru showed no emotion. He looked as though he was half dead already and showed no interest in what he was doing. Pity flickered in my heart for him.

It was dangerous to feel that way, after all, he was trying to kill me. But I stopped all such thoughts when he rushed at me and with much enthusiasm swung his sword at my head. I ducked in time, jumped to the side opposite his swing, rolled out of the way, barely missing Heru's second swing at the floor and my legs, and came again to my feet in a half crouch, ready for his next move.

The audience cheered wildly at this point, most for Heru, but I did hear the name Janus being shouted by a few in the crowd. It had an exhilarating effect on me. I was stronger for it and ready for anything.

Bartu had told me if my opponent wasn't holding his sword straight, that he would give away his intentions because he would have to correct the sword's position before he could use it effectively.

Heru advanced on me again. He pulled his sword slightly towards himself before he swung it at me. I jumped back. He continued to swing at me and I jumped back each time until I hit up against the table with my back. I used my momentum to carry me up and over the table and landed among those sitting there. I heard, but didn't see, Heru's sword hit the table behind me. Food and platters flew everywhere. Sauce rolled down my back and onto my legs.

I walked around to the other side of the table. Heru just stood and waited for me. When we were both back in Malux' view, Heru rushed at me and swung, but instead of jumping out of the way this time, I gambled by ducking, then rolling forward past his legs. Heru barely missed hitting me with his shield. I swung backwards with the ax at his legs as I went by. The point at the back of my ax found his shin and entered, tripping him.

I rolled back and struck at him with the edge of my ax but he avoided my blow. He was quick to slash his sword at me while he was lying on his back. I spun away but the sword came down on my arm. It hit the folds of the robe and cut me, not deeply, but enough to turn the robe red as I rolled away.

Heru got up quick and tried to hit me on the ground. I could see his pattern of hesitation just before each of his swings, as I rolled side to side avoiding his sword. Again I gambled, by rolling over my ax and onto my back, and then suddenly throwing it at Heru just as he began his swing. This caught him by total surprise and the ax hit him right in the forehead ... the back point of the ax stayed in. Heru fell backwards and released his sword as he fell. He weakly rolled onto his side and tried to pull the ax out.

I leapt up, grabbed his sword and looked around.

The air was filled with many cheers and boos, but mostly the chant 'death, death.'

The General's face was grim. He merely nodded his head once in the affirmative.

Malux looked at me. His face was a mix of rage and an evil looking pleasure.

Heru was now looking up at me. He ceased to struggle. Our eyes met. Through the blood his eyes conveyed the message, 'quickly now, I wish to rest.'

I hesitated a moment, then quickly plunged the sword into Heru's throat and twisted. Blood spurted far from his body and he convulsed for a second or two, then stopped moving, giving out a horrible gurgling noise before dying.

I dropped the sword and looked at the mostly cheering crowd. The General came up to me and hugged me and whispered, "You had to do it. Now stand up proud and be silent."

The General let go of me and turned to Malux and said, "Is he not as good as I claim, Master?"

Malux looked at the General and spat out the words, "The boy has earned the right to live. See to it General that he is well trained and does well in my service, but also make sure that he is kept out of my sight."

With all the rolling around my black felt nose must have fallen from my face. It was hard to concentrate on looking for it with all the chatter that broke out among those seated, and with the servants running up to clean the blood, I could not find it.

"Can I go see that Janus is attended to before we talk more, Master?" the General shouted above the commotion.

The room grew quiet and Malux said, "Very well, be sure that you are back for the evening meal. I would know the progress for the campaign through the wild lands. Now go."

We both bowed then the General led me by the arm out and through a crowd that had gathered at the entrance to the dining hall. Rumor of the fight had spread throughout the castle. Brun was there. He took my other arm and pushed away the crowd then they half led me, half dragged me totally naked to the General's tower, up into his bed chamber.

When we got into the room, the General said, "I'm sorry Janus, next time I'll ask for a sword for you to demonstrate with." He then smiled at me.

Brun handed me a new robe and said, "The lad did well enough. I saw it from the doorway."

"No, he was lucky. If he had missed with the throw of his ax, we would be burying him right about now."

The General looked long and hard at me then continued, "No … perhaps it wasn't luck after all. Maybe his ax was guided …"

Brun interrupted. "Master, before we blabber any more, let's get this robe off of him and stitch him up."

Brun made me sit and then carefully unwrapped the robe to reveal a small gash on my forearm.

"Ah boy, you've got too much blood in you. How can you bleed so much from such a small wound? All this needs is a good binding. I'll not need my needles for this."

He poured some rye alcohol on the wound before wrapping my arm. I yelped in pain.

"Hush boy, or I'll put these bandages over your mouth. Yelling in my ear. Is there no respect for the elderly these days?" Brun scolded me.

"You're not that old Brun," the General said with a laugh.

When he stopped he said to me, "Janus, you do not have to keep silent any more. You can talk if you like."

I looked at him ready to cry and said, "When I looked into Heru's eyes, it was as if he were glad … to die."

The General put his hand on my shoulder.

"Janus, there are many here who are glad to die. No one much talks about it, but many men in this city and fortress take their own lives every day. This place is torture to the soul and you have just experienced only a small piece of it. You will be better off than most. I have been ordered to keep you out of our Master's way. You do not really know how lucky you are.

"Keep it in your heart that you did the only thing that you could do. Heru is now in a better place, free from the horror of his daily existence. He was one of Malux' play things and a pretty good fighter to boot. If he had been trained better, you might not have won. Fortunately for you, the fortress soldiery are not trained by me or my trainers. Drux' hatred of me keeps them out of my command.

"So perk up, things have just got better. Do not dwell on past deeds over much. What's done is done. Live now as best as you can. Take delight in the small pleasures of being alive. It is how I get through each day."

Tears had started to slowly fall down my cheeks. The General smiled and I smiled back.

"That's better. Now I must leave you. There is much to do. It takes a lot of work to prepare a campaign."

The General left quickly.

Brun rubbed my hair after he had bound my wound and said, "I guess that you are not so bad to know after all, but you'll have to tighten up a bit. You're an open book. It's easy to tell all there is to know about you with just a glance."

Brun smiled at me then left the room. I made my way to the bed and fell onto the cushions.

What Brun last said made me giggle. Then laughter came out of me loudly and uncontrollably. 'Know all about me with just a glance.' If Brun only knew what was going on.

I laughed hard and long, but my laughter then turned to tears. I cried for the memory of Heru.

Vowing to avenge him and all the other innocents in this place who died at the hand of Malux, I cried then fell asleep, slept through dinner, through the night and didn't wake until morning.

20

War

Brun woke me the next day, and introduced me to my duties and to my training schedule.

Brun taught me about numbers, languages and administrative duties.

The General taught me about war and introduced me to many different weapons of war. His arsenal of weapons was much larger than Cliff's. When the General couldn't teach me about weapons, Anu took over. He seemed to delight in telling me the difference between each weapon and each of their strengths and weaknesses and how each weapon could be used to inflict the maximum damage upon the human body.

Bree taught me about stealth, how to get from place to place without being seen and how to overcome obstacles that are designed to keep people out, such as barred doors and windows.

Dux was a surprise. At first there seemed something wrong with him. He was a little slow and seemed stupid, yet he taught me how to be observant. How to see things that are not at first apparent. He wasn't slow. It was more like being constantly distracted by everything that was going on.

He remembered everything and could tell you all that happened in a busy room. He didn't miss a single detail. Dux was amazing. He didn't take the time to talk, because he was constantly watching all events around him and just had to be coaxed to tell what he knew. Of all my teachers, he was the most interesting. Much more interesting than learning twenty different ways to kill someone with a war spike.

Vex and Stir were Dux's closest rivals as the best teachers however ... they taught me how to lie down and do nothing. That only happened though when we were left alone ... which was almost never.

The General kept me in his tower, rarely letting me out. I fought in the tower, learned to write there, and literally learned how to climb the walls, inside and outside the tower. It was while climbing the outside wall that I found out that the appearance of the castle and the fortress was merely an illusion that Malux had cast to impress his enemies. It was really made of individual stones and his magic made it look like the entire structure was one piece.

The only times I got out of the tower were to be trained for fighting on horseback, to learn archery and to learn about how to raise, train and field an army. The General had captain Krue teach me to fight on horseback. He had another captain, Houk, teach me archery. The General himself taught me about armies.

At first Krue and Houk showed their displeasure in having to teach me, but when I showed a great capacity at mastering the skills being shown to me, they began to enjoy our sessions.

I threw myself into learning all that my teachers were showing me, with great enthusiasm. The same enthusiasm Bartu had instilled in me during my training with him.

Six months went by ... I was constantly moving from one teacher to another, while preparations for the next campaign were being made.

There was an air of excitement in the castle at the prospect of going to battle an enemy, and it was very contagious. The strategy and tactics used to wage a war fascinated me.

It was two weeks to the General's departure. We were sitting and having one of our usual after dinner discussions.

"Well, Janus. I hear that your armor has finally been finished and that it fits you like a second skin," the General said happily.

"Yes. It took the armorer a long time to get the elbow and shoulder joints just right. Now I can move without any hindrance."

"Good. Your problem is that you are growing too much muscle. At the rate your are growing, we'll have to get you new armor every six months."

There were laughs from those sitting at the table.

"Krue tells me that you have mastered fighting on horseback," the General continued.

There were a few more laughs.

Brun added, "Captain Krue told me that he doesn't want to see Janus on a horse any more, unless it is when we are fighting the enemy."

"Why is that?" Bree asked.

"Because he unhorsed Captain Krue during his training yesterday. The Captain will have a sore behind for a few days."

This time the General laughed the loudest.

When the laughter subsided he said, "That's good news, yet not all your training goes well."

I looked down.

"Your archery for instance."

"I do not know why but always my first arrow goes wide to the right or left. My height is right, but the target evades me on my first shot. I always hit on my next shot. It is strange but to correct my shot I move my arrow in the direction of the miss. Captain Houk can not tell me what I am doing wrong. He is as frustrated as myself."

"It is said that the first shot is usually the most important. Maybe you just were not meant to be an archer."

"No. I will improve. I promise."

I would do anything to get out these days and didn't want to stop the archery, because it would mean not being able to get out as often.

"Very well. But Brun also tells me that you are not doing as well as you should in your other studies."

"Ay, the lad just doesn't keep his concentration," Brun said for all to hear.

It was because of Brun's lessons that I would do almost anything to get out of the fortress. He was the worst of my teachers. He hounded me and was always pushing me to try harder. There was no satisfying him.

The General thought for a moment then said, "Perhaps Janus needs a break from all his training."

"Master, this one will just go lazy the moment we stop teaching him. He would just lie around with the dogs and daydream all day long if we would let him. No, keep his nose right in it I say," Brun said.

The General smiled at Brun then looked hard at me and said, "No Brun. I think he will go with me. Not that you would not have done a wonderful job with him while I was gone ... and I'm sure that you could keep him safe ... but no it would be better for him to stretch his legs and learn what real battle is all about."

Brun frowned then smiled at me. Brun had become fond of me in his own way. But when he was assigned a task, he paid utmost attention to it and took every one of my failures as a sign that he wasn't trying hard enough. He could drive anyone crazy as he strove for perfection. In his heart he wanted me to succeed.

To tell the truth I was extremely happy at the thought of going and smiled openly. I longed to leave the fortress.

The talk turned to other matters. I paid little attention. The weeks would not go by fast enough for me.

They did go by however and eventually I found myself riding behind the General and Krue. We were making towards Finirton. This did not make me happy, but I was powerless to do anything about it. The General's orders were to bring under Malux' control all the lands to the west of his current boundaries, having already brought all the other lands on this continent under his sway.

This was not going to be much of a campaign as I understood it, because the population in the wild lands was small. There were no powerful lords out there, so the opposition would not be strong. The General did tell me though that we would probably be gone from the fortress for a year, because of the large distances we must travel.

It was more than a month's travel before we came to Cliff's mountains but we were south and on the opposite side from where he lived, but it was still almost two weeks travel from here to Finirton. There was only one pass that could be used by such a large group unless we traveled south where the mountains trail off into many small hills. There were a few rich sea towns there which the General had destroyed under Malux' orders. On his northern swing he came to my village and then turned back to Malux' city and fortress. So Finirton had been left alone up until now. At the pass through the mountains, the General had established a small fort and garrison many years ago. The General said we had to stop and attend to business before making our way west to the very edge of the continent and to the ocean.

We arrived at the small fort. It held just under fifty men. The General, Krue, myself and ten of the General's guard went to talk with the garrison captain. Wily was his name.

He was waiting for us at the gate. The General had a grim face on.

This was confusing. The General said that he and Wily were friends, yet they looked nothing like two friends who were about to greet each other.

We got off of our horses and approached the gate.

"Greetings General Harauld."

At that moment the strange tingling feeling came on my back and in my belly again. Magic.

The General sensed it too. He suddenly stood straighter.

"I'm afraid that greetings are not enough," he barked. "I have been sent here by our master to relieve you of your command. Hand me your sword," he added sternly.

Wily hesitated then asked, "Why, may I ask?"

"It has been reported that your men have been going into the wild and raiding villages for the purpose of bringing women back to the fort. The rules are clear. Women are to be killed on sight."

"That's a lie," Wily said vigorously.

"Drux says otherwise."

The General winced at the sound of Drux' name.

"Give me your sword," the General said with emphasis, "Or do I have to take it from you?"

Wily looked for a moment like he was going to attack, but something in his eyes showed that he was tired. He surrendered his sword without a fight, handing it to the General.

"Now hang him," the General said to his men.

Wily's eyes widened and he struggled as the guards grabbed him and dragged him to a hanging post.

"Untrue! Untrue! All lies!" he yelled until they pulled him up by his neck. He made horrible choking noises before he stopped his struggles.

The General merely stood and watched until it was over, then said at a barely audible level, "I know, my old friend."

The General turned to the second in command and said, "Steth, get your men ready. You will join my infantry on our campaign. I will appoint a new Captain and leave a garrison here from my own troops. Now go, we leave in the morning."

The tingle of magic left my body.

The General dismissed the guards then said to Krue, "Tell the squad leaders to pick out all the trouble makers and malcontents and have them stay here for the garrison, then go tell that idiot Gryt that he is now the garrison leader. He always was too close to Drux for my liking."

The General smiled then continued, "I should be able to get away with this one. I can tell our Master that I wanted to keep an eye on these men myself, and replaced them with men I knew were true to the cause.

"It will help me to clear our army of those that do not want to be here, and we will be short one spy as well. Now go."

Krue left, then the General said to me, "Though it hardly evens the score between Drux and myself."

I shook my head in agreement and stared at the dangling body of Wily. I said to myself, "Yes. One more senseless act to avenge."

We went back to the troops who had set up the General's tent. We slept out here instead of in the fort. I think the General didn't want to see Wily. The body would stay up there for a week before anyone could cut it down. Malux wanted all to know the consequences of disobeying him.

Our journey to Finirton continued the next day but it was uneventful.

It was a surprise when we got there that the town was mostly deserted. There were only a few elderly folk left who refused to leave. Malux' standard orders were to kill all who could not be of use to his cause, so they were burned inside their own homes for their stubbornness. I had to leave the town because I could not stand to listen to their screams. All that was left that was useful was taken, and the rest was burned.

The 'campaign' was starting with less than great success. Malux would not be pleased. The General led us further westward. There was a small trade road that led to the coast from Finirton. The General had said that it would be an easy ride with little of interest on the way, but we came to an obstacle early. We found that a bridge that crossed a fast river had been destroyed by fire.

The General was mildly annoyed but he said to Krue, "Well, what do you think?"

Krue replied, "I think someone has heard that we are coming."

"And they are trying to stop us? This is only a minor delay. They can not stop us, so they must be trying to delay us.

Probably to prepare a defense. So we must try to get across this river as fast as we can. Instead of rebuilding the bridge we should try to find another ford to cross it and then make our own road to it. Send out scouts both ways."

Krue left to give the orders.

"You used to live in these parts, Janus. Did you ever hear about any leaders strong enough to unite the towns around here?"

I paused here as if in thought, for Janus would not have known that information. But as Einu, there were many stories about the resistance against Malux in this area from all the strange visitors that came to visit Cliff. I was torn as to whether or not to tell the General anything. It would make my current existence much easier if the General had an easy campaign. Yet many of those people that I met at Cliff's would die because of any stray words.

The General waited patiently for me to say something.

"No. I don't know of anybody like that."

I decided once again that it would be best to act only as if I were Janus.

The General gave orders to make camp here for the night, because it would be impossible to know how long it would take for the scouts to return.

It was in fact not long before the scouts who had headed up river came back. But only half returned. The leader had an arrow in his leg and had been carried by his companions. The General went up to the scout and demanded, "What happened?"

The scout said, "We found a ford about a mile and a half up river. There was a small trail leading there that someone had tried to hide. When we tried to cross, we were shot at by archers who were hiding on the other side. We lost ten men before we could find safety in the trees."

"How many were there?"

"I'd guess about thirty, General."

"Get him to the surgeons!" the General shouted to the two scouts carrying their leader.

Then I could see the General's mind in action as he yelled, "Krue, I want the fifty best archers we have, and about one hundred foot and one hundred horseman assembled at once. I want that ford secured now." He then turned to me and said, "Janus, I want you to stay here."

My face flushed with anger. His words made me feel like a small child.

Before he turned to leave, I burst out, "General, I want to go. Have I not proved myself worthy with my sword?"

"You have Janus. Your sword is worth more than twenty of the common soldiers. But you are being honed for a purpose, not to be lost by a stray arrow in an ambush."

I stared at him with hurt in my eyes and said, "Very well."

The General paused for a moment, then relented, "You can come. You will have a body guard and will ride in the rear."

There was barely enough time to get my armor on before the signal to ride was given. He had assigned six husky soldiers to ride around me. The General led the small force with the horseman in the lead, followed by the archers, then the body guards and I followed the hundred foot soldiers down the crude path. It was being widened as we rode. The General had ordered the felling of all the small trees so that the path would be wide enough to allow the carts and wagons that carried our supplies to eventually follow us.

The path generally followed the river and was mostly flat except at one point where the river passed between two hills. The path curved around the hill following the curve in the river. It then opened up onto a small marshy clearing as the slope of the hill eased and some water from the river seeped into the low ground here.

The steady noise of the soldiers' marching was broken by screams in front of us. Our soldiers were falling like flies. Arrows were being shot into their midst.

Men were shouting, "Ambush!"

Then lightly armored men ran down the hill and others jumped off of rocky overhangs onto the remaining foot soldiers ahead of me. Before my body guards could react I spurred my horse forward to help our soldiers. There were shouts of 'wait' behind me, but the guards quickly followed.

The attackers easily outnumbered our forces and we were hard put to stay our ground. There was not much fighting room here. Between the steep hill and the river there was at most ten feet of maneuvering room. I quickly approached the fray, but a line of our soldiers blocked my path. Ahead of us in the distance were dead soldiers, and other enemies hiding in the forest. There would be no immediate help coming from that direction. Anyone rushing to our aid would be slowed by the marsh and would be easily picked off by their archers.

Now that I was among the trees it was a disadvantage to be on horse so I jumped off with my sword in one hand and hand ax in the other.

The line of foot soldiers in front of me broke as more of the enemy came jumping down from the hill above. I was suddenly in a mass of fighting. One enemy charged me. I rolled to one side and chopped at his leg. It came off beside me, and the man flew through the air into the river.

I came to my feet just as another charged me and easily avoided his blow then side stepped his charge, letting his own momentum cut a deep gash in his side as I simply held my sword point in the direction of his movement.

My body guards charged into the melee from behind me, sending everyone out of their way as they passed.

One went down as an enemy jumped on him. Another went down with an arrow in his back.

The others tried to turn, but either they or their horses were taken down.

I turned and saw that there was a lone archer standing up the path, nocking another arrow. He was about twenty feet away. It was impossible to reach him before he could shoot me. I was his only clear target, so I stuck my sword in the ground, transferred my ax to my throwing hand and threw. The archer tried to duck but it hit him squarely on the shoulder and he went down.

I grabbed my sword and turned in time to meet the charge of three more enemies coming at me one after the other.

It could have been a choreographed dance as I wove between the three and brought them all down, each with one stroke of my sword, turning right then left then right.

It was over quickly, but other enemies eyed me. They were all without opponents.

I could not outrun the lightly armored men nor escape via the river without drowning.

There was no other option but to fight and I backed up under an overhang of rock so that no one could come at me from the rear or above and waited.

I grabbed a broken spear on the way and threw off my helmet so as to see better.

A group of ten men stood in front of me.

One said, "He's only a boy."

Two surged forward at me simultaneously, swinging their swords as they came. I parried one with my own sword and took the other's swing full on my side, trusting my armor would hold his small sword, and stabbed him in the face with the spear.

My armor did hold, but the blow gave me a nasty bruise. The other man tried to take my head off, but I ducked just in time, losing a few hairs that stayed in the air as the sword passed over me. I brought my sword firmly to his chest then pushed with all my might upward.

He went down and fell off my sword. The group of soldiers had become larger but I could only hear my loud breathing as there was silence among the enemy.

One of them said, "We do not have time for this. Are there any archers here?"

There were only a smattering of no's, then the same man said, "Well, find one."

I waited for a few seconds to catch my breath and looked out from my small protected area into the eyes of these men. Then a thought occurred to me. I should be trying to help them, not kill them. What was I thinking? Malux was their enemy as he was mine, but all that was going through their minds was the thought of my death. It would be only a short moment before an archer showed up and stuck his arrow in me.

I thought of trying to talk to them, but dismissed that. Why would they believe someone who was just trying to save his own life? I grabbed the short sword of the man I killed with the spear and decided to charge. What else was there to do? Better to die fighting than picked off like a helpless animal.

Suddenly an archer appeared with arrow ready. His arrow head was painted red and my death was upon it. But looking at the eyes of the archer, I recognized him. It was Jocko.

"Jocko, it's me Einu!"

I quickly realized my error then said, "No, I mean Janus."

The archer had hesitated upon hearing the name Einu, but finally did recognize me as Janus.

The man who had spoken early said, "Shoot, what are you waiting for?"

Jocko replied, "I can not. He's a lad from my village."

"It must be a trick, the lad doesn't even know his own name," the man said.

"No, it is him."

"Give me the bow, I will do it then. We've wasted enough time on this one."

Just at that moment there were the sound of horses coming up the path on which we had come before the ambush. The men in front of me shifted nervously.

The man said, "Damn. To the river. Leave this one."

Jocko shouted to me, "Come on Janus. Come with us."

The man shouted to Jocko, "Leave him. He's one of them. He would only betray us."

He then dragged Jocko to the river and jumped in just as Captain Krue arrived with many horsemen. He stopped when he saw me and shouted for the others to pursue the archers that were now trying to get from the hill to the river.

He offered me his arm and pulled me onto his horse and said, "I'm sure the General will be glad to see you alive. He ordered that I follow at a discreet distance and we rode like the wind when we heard the distant shouts of fighting."

The horses that rode by made little noise. Their hooves had all been muffled.

"Thanks," was all I said.

"You must have put the fear of your sword in them lad. There must have been over twenty of them standing there afraid to attack you. How many did you get?"

"Seven. I think. No, eight with the archer."

"Eight. I'm impressed. At the age of fifteen, I was worried more about not having to kill chickens for the family meal. Here you are casually talking about taking down eight grown men in your first battle. The General sure knows his business. Ah, and speaking of the General, here he comes now."

Jocko and the ambushers had cut and hidden logs then tied them to the bank. They were now using them for their escape, swimming with the logs to the far bank as our soldiers watched helplessly, unable to stop them. By the time our archers showed up they were all out of sight.

The General rode up beside Captain Krue.

"I'm glad you got here in time, Krue."

The General looked about.

"Janus, was the rear guard totally wiped out?"

"Yes."

"None but you survived?"

"None."

He saw my dead body guards as well.

"Did your guards die well?"

"They protected me to the end."

We all dismounted and started to walk in the direction of the ford. The dead and the dying made for a horrible sight. I suppressed the urge to shake but couldn't get warm.

"I saw what happened at the end though," Krue added.

My pace slowed.

Krue continued, "The lad tells me that he killed eight enemies. They had pinned him up against the rock, but they wouldn't attack. He had made them fear his sword. I'm sure glad that he is on our side."

The General shook his head and said, "Yes, I'm glad that he is on *our* side."

I stopped walking. General Harauld and Captain Krue noticed and stopped as well.

I sat down in the middle of the path and put my knees up to my chin and wrapped my arms around my legs and started to rock slowly back and forth. I still held the swords in my hands then saw the blood on them. After dropping them, tears slowly fell down my cheeks.

Something strange was happening to me … a distinct duality … the part of me that was Einu suddenly felt very separate and was apart from Janus.

The part that was Janus was in pain. He was upset. Turmoil went through Janus' body as he tried to cope with killing. I had gone through this myself while at Cliff's home and tried to comfort the part that stopped responding inside of me. Janus just wanted to stop, but couldn't figure out how.

This was the first time that Janus was a separate entity. I was in awe of this feeling and just watched. Janus' body had reacted always as if it were my own, but now I was just an observer.

Janus wouldn't move and I couldn't move him.

"Janus, it's okay. You'll be okay. You survived. You did what you had to. This feeling will pass," the General said.

I heard a sob come from my throat and wanted to say that I'd be okay, but nothing came out. Janus' extreme emotions had paralyzed him. All I could do was wait.

The General ordered a small group of horsemen to take me back to the camp. I rode double in front of one of the soldiers. Someone helped me out of my armor before I fell into the General's cot.

Deep sleep overtook me immediately.

I slept for two days.

155

Upon waking I was disoriented, and remembered dreaming, but this time the dream had more depth. That women was talking to me again. She definitely was my wife and we had talked for a long time. Part of me understood what was said but part of me did not.

I thought briefly that Maru was my wife and saw her very clearly. Memories that were not my own came to my head. Deep emotions and embarrassment flushed over me, for peeping at two lovers, before I shook myself to break the spell.

I was extremely hungry and the hunger made me feel like myself again.

I looked about and saw daylight through the open tent door. We were no longer by the river. Inside the tent, the General was sitting at his table.

After I got up, he said, "Joining the living again are you?"

He had an empty plate in front of him. It had obviously just held some food.

"Yes, but it was strange, I was somewhere else before being here."

He looked serious when he said, "Tell me, where were you?"

"I don't know. It was a strange place, full of magic and wonders. Even where I lived was strange yet somehow … familiar."

The General stared past me and said, "I too dream of a strange place that I go to when asleep. It feels like I belong there sometimes more than here …"

His voice trailed off, but he shook his head then said, "Enough of that. Eat something. We will be moving soon. There is no sign of our enemies. We must hurry to the coast. Harfton is our first target. I want it to be sacked in the next seven days, or Apprentice Drux will tell our master all about my incompetence again."

We ate quickly and were ready to move in an hour.

We traveled without much incident, except for the many trees that had been felled across the road in inconvenient places, there were no more ambushes.

I was glad. The feelings from the battle left me with little will to fight.

We got to Harfton in six days to find that it had already been burned to the ground. The General was not pleased.

This just made him worry, because someone had obviously done this with a purpose and he worried what that purpose might be.

After spending a day scouting around Harfton, we headed north to Karff.

The General knew from the reports that this was a town that had been built on a protected plateau overlooking the sea. There was also an old keep there that could hold back attackers. The General feared that we would find the residents of three towns there to defend it.

When we arrived at Karff, the General's fears were realized and were much worse. The town had two distinct geographic sections. One was at sea level and contained the port, but this was now burned to the ground.

The second was high up on the plateau. The keep was up there but now stone walls had been built around the plateau, the highest walls found on the easiest approach to the plateau. A steep slope with a winding road led up to a gate.

We laid siege to the town while the General ordered ladders to be built.

The General watched the enemy up on the walls for hours on end. He scouted around on each side of the plateau except for the side that faced the ocean, and he cursed each time when he came back to his tent.

Before he ordered the attack, the General, Captain Krue and I were inside the tent, discussing what could be done.

"There just doesn't seem to be any weakness to the defenses," the General said to Krue.

"No, there isn't. We will have to try a direct assault," Krue said.

"We will lose half our men that way," the General said disgustedly.

"Well, better that than losing our heads for not doing anything at all. Our Master will not tolerate these people defying us."

"Krue, I know that you are right, but do hate such waste of lives. I wish to know who was behind this. Whoever it is, he has made my life more difficult. Our scouting reports never mentioned the fact that we would come across any defenses. I would have brought siege weapons if that were the case."

"Surely the sorcerers would have known something?" I asked.

"Oh, they knew all right. They just didn't tell us anything. That's their way of having fun. They've been watching us closely for the past couple of days seeing what we will do next. They are going to delight in the upcoming carnage and loss of life. I'm sure that Apprentice Drux is going to cheer for the enemy. He would just love to see me fail."

"Don't worry so much General, we will prevail," Krue said proudly.

"It just feels sometimes that more than just the fate of the lives of our soldiers is in my hands, and if I fail at any time, then the world will be plunged forever into darkness," the General said then paused and looked into my eyes as if looking for something.

I felt cold. The General had voiced my exact feelings.

Krue said, "If you let your fears stop you then you will never accomplish anything, will you?"

The General smiled then laughed, "You're right old friend. Let's get some sleep tonight and have faith that everything will be okay in the morning. Without faith I would have succumbed to the darkness long ago. Let's wait for the morning and see what happens."

Krue left and the General went to his cot and it seemed like he fell asleep immediately. He didn't waste time. When he decided he was going to do something he didn't hesitate, and falling asleep was no exception.

I on the other hand couldn't sleep and didn't want tomorrow to come. Many would die tomorrow and I wished there was a way to stop the fighting. I had lost all my earlier excitement about coming with the General to experience battle strategy and tactics firsthand.

Campaigns turned out to be mostly weary traveling, moments of thrill and terror while fighting, not knowing if you'll survive, then disgust after the fighting is over and the result of battle is there for all to see.

I wished again for it to all go away, but I was still Janus, lying in a now dark tent, listening to the wind and the sounds of the night slowly lulling me to sleep.

Then I found myself sitting in a strange room with odd chairs with large cushions on them. To my surprise the woman who I knew as my wife entered.

She came up to me and said, "What's the matter?"

"I am somewhere where I do not want to be, doing something I do not want to do."

She looked into my eyes.

Her eyes were the most beautiful eyes I had ever seen. I could get lost within them forever and not complain one moment ever again.

"Sometimes we must do things that we do not like to do. Just get it over with, then come back here. I will be waiting for you."

She got up then left the room.

Then there were loud noises. It was morning. The General was already gone. There was an excited bustle going on in the camp. Battle was being prepared for.

I hurriedly put my armor on and my sword with scabbard then put a hand ax in my belt, grabbed one of the General's shields and went outside. The General gave orders for battle. Ladders were being grabbed, lines formed and weapons readied.

When the General saw me, he said, "Ah good Janus, you are up, so no one will have to fetch you after all. I am going to lead the charge up the plateau myself and can think of none better to be at my side. Will you come with me on this fine day?"

It was surprising to be asked.

"Of course."

The General laughed then said, "I knew you would, besides our Master would be watching, and what better way to show him that you are trained for battle then by being at my side when the fun starts, right? Besides I don't want you to get out of my sight again. If you're going to pick a fight with fifty men again, I want to be there to see it."

Ever since that day at the river, the story has grown about my deeds. The General exaggerated as well. He must be trying to manufacture a reputation for me. Because there were at least a dozen different version already, all with greater deeds than were actually performed.

"When do we attack?"

"Do not be so eager, Janus. Soon enough." the General said then softly added, "Too soon I fear."

Again I wanted to laugh, but held back. I was anything but eager.

It was not long before he gave the order to advance. All that could be done had been done. We walked up the steep slope like ants swarming over a sugar pile. When we were about half way to the walls, a horn blew and arrows started to fly. We held our shields above our heads as the arrows came down.

Screams came from all around me. Orders were shouted and we quickened our pace upwards. There was the panting of hundreds as those around me strained carrying their burdens of armor and ladders. When we approached the top, enemies popped out of covered holes. They ran to loose piles of rocks and hit chocks that had prevented the rocks from falling. After hitting the chocks they ran to the walls and were pulled up by ropes that had been lowered for them.

The rocks slid down and had a terrible effect on our ranks. They gathered more material as they came down, sweeping along all who could not get out of the way.

I was near the top and off to one side where the slide was not as dramatic. The rocks went down the slope on either side of me. Hundreds must have been lost to the slide or in the trample to get out of the way. The sounds created by this event were a combination of a deafening roar and barely audible shouts and screams of terror.

The General cursed and shouted loud after the noise from the slides had stopped, "Run! Charge! Death to our enemies!"

Our forces surged forward, running and shouting battle chants as they scrambled as quickly as they could up the slope.

The General reached the top first then shouted to the rest to hurry and put up the ladders and scale them.

I stood beside the General with my shield above my head waiting for enough to join to start up the walls. The archers on the walls concentrated on those carrying ladders.

When our ladders finally started to go up, rocks were thrown from above at those climbing. Others with long forked branches pushed the ladders from the walls. Death fell from above. Bodies started to pile up around us.

When enough of our archers were near the top. The General ordered them to concentrate their fire at the those above the gate. He then ordered all those coming up the hill to raise their ladders there. When they had climbed half way up, he ordered the archers to fire at either side of the main assault.

Our forces were quickly up the fifteen feet to the top and fighting.

There wasn't much of a contest, once the hand to hand fighting started between the defenders and our forces. Their numbers were not sufficient to stop the attack and those who resisted were only lightly armored with only wooden shields and had poor weapons.

When a steady stream of men poured over the walls, the General ran to a ladder and started climbing. I followed but was surprised to see how fast the General could run and climb. It was hard to keep up with him.

When we got to the top, the General was already giving orders to clear the barricade that was set up in front of the gates. In the town, all of the enemy was running towards the keep at the center.

Archers from atop the keep helped in their retreat, but the fleeing enemy were forced to turn and fight as there were too many of them to get through the one small iron door.

When there were sufficient numbers of our forces to threaten to break through the open door, it was shut, leaving those outside cut off. Ropes were thrown over and many threw their shields and weapons down and started to climb up. Some remained behind to protect the climbers. Most made it up the ropes. Some were picked off by our archers who made it through the now open gates at the wall. None of the enemy that fought at the bottom were left standing.

A few of our soldiers who tried to climb up the ropes after the enemy, fell back as the ropes were cut.

When all the fighting had stopped the General ordered a search of the town and set up a ring of soldiers around the keep. The keep at forty feet in height was too high for ladders, so the General ordered the battering ram he made to be brought forward.

We waited for it to arrive, but our enemies did not wait. They had a catapult atop the keep and it now shot burning balls of fire into the town. The thatched roofs burned quickly and soon the entire town was on fire. The General ordered everyone back to the walls. We now had to wait for the fires to go out before we could attack.

After about an hour after the fires had started, shouts were heard from near the cliff. Messengers quickly came and told the General to come to the cliff's edge. When we got there we saw boats. Boats of all sizes were coming out of the cliff itself. A hidden cove must have kept from view a large armada of craft that could be accessed from the keep. We watched helplessly as they sailed away. Then we heard more shouts. Smoke was coming from the keep. The enemy was escaping and they burned all that they could in their escape. The General was not pleased, but in the following days we pieced together all that the enemy had done and how they had done it.

We found holes in the ground in front of the walls where a single man must have stayed until we attacked. We found food and water in there, but it must have been a cramped stay, because we never saw any outward sign of these covered holes. We didn't see their men until they ran out to start the rock slides.

When we examined the keep we found it had been stocked with all manner of supplies, though most of it was burned when the enemy left. More interestingly was the tunnel leading down to a cavern with a dock for holding boats. It was a natural cavern that had been enlarged by its inhabitants. It was quite invisible from the land and I would imagine also hard to find from the ocean. One had to sail around a jut of rock before coming to open water. It would look like no more than a large crack from the ocean, certainly not large enough to sail a ship through. Yet many ships were hidden inside here. The General estimated that there had been thirty ships of all sizes, and at least three hundred of the enemy escaped in them.

We saw no signs of women or children during the attack or during the escape. The General figured that they must have established a refuge either further north or on some small remote island out to sea.

Indeed, the defenders definitely did not make the General look good.

"We have over eight hundred dead or still dying, General," Krue said.

"Not good. That was far too many men to lose," he replied.

"We still have over twelve hundred ready and fit to fight, and another couple of hundred wounded who could fight if pressed," Krue said.

"What do we do now General?" I said.

"Well, we certainly cannot follow our enemies, so we go home. We will leave at least two hundred able bodied men here and the most seriously wounded.

"Tell Steth that he will be in charge of the garrison, he's had experience in these parts. Oh, and make sure that of the two hundred there are at least fifty archers. I don't want the enemy to be able to take this place back.

"If I had known more, I would have insisted on some warships, but all of the fleet is preparing for the next campaign. If we are going to invade another continent, I'll want better information than we had before this campaign.

"Well enough said. Make the necessary preparations. We ride for our Master's fortress tomorrow," the General said sadly.

He patted my shoulder as he passed me, then he walked to the edge of the cliff and watched the sun set into the ocean.

21

Plot

"I worry for our master, Janus," Brun said.

He sat at the dining table wringing his hands.

"General Harauld should have been here by now. Master Malux must be punishing the General for the failures in the campaign."

"You worry too much Brun. Our master will be okay. If anyone can convince Master Malux that he was right in what he did, it is our General," Bree said.

"Master Malux enjoys the rivalry between Apprentice Drux and our Master. I doubt that he would let anything stop the pleasure he derives from their fighting. He would not allow either to get the upper hand for very long. The General will be back and he will be whole. Mark my words," Dux said.

We all turned to look at him in amazement. This was the longest he had ever talked. Usually he said one sentence then stopped.

"I only hope you are right Dux, but Master Malux might do anything ... I do so hope that you are right," Brun expressed nervously.

We sat and thought in silence for a moment. These thoughts were disrupted by the sound of someone running up the stairs. Anu came up to the table and said, "The General is coming. I took the long way back here from the main stores past the audience hall and saw a guard who I knew at the doors and asked how it goes inside. He said that he heard a lot of shouting and that Master Malux was in a foul mood and that there was a lot of magic in there. He saw Master Frar being carried out. He was singed and was not breathing when he left the audience hall. It was much calmer after that. The guard saw the General with a half smile on his face and saw Apprentice Drux' face. The Apprentice looked like he was ready to explode."

Brun said cheerfully, "Frar dead? I don't believe it. He was one of Master Malux' most trusted advisors. The General must have said something real good to have caused such a turn of events. Ha! We must find some wine to celebrate with."

"Why would Master Malux kill one of his advisors?" I asked.

"Didn't like his advice?" Bree said playfully.

"Who knows lad. Master Malux likes to kill one of his advisors once in a while just to keep them on their toes and to get new blood near him. The only ones who seem to be safe from death are his apprentices. Even though he punishes them cruelly sometimes, he never kills one," Brun added.

Brun got up then continued, "Now Bree, we must find some good wine. Have you got some somewhere?"

Bree got up as well and said, "Yes, I found some on my last expedition through the cellars."

"No one saw you?" Brun asked seriously.

Bree feigned insult and said, "Master Brun you wound me, I am more careful than that. The day someone catches me I will be dead."

"I am not your master, you pig's brain, but I will whip you myself if anyone ever catches you. Now let's get the wine."

Bree and Brun went down the stairs, arguing all the way to the kitchen.

Dux, Anu, and I all sat in silence waiting for them to return. We heard two people coming back up the stairs, but to my surprise it was the General and his advisor Goryl. They both looked quite pleased.

The General looked at us and said, "Good news, but where are Bree and Brun? They should hear it as well."

"They went to get some wine for the celebration," I said.

"You know?" Goryl said.

"We've only guessed. We know about Frar, and figured that in itself was cause enough for celebration," Anu said.

"News travels fast. You certainly are good at gathering it Anu. That is one of the reasons that you are here. I guess that I should not be surprised."

Brun and Bree came up.

"Master," Brun shouted, "How goes the battle?"

"The battle is won. Master Malux has agreed to all that I proposed. I am now in charge of the entire campaign, down to the minutest detail. No one else has a say in how to prepare for the invasion of our neighboring continent. I have the entire army, including the fortress garrison ... the fleet ... all the workers and the fate of our allies as well, at my disposal."

"He's not going to turn on the barbarians?" Brun asked.

"No. That is the part that I find most amazing. He agreed that we should leave them alone until we conquer all the kingdoms on the next continent."

"I thought that the barbarians were to be converted. That all their women and girl children were to die when all was conquered on this continent," Brun said.

"That was the plan. But now the General decides what is to be done and Master Malux agreed that the barbarians fight better when they have women among the spoils," Goryl said.

"Master Malux must be getting old. He's slipping," Dux said.

"It's too good to be true. I can't believe that there is not some other motive behind our Master's change of heart," I said.

"Believe it. This *change of heart* was just what I had been hoping for."

The General looked into the eyes of all of us.

The General then shouted, "Now Bree, let's see what your hands have brought us."

"Only the best. Only the best."

There was plenty of wine to go around.

Everyone was merry and drank until they fell asleep. I was not as happy and did not drink more than one glass, but no one complained.

To all in this room, this was as good as it ever got. However, I was not content and had the haunting vision of a beautiful pair of eyes that did not leave me all evening.

The next day things went back to normal. I resumed my training, and the others went to their chores. The General was busier than ever making preparations for the biggest campaign of his life. He told me that it would be years before we would be ready to go. We didn't have half enough ships to carry the amount of soldiers and supplies that the General wanted to take with him. The General wanted three hundred warships and another three hundred smaller vessels before he would set out.

He said that such a fleet would take three years to build. There would be plenty of time to hone my skills as a warrior. He would be busy overseeing the construction and making sure that all the supplies necessary to launch such a campaign would be ready all at the same time.

So time went by as it did for everyone else. I missed my unique perception of time. Stopping it as Einu had seemed so natural, and now it felt natural for it not to stop as Janus. My existence as Einu was exotic and more dangerous. Even though now I was in danger of my life being terminated any day, by virtue of living in a tyrant's fortress, this life felt ordinary.

Life was routine. Everyday, I would practise with the sword and other weapons, remembering what Bartu had told me and paying attention to my other teachers. Eventually only the General would teach me anything about fighting. It became easy to defeat Krue and the other substitute teachers. They gave up easily and were nothing more than sparing partners for me. Only the General could hold his own with me. It wasn't because he was better than me, it was more because of his presence, his unpredictability and his desire to win that he was still able to teach me.

I knew that as Janus I was a much better fighter than I was as Einu. Janus had a much smaller, quicker body. As Einu, I was larger and a bit slower, but made up for those faults with an accurate eye and a longer reach, but in a fight between the two of us, Janus would eventually win.

Night after night I thought about my situation. Bartu had always said to me to be prepared for anything, yet how could anyone prepare for not being themselves? I wondered if the reason I had been a timestopper was to become Janus and then find a way to kill Malux by myself. It became a hidden pressure, the feeling that I had to accomplish this. But the thought of it put fear into my heart. I wished that somehow Cliff or Bartu could advise me, and dared not to tell the General of my secret desire.

The nights also let me learn more about myself. I still felt the separateness of being, for I had lived as Einu much longer than as Janus. Yet as time went by, being Janus became the most comfortable persona, and after almost four years of being him, I wondered if I ever would be Einu again. Sometimes the memories of being Einu were remote and dream-like. It was only the different memories of Maru and the haunting visions of a wife and family that reminded me that I was not Janus.

So it was I found myself sitting alone, three years after coming back from the first campaign, looking out from the tower with Vex and Stir by my side.

Not much had changed in that time except that everyone was older. Preparations for the big campaign were almost complete. The General had said that we would set sail in one month's time.

There was a noise, the almost imperceptible steps of Bree coming up behind me.

"What is it Bree?"

"I'm sure glad that the guards in this fortress are not like you," he replied.

I turned and saw him about ten feet away. My mind must have been distracted, that was the closest he'd gotten in a long time.

"The General wants to see you."

"Where is he?"

"He's just outside the city. He told me he wants to meet you out by the caravan staging area. Bring your horse, but no armor. Look casual."

"What's going on?"

"I never question anything that goes on around here."

I laughed. Anu and Bree had to be the two nosiest people around. If you relieved yourself one extra time in a day, they knew about it.

Bree just barely closed his eyes and nodded his head very slightly. This was the signal we used that something very important was afoot.

"I guess I'll just have to go and see for myself."

Riding through the city was always unpleasant. It was a place of much sadness and misery. There was no hunger, and not much crime, but the feel was wrong. The place was unnatural and it constantly made me anxious when I passed through the dirty streets. The looks that the inhabitants gave me riding through were very chilling. You could see outright hatred in some faces, and a complete lack of spark in others. There were very few through the city who wore the white robes with the red collar. When leaving the fortress on all my recent excursions, I'd been allowed to wear armor with a red scarf. I definitely missed the sense of protection of having armor on right now. I hastened my horse to get through the gates. The guards no longer stopped me, probably because they feared that I could get them some unpleasant job to do in the upcoming campaign. Their fear was unfounded but I didn't do anything to break it either.

The General was with Goryl and a few of his most trusted guards, inspecting the wagons that were leaving for the port city Horve where the fleet was assembled. The General was paying attention to the smallest detail as usual. He was shouting at one of the drivers for not tying up his load properly. One of the barrels he was carrying was damaged from shifting too much.

I waited until he noticed me, then said, "It's good to see you in a good mood today, Master."

"Don't start with me, this shipment should have been on its way already," he said gruffly.

His mood quickly shifted and he said to Goryl, "See to it that everything is as it should be and report back to me when you've finished your inspection. Take the guards with you, they'll put anyone straight if they give you any lip."

"Is it advisable for you to be alone General?" Goryl said worriedly.

"I'll have all the protection I need with Janus here," he said with laughter in his voice.

Goryl and the guards left.

"What was all that about?"

"Someone has been sabotaging our efforts to leave on schedule. Supplies are missing or wrong. With all the other rumors circulating in the fortress Goryl thinks that someone might try to get rid of me."

"No one would dare," I scoffed.

"My position is not as secure as it seems, even though no one will attack me openly any more. I'm sure that if some accident does happen to me, our Master would not severely punish any of the apprentices if it could be linked to them. So I've been watching my back lately."

To emphasize what he just said he turned and looked behind him. "Let's find some place where there is no one around."

We rode down the road a bit then turned off down a small path and came to a clearing. We let the horses graze and the General sat on the ground and motioned me to sit beside him.

He started talking in a hushed tone, "We will be leaving in less than a month and I have been thinking. Unless we act before we go, it will be years before we come back. I have been watching you, and think that you are ready now."

"Ready?"

"You are one of the best fighters ever. There will be no benefit in you going to war. The only thing that may happen is you are killed in some freak happenstance."

This was confusing, wasn't the purpose of my training to make me the best fighter in Malux' army?

The General looked all around very carefully before returning his eyes to mine.

"I have not been telling you the truth about why you were being trained ..." he said just above a whisper.

I gave no reply, waiting for him to finish what he had to say.

"The reason I chose you four years ago was not to fight for Malux but to fight against him."

I sat there for a few seconds as his words sank in, then burst out laughing.

The General appeared somewhat agitated at my reaction to his news and quickly looked around again.

"Janus this is a most serious matter. I intend to kill Malux and want you to help me."

I grinned.

He scowled.

"Forgive me my merriment General, but I find that to be most amusing ..."

The General wanted to talk but I cut him off.

"... *Remember* I had told you that Bartu had been training me to fight?"

"Yes."

"Well his purpose in training me was the very same as yours. I have been trained by two excellent teachers for the same reason."

He paused for a moment then it was his turn to laugh.

We both sat there and broke out in renewed laughter each time we reconfirmed what the other was planning.

The years of tension that our secret purposes had built up

in ourselves ... burst like a dam ... to our great relief. I felt closer to the General now than ever before. It was as if I had been waiting for some sign and this was it. I was about suggest to General Harauld that we should go right now and get it over with, when he said, "I have planned this long and think we will wait until the last day. The day when we are to depart for the campaign. In that way it will not seem unusual to be walking around in armor in the fortress. Departure day might just give us an excuse to see Malux in his tower. His tower is isolated from the rest of the fortress and help can not get to him quickly. Of course we will have to get by his guardians, but we will not try this alone. We can count on Brun, Anu, Bree, Dux and Goryl and maybe others as well. But who, remains to be seen ..."

When the General started to talk I noticed something strange happening to me. It was almost as if I was becoming detached to the whole scene ... the birds singing, the insects that were crawling at my feet, the wind in the tall grass and the General's voice ... all these things became equal to my awareness. It was as if I was paying attention to all of them at the same time and not just listening to the General's voice.

Then the strangest thing of all happened. Time stopped.

I was surprised that I was still aware. I never thought I would again experience stopped time.

There were voices. The usual voices when time stopped, though two were stronger than the others. One was a woman's voice. She was calling a strange name. The name sounded like none that I heard before. The voice was very familiar and hearing her call this name sent chills down my back. It was a magical sound.

The other voice was getting louder. It too was familiar, a male voice, and it was calling my name.

"Einu!"

The voice was right in front of me. All I wanted to hear was the other voice, but could no longer avoid paying attention to this closer one. His voice sounded like a slap and with it came a sharp pain in my shin.

Suddenly I recognized the voice. It was Cliff's. At the moment of recognition, I felt a severe disorientation.

I was back in Cliff's home. He was kicking me in the shin and yelling my name.

"Einu, snap out of it!"

I jumped back and found myself taller.

TIMESTOPPER

Looking down at my body, I saw that I was myself again.

22

Einu Again

"I hate it when that happens," Cliff said with much annoyance in his voice.

"What?" was all I could muster.

I was confused. I had been very used to be Janus. It was a shock being myself again.

"Just start time again, before you drift away somewhere else."

I was so confused that it was easy to forget that time was stopped. It felt for an instant that I could see normally. It took Cliff's words to remind me that time was still stopped.

"That's better," Cliff said when time restarted.

"Now enough foolishness. We have to decide what to do with you. Bartu thinks that you are ready to go fight Malux. Your antics of today suggest that you are less than ready. Just what have you been up to Einu?"

"Is there something I should know?" Bartu added.

"The lad here just got lost. He drowned himself in the voices and it took me an eternity to get him back," Cliff said to Bartu.

They both looked at me as if waiting for an explanation.

"I ..."

What would be the best way to tell them what happened?

"Yes, what is it?" Cliff asked.

"I ... I'm back."

"That is obvious. What are you back from?" Bartu asked.

"I was Janus."

"What? Are you sure?" Cliff said excitedly.

"Yes."

"He *is* ready," Cliff said to Bartu.

"What?" was all I could say again.

"Tell us what happened and don't leave out a single detail," Cliff said to me in a serious tone.

I began slowly at first, but as memories of my life as Janus came back to me, the story was easier to tell. We were interrupted briefly when Maru came back from her bath. I stopped and just stared at her. She looked just as beautiful as I remembered, but Cliff instructed me to continue. Maru listened with great interest when she realized what I was talking about. She was the only one to ask me any questions and eventually Cliff told her to be quiet. He said it was more important to get the whole story out because there was a possibility of me forgetting it. So they listened in silence to the rest of the story of my life as Janus.

After finishing telling about my final conversation with the General, Cliff said, "Well, that is quite a tale. I would not have expected it from a timestopper so young but again you prove to me that you are a timestopper like no other. You discovered one of the secrets of the voices, and on the moment of discovery you immediately used that knowledge to go to the place where you could gain the best information to complete your quest."

"What secret?"

"I'll have to tell you later. Right now we have to figure out what to do," Cliff said casually.

We all were silent, in deep thought.

My thoughts were of the distinct difference between my life and the way that I felt living Janus' life.

"Cliff?"

"Yes, Einu?"

"How come I feel so different?"

"What do you mean lad?"

"Well, now that I am myself again, Janus' existence seems really boring. I mean that a lot of things happened to him but there was something about his life that was not describable. Can you help me?" I asked perplexed.

"You mean his life was ordinary."

"Ordinary?"

"Yes ordinary. You now know what it is like to be like everyone else and to not be a timestopper."

"Is that it? The ordinariness is gone?"

"Yes I'm afraid so. Most humans bottle themselves up and ignore the vastness of the universe that is readily available to them. To you that is boring, because you can see more than the rest of your kind can. You are lucky that you were born the way you are. More aware."

I digested what Cliff said to me for a moment then thought of the situation Janus was in.

"But tell me now, what happens to Janus?"

"What do you mean? Nothing happens to him."

"But I was him for four years."

"So?"

"How will he carry on with the General's plan?"

"Just as you would have."

"How? I don't see how."

"What's your problem? Janus will continue on as if he had made all of the decisions himself. His lack of awareness will keep him in the dark as to how he accomplished all of his deeds with your help. To him it will seem that he made all his own decisions. He will put down all of the knowledge he gained from you as instinct or maybe luck. Janus has definitely benefited from having had two points of view at his disposal. He would only be able to absorb the concepts that the two of you could easily share, and would have a hard time with the concepts that you have running around in that mind of yours. They would be alien to him. Even though they are now part of his psyche, he may never be able to draw upon that knowledge. But don't worry about Janus. He will be okay. The only danger he faces is if you two ever meet face to face and look deeply into each others eyes. He may then remember what happened and he could lose his sanity. His ordinariness will be his best defense."

While listening to Cliff and not fully understanding what he had said, I reached up to feel for my nose. It was so good to have one again. My worry about Janus increased when I realized what he was about to do. He was going to attack Malux with the General. But when? What day was it?

I jumped up.

"What is your problem now lad?" Bartu said.

"Didn't you listen to my story? Janus is going to attack Malux. We have to stop him!"

"You mean help him," Bartu said.

"What?"

"Help him, he said. Sometimes I think you're deaf or dumb. I haven't figured out which yet and I've only known you all my life," Maru said.

When I thought about it, I knew she was right. It was time to go to Malux' fortress.

"Right. We've got to go."

"Sit down lad, we'll leave in the morning," Cliff said.

I sat, somewhat confused at the casualness of Cliff's statement.

"But when is Janus going to attack?"

"You said so yourself. In three weeks," Cliff said.

"But how do you know that?"

"Well, as your shin can tell you, I had been trying to rouse you from your trip out of your body for quite some time. If you had actually been more aware you would have heard me. You had just the right amount of awareness to actually be able to transfer your consciousness to Janus but once there you seemed to go dumb and couldn't see me any more. So it took until you came back to the moment that you left your body that you realized that something was different and you became aware of me."

"What was different?"

"You were about to switch time modalities."

"What?"

"You were about to enter from what was, to what would be. Or from your perspective you left to go into Janus' past and when enough time had past that his present matched yours, you were about to go into his future. If you had actually stayed with Janus, you might not have come back, you would have shrugged off the recurring strange feelings and time would have started for you again. Fortunately, you had just enough awareness to get back. Seeing the future is slightly different than seeing the past. Not that much different as you might think, but it is different. In that moment your awareness served you by allowing you to see the horizon coming at you ... that junction point where your consciousness would have actually changed where it drew its energy from.

"But that is history now as well. Your flow of consciousness is back with Einu, as it should be."

Cliff emphasized his last point by putting his finger onto my chest.

"So that is how I know that Janus will attack Malux in three weeks, because the conversation that you as Janus just had with General Harauld, had just taken place when you began your story about you being Janus."

"So what do we do now?"

"We go to Malux' fortress, of course," Cliff said.

Bartu added skeptically, "It takes at least a month to get there on horse. It will take a week to get to the mountain pass and somehow we will have to get past Malux' garrison stationed there, then we will have to ride hard and hope we do not meet any patrols. If our horses do not falter, there is a slim chance we will get there,"

"I could stop time."

"And what, carry Bartu all the way there? Lad, you can do that if you want. I'll have no part of it."

"So what's to be done?" I asked in frustration.

"Put on some tea."

I looked at Cliff like he was crazy.

"What?"

"Put on some tea, we have guests arriving."

Cliff cocked his head to one side, then said, "Ah! They're here. I'll fetch them."

Cliff jumped up enthusiastically and ran out the door.

Maru got up and started to make some tea. Bartu just smiled at me and shrugged his shoulders. I was feeling restless and wanted to move about, to do something, at least prepare for our departure, but instead I just sat and waited.

Bartu finally said, "Get the ants of out your pockets lad. Just wait and see what happens. Besides if you want to know, we have everything already packed and ready to go, we have been ready for weeks. All we have to pack is the food, and we will do that before we sleep tonight, so just have patience."

It wasn't much longer before we heard footsteps approaching from the corridor.

The first man through I recognized as the one who had led the ambush by the river against the General. Next came Cliff, then following him a very skinny man. He looked more weather-worn and older than I remembered, but there was no mistaking Jocko.

23

Jocko

"Jocko!"

"Einu?"

I got up and embraced him like he was my long lost father.

"I'm sure glad that you didn't kill me by the river," I said mischievously.

"What river?" Jocko said confused.

"Remember when you ambushed Malux' army by the river, three years ago?"

"Yes, lad. What of it?" Jocko said suspiciously.

"Remember seeing Janus surrounded by your companions and him saying, 'Jocko it's me Einu ... no I mean Janus.'"

"Yes I remember that very well. I've been thinking of Janus, you and the other lads from the village these many years. But again I ask what of it?"

My grin stretched from ear to ear when I said, "It was me."

Jocko looked at me like I was a truant boy. "I'm most sure Einu, that it was not you, that it was Janus."

"No it was me. I can tell you everything that happened at the river."

The other man said to Cliff, "Gnome, what does he mean? Is he a sorcerer? I'll have nothing to do with sorcerers."

His voice rose as he kept his anger barely in check.

Cliff said to me, "Einu. What is appropriate behavior when you haven't seen someone in years? Don't you say, how are you? How have you been? Or something like that? Do you have to put someone on the defensive right away? You have no idea what has been happening to Jocko since you last saw him. Take the time to find out. Don't confuse him with the first words out of your mouth."

I stopped smiling then said, "Sorry Jocko, I didn't mean to upset you or your friend."

The other man said, "Besides, I am not daft and can tell that this is not the same lad at the river   that day, unless he became about a foot taller and grew back his nose."

"You're wrong Sir Hamard, this is the same lad."

He reacted with a deep scowl.

"And no, he is not a sorcerer. He is a timestopper," Cliff continued.

"A what? I've never heard of a time stopper. Are you trying to trick me, Gnome?"

"No Sir Hamard. Perhaps a quick demonstration of the lad's powers will convince you.

Cliff turned to me and said, "Einu, do it."

I shrugged my shoulders and stopped time. Cliff watched as I walked behind Sir Hamard and took his knife from his scabbard then stepped back and restarted time.

Hamard gasped as he thought I had disappeared. He turned and saw me behind him. He noticed the knife and quickly looked at his belt and saw that it was his.

"Sorcery!" he half shouted.

Cliff said to him, "I can assure you that it is not. The lad has no more ability to cast spells than I do or Bartu here or Maru there by the fire."

Sir Hamard looked at Cliff, Bartu and Maru with suspicion, then he pulled out his sword.

Cliff said, "You have not entered a den of sorcerers like you fear, Sir Hamard."

"Put away your sword or you might get hurt," Bartu said.

"I will not. Even if you are not sorcerers, you say that

this was the lad who fought with the enemy. Then that makes you my enemy. That lad killed one of my dear friends that day."

"Sir Hamard I can assure you, that Malux is *our* enemy, as he is yours."

Cliff walked up to the tip of Sir Hamard's sword.

"Just why did you come here today?"

He shifted uneasily then said, "I heard that gnomes and sorcerers were mortal enemies and upon hearing that a gnome of high repute was dwelling in these mountains, I came to seek his aid in our fight against Malux."

"Well, you heard rightly."

He turned to me and said, "Einu."

Cliff rolled his eyes. I didn't understand.

"Oh you're so dense, just stop time."

I did.

"Now get the sword."

I pried it from Sir Hamard's hand.

"Give it to me and restart time."

Sir Hamard yelled, "Treachery and sorcery."

He backed to the door. Jocko slowly went with him.

"Sir Hamard, the only treachery comes from your own mistrust. Here is your sword back."

Sir Hamard reached for it, but Cliff pulled it away.

"Providing that you promise to sheath it."

He nodded his head and Cliff gave it back.

"Now you are free to go if you want, providing that you promise never to tell any agent of Malux where my home is. Yet, if you would wait just a few minutes we are just making our plans to attack Malux himself. So if you are interested in the death of our enemy, I suggest you stay for a while."

Sir Hamard looked about, then sheathed his sword and said, "I will stay and listen."

"Good."

Then Cliff turned to scold me, "See what a few misplaced words can do. I hope this teaches you something. Get out of your head once and a while and pay attention to others."

Maru brought over some cups full of tea on a tray. She placed it on the table, then turned to me and slapped me on the head.

I winced. She went to Jocko and hugged him then said, "It is good to see you again."

Bartu laughed with great gusto.

Jocko returned Maru's hug but seemed very confused with what was happening. Maru then returned to working on some clothes she had been mending.

I felt very uncomfortable. I was mortified for never having thought that I might have killed someone that Sir Hamard knew.

"So what is the plan?" Bartu said to Cliff.

"Well, we go the fortress and try to help Janus and the General. They seem to already have a plan ..."

"What? Help the General? What kind of a plan is that?" Sir Hamard said loudly.

"If you would just listen for a moment, you will hear what we have to say. Now where were we? Oh yes, the plan that the General has for killing Malux is the best. Surprise. If we can surprise the Sorcerer in his tower than we have a good chance. With the General's group and our own working together, we have half a chance of killing him. Now the only problem we have is getting to Malux' fortress in three weeks."

"Why three weeks?" Sir Hamard asked.

"Because that's when the General plans to attack him."

"How do you know this Gnome?"

"We gnomes have our ways of knowing things."

Cliff just smiled then continued, "But what I know is not as important as the problem of how to get there. Is there anyone who can think of a way to do it?"

There was a moment of silence then Jocko said, "I think I know how."

He paused for a long moment then Bartu said, "Well, do not keep us in suspense. If you know something my good man, then tell us."

"There is a pass less than a day's ride north of here. If we take it, we can save the time it takes to travel to the main pass up and back. It is almost directly in line east to the fortress."

"How do you know this?" I asked.

Jocko replied, "Well lad, after our village was attacked I had nothing to do. I worried about what was going to happen to all of the lads in the village and wanted to follow them, but was afraid to take the main pass because I thought that it would be well guarded. So I went to the mountains to find another way and found one. It is a very dangerous pass. It was formed very recently by a rock slide. The whole side of a mountain fell away, leaving a very gentle slope to climb. The footing is still loose and treacherous but with some luck we can get horses over it and be clear to get to the fortress in time. I had actually made it to the fortress, but saw that there was nothing that could be done so I made my way back and joined up with Sir Hamard here in his fight against Malux."

"And fight him I have, but we have no real chance of winning or surviving much longer in the cold north unless we can do something about the sorcerer. Curse him. That is why I came here and if you are serious about killing him, then I will come with you," Sir Hamard said.

"What is your grievance with the sorcerer?" Bartu asked.

"Who doesn't have a reason to want the sorcerer dead? But I will tell you the cause of my hatred. Before coming to live in the wilderness, I was a baron of King Ott and was called to fight against Malux, but as you know we lost. I managed to escape from his armies, to return home to my keep, but found my wife and two daughters dead. If that is not enough reason to hate him, then tell me of another and I will hate him for that as well. For there are many stories about what Malux has done to others. That is why I have now under my care a few hundred that would escape from his tyranny. There is nowhere left to run. The time has come to strike. The last desperate strike of a hunted animal can sometimes be lethal. That is my hope and that is the reason for coming to you today. I have brought with me a few men with horses. There are enough horses for all here and a couple for provisions, but not enough for all of my men."

Cliff smiled and said to him, "They can stay here or can go back on foot as they desire. They will be safe here if they stay. Gnome's homes are never left unguarded. We have many friends in the world and some from without."

Sir Hamard looked closely at Cliff. A small smile eventually crossed his mouth and he said, "I do like you Gnome, so will come with you, to make sure that you come back."

"Do not fear for me. We gnomes are different from you humans. If you truly like me then call me Cliff. Now let's finish our tea. We have much to discuss before we go."

The talk turned to the actual hows and whys of travel. I was not much interested in the talk and soon fell asleep.

Someone shook me until I awoke.

Bartu said, "Come on lad we are going very soon, gather your things, and do not forget your weapons."

After sleeping the entire night at Cliff's table I was stiff but quickly got up and prepared for travel.

The predawn air was chilly. There were swirls of mist passing eerily by as I joined the others. The horses had been made ready. We would be off in a moment.

Maru was there. She was saying good-bye to Cliff and Bartu. She noticed me then came over. She said nothing. She merely stood in front of me in silence.

Suddenly she reached up and grabbed my tunic and pulled me down to her. She kissed me quite passionately for a brief moment, then said very slowly and with emphasis, *"Don't do anything stupid."*

She then walked backed into the cave and was gone from sight.

I stood shocked and didn't know what to make of her.

Bartu laughed when he saw me stand in confusion.

All he said was, "Virgins."

Sir Hamard said to his men, "Kenard, I expect you and the lads to stay here to protect the lass and to be on your proper behavior. Understand?"

Kenard nodded.

"I'm sending Houth back to let everyone know what is going on and to expect the worst if I do not come back."

Sir Hamard got onto his horse. We all followed suit. It was funny seeing Cliff sitting on a horse. The horse however seemed to enjoy having such a light load and he obeyed the slightest command that Cliff gave it.

Bartu rode up beside Sir Hamard and said, "I'm worried about Kenard and your lads."

"Why?" Sir Hamard asked.

"Who's going to protect them?"

"From what?"

"From the lass. If she doesn't have them groveling and begging her not to be cruel to them before we get back, I'd be surprised."

Bartu smiled and rode off after Jocko. Sir Hamard had a strange look on his face. He looked at me. I gave him a half smirk and shrugged my shoulders, then we rode off.

The trip to the pass did not take long, only one day as Jocko had said. It took half the next day to go up, then the rest of the day to come down. The footing was loose but Jocko's lead was true. We camped our second night on the other side of the mountains. It was then that I had a feeling like something out of my past was coming towards me, yet I did not know what it was.

I said nothing, but as more days past, the others noticed my odd behavior.

"I told you to leave your ants back at Cliff's home. Did you not heed me lad?" Bartu said.

"They didn't want to get out of my pocket," was all I could say.

We were a week out from Cliff's home. We were resting and eating a frugal meal, when Cliff suddenly jumped up.

Bartu unsheathed his sword. Everyone followed his lead.

"What is it?" Sir Hamard whispered.

"Trouble," Cliff answered quietly back.

The feeling that something was going to strike at me got stronger. I was on edge and wanted the feeling to stop.

Cliff looked at me and said, "You are our only hope. You must face him alone."

Cliff's words coupled with the odd feeling made me want to scream. What could be coming that had even Cliff worried?

We heard a horse approach and it came quickly from around a large rock, with a rider on its back.

I recognized him immediately. The sight of him was like an arrow piercing my heart. I grew calm and cold and knew why he was here.

I didn't want it but knew that a fight was inevitable.

He got off of his horse and approached me.

"Caines," was all I said.

24

Caines

"Have we met?"

"Yes. You killed my uncle Jauru."

"Ah yes, the *brat* with the ax. I thought that there was something different about you, but didn't suspect that you were a timestopper."

I didn't want to show any weakness and was glad that he hadn't noticed that I had fainted when he killed my uncle.

"What do you want, timestopper?" Cliff asked.

"Just the nephew. If I'd known about him that day then I wouldn't have been chasing him through those mountains for years. Did you have something to do with hiding him, Gnome?"

"Me? I did nothing. The Earth did that on her own."

"Keeping him underground and growing him like a mushroom were you? Well, I'll soon chop his top off."

Caines got off of his horse and carefully took out a long cloth, and slowly unwrapped it. Eventually a well polished sword emerged.

"Now what do you think you're going to do with that?" Sir Hamard asked.

"Quiet and I might let you live," Caines warned with controlled anger.

Bartu put away his sword and said, "Leave it alone Sir Hamard, there is nothing that we can do."

"Are we just going to let him take the lad without a fight?"

Bartu smiled and added, "I doubt that he can just take the lad anywhere without Einu himself having a say in it."

Bartu went over to the horses and watched from there.

Sir Hamard and Jocko reluctantly joined him, but they refused to sheath their weapons.

Cliff came up beside me and said softly, "I could help you if you like."

"No. This is my task."

Cliff went over and joined the others. I pointed my sword straight at Caines' chest.

"You die today boy, just the same as your uncle did," Caines said just before he stopped time.

Anger rose up within me. I wanted to kill Caines.

I heard Bartu's teaching voice inside my head say to me, 'Do not fight angry, you will be unbalanced. But if you can not avoid it, then use your anger to finish the fight quickly or else you will use too much energy towards it. Instead, harness the anger and use it to serve you.'

"Ready boy? I will not attack anyone who is not ready."

I stood motionless, aiming my sword straight for his chest.

"I'll take that as a yes."

He slowly moved towards me, his sword in his left hand pointing at my chest. He inched forward until the points of our swords were over one another.

He suddenly lunged. I deflected his sword down and to the right, but not far enough. His sword slid by my right leg and cut me. Moving forward I kept our swords locked at our sides.

We crashed together. Caines tried to hit me in the throat with his right hand, but it was low and hit me in the upper chest. I brought my left elbow down hard onto Caines' face, hard enough that he fell.

Caines tried to hit me with his sword as he went down. It was a feeble attempt. I easily leapt over his swing and brought my sword down on his left hand. He dropped his weapon and yelped in pain. I stood on his sword and placed mine at his throat.

I wanted to plunge it in and avenge my uncle but something stopped me.

"Restart time," was all I said to him.

Time resumed.

"You should die for all that you have done. Instead you shall have my mercy, just as you had my uncle's."

I took my sword away from his throat.

"Still, you should not go totally unpunished."

I bent down and picked up his sword and went over to an outcropping of rock and wedged it deeply between two rocks, then sharply pulled on it until it snapped, and threw the hilt at Caines' feet.

Caines had been sucking on the wound on his hand. Through a mouth covered in blood he said, "You will regret this some day."

He then got up, jumped onto his horse and immediately rode off.

Suddenly I felt the pain in my leg. I looked down to see my entire pant leg was covered in blood.

Bartu came up to me and said, "I knew you would win, but you did not pass unscathed. So let us bandage you with all haste."

Bartu ripped open my pants and cleaned and examined the wound.

"Not deep," was all he said and proceeded to put a plaster on it.

Bartu looked at Cliff and Cliff said, "Over on the first pass, not too much to talk about. Einu just used his superior height to his advantage, but his parry was a bit slow. You should work on that with him some more."

I groaned and could see Bartu getting me to do parrying exercises all the way to the fortress.

Bartu closed his eyes slightly as he looked at me, but then quickly smiled and said, "What is the worry? You survived and that is the important part. Every battle that you win makes you wiser."

"It's not the ones that I win that I'm worried about," I replied.

Bartu started to laugh and the others all joined in and then everyone slapped me on the back. We went back to finishing our meal, then continued on our journey. My wound healed over the next two weeks, and the uneventful journey was over quickly.

We had no more problems than saddle sores from riding so long and so fast.

The city and the fortress loomed up in the distance.

Cliff stopped us and said, "I think it best to send Einu in alone and try to find the General. He knows the ways of the city and fortress better than any here, and it is least likely that he could get caught and most likely that he could get away."

Cliff turned to me and said sternly, "But stop time only unless you must."

I got off my horse and sat down to take off my bandage. The wound was sufficiently healed that it wouldn't bother me any more. I put on my spare pair of breeches and tunic from my pack, so as to hide my travels. I then set out on foot towards the city.

25

The Sorcerer's Tower

I had taken my sword with me, hoping to pass as a young soldier in training. My height worried me a little bit, because someone this tall would certainly be remembered. I slouched a bit.

I walked up to the city gates and passed right in with another group of young soldiers. The guard was very lax, nothing of significance had happened here in years. But getting into the fortress would not be as easy.

As I walked toward the fortress an ominous weight grew in the pit of my stomach. I tried to ignore it, but it was slowly building in pressure with every step. I felt very visible but I then remembered something that my uncle had told me. He had described this feeling to me and said to let it fall to my feet and it will pass.

I stood there for a moment and tried to let it fall, then heard Cliff's voice in my head, 'Do not fight it. Embrace the Earth and she will protect you.'

I became aware of the ground and knew it was aware of me. There were lights and a faint sound coming from beneath my feet. No one else seemed to notice.

The weight in my stomach traveled down my legs and with a burst of light and sound disappeared into the earth. Whatever spell Malux had cast against timestoppers left me.

Suddenly, feeling energized I looked up and to my surprise there was Brun. He had someone pulling a small cart behind him.

I shouted, "Brun."

He stopped and watched me run up to him then said, "You will address me as Master Brun, lad or I will find out who your real master is and have him pull your ears off."

Brun's words took me aback a moment. I forgot for a moment that I was no longer Janus, and that he would have no idea about me.

"Sorry Master. I forgot myself."

I half closed my eyes and slowly nodded my head.

Brun tried to show no surprise at my use of 'the signal' but it was clear to see that he was shaken.

He said to the man who was pulling the cart, "Git back to your master, this one will pull the cart."

Brun waited until the man gladly left and said, "I don't know who you are but do as I say or else I will call the guard and have you strung up by your toes. Now grab that harness and follow me."

Brun took me just where I wanted to go. We entered the fortress with no problem. He told me to leave the cart and instructed some servants in the fortress to bring the goods up to the General's tower.

Brun led me straight to the General's top floor. Bree and Anu were there. They were dressed for battle. They had leather armor and some wicked looking scimitars at their sides. Bree in fact had two, one on each side.

Brun said to them, "Hold him."

They grabbed me and Bree took out a knife and said, "Hold still or I'll slit your throat."

I laughed. This was not what they had expected.

Brun said, "Hold your tongue boy or we'll tear it out. Now I want some answers. Who are you and what do you know?"

"Okay, I'll give you answers."

I stopped time and loosened myself, took the knife from Bree and went behind him and placed it at his throat. They all gasped when I started time again. Bree stiffened immediately when he felt the knife.

He said, "Easy boy, we were just playing with you. Be careful with that knife. We wouldn't want to go and hurt somebody with it now, would we?"

I laughed again and said, "You don't know how often I wanted to do this to you, after all those years of training to be aware of you coming for me. Creeping up silently and scaring me half to death."

Bree said confusedly, "Do I know you? I don't remember ever doing that. And I can assure you that I meant no harm by it …"

At that moment the General and Janus walked in.

My heart skipped a beat at seeing Janus standing before me.

I lowered the knife and said, "Janus."

He looked at me and recognized me. We moved quickly to each other and hugged.

"Einu. How did you get here? *What are you doing here?*"

We moved away from each other but still held each others arms and in spite of Cliff's warning we looked deep into each others eyes.

In the depths, his memories and mine were the same. He felt it too. Janus' eyes welled with tears as he understood.

The General interrupted us, "I understand now. You are the other face."

He was looking straight at me when he continued, "You're the timestopper that got away that day when we raided Janus' village four years ago, aren't you?"

"Yes. But I am more than that, isn't that so Janus?"

Janus stood in shock. He shook his head numbly and quietly said, "Yes," then looked at the floor.

"Janus and I were as one for the past four years, and I know all that he knows. All about the plan."

Brun, Anu and Bree all looked at the General, waiting for his lead.

The General said, "What do you plan to do about it?"

"I'm here to help and I've brought friends."

"Who?" he said commandingly.

"Bartu."

The General's eyes lit up.

"The leader of rebels from the north woods, Sir Hamard."

The General nodded his head and put on a slight grin.

"Jocko, a friend from my village and expert archer."

Janus became animated when he heard Jocko's name and looked at me again.

"And a very special friend of mine, Cliff. A gnome of high repute."

The General laughed as only he could laugh. All but Brun visibly eased with the General's laughter.

"All is well then. It appears that we won't have to try and kill you after all. Indeed this is a great day. My prayers have been answered."

Brun finally relaxed.

"In fact this has exceeded my expectations. A timestopper, a gnome, an archer, a great strategist and a fighter of great renown, all come to me on this day to offer me help. Never would I have imagined it. But the creator works in strange ways. There is no need to question your integrity. We must find your friends and invite them to the party ..."

The General was interrupted by the noise of steps on the staircase.

In short order, in came Dux, Goryl and Krue.

"Ah Captain. You might be wondering why I have asked you to come here."

Krue looked suspiciously around. He was no fool, he knew when something was amiss.

"Yes General, I was busy getting the horsemen ready when your servants came to get me."

"Well Krue, the truth is I have a proposal for you."

The General let those words sink in before he continued, "Remember all those years of battles and how, after each, we would sit in our tent and dream about how things could be different?

"Well, today is that day. We're going to kill Malux. Would you care to join us?"

Krue was taken aback by the General's words, but he soon smiled and said, "Might as well, things can only get better. If we win, we change the world. If we lose, then we are dead."

The General laughed. "Then we are decided?"

Krue said, "Yes."

The General turned to me and said, "Well Einu, we have five more fighters, two rogues and a fishwife to throw into the mix."

"I'll not be called a fishwife," Brun said angrily.

Everyone in the room burst out laughing, all the while Brun shouting at everyone to stop. He even threatened to call the guard. We all had a good laugh at his expense and the tension in the room had been lowered greatly.

Brun sulked when everyone stopped.

"Now Einu, would you lead Brun, Dux and Goryl and figure some way to get your friends back here. Send for me if necessary, we'll stay right here."

Before we left the General's home, Brun took some tunics and breeches and some sacks from his stash of supplies.

We left the city without any trouble and we made our way to where Cliff and the others were waiting.

When we found them. Bartu said, "You took your time."

"A lot happened," was all I said.

"This is a fine lot that you brought with you lad," Brun said.

I introduced everyone to each other.

Then Cliff said, "Shouldn't we be getting back?"

"Yes, let's hurry," Brun added.

He took out the clothes he had brought with us and said, "Now put these on and put your things into the sacks. I'm afraid that the best way for you master Gnome to get into the fortress will be in one of the sacks."

"I'll not be carried around like a sack of potatoes on the back of one of you. You'll more than likely drop me."

Bartu laughed then said, "Just pretend that your playing one of your tricks. We can carry you all the way to the sorcerer and you can jump out and scream. Maybe the sorcerer will drop dead from fright and we won't have to fight."

Cliff directed a scowl at Bartu.

"I'm afraid I can think of no other way to hide you. You are kind of obvious master Gnome," Brun apologized.

"All right, but the first one to drop me will live to regret it."

We took it in turns to carry Cliff. He was much heavier than he appeared and complained about his ride until Brun pointed out it wouldn't look good to be carrying around a talking sack. So instead, Cliff would give a poke to whoever was carrying him if he didn't feel the carrier was being as careful as possible.

We eventually made it back to the General's tower.

The General had been telling the rest what he expected of them. When we came in and let Cliff out of the bag, he looked all of us over and said, "We make quite the group now don't we? Bartu, I had always wished that you would be here at my side on this day. That was the reason I always wanted you to join my army."

"Ah but General, you see I had to decline. I could not have stayed away from women that long. Besides you do have your wish after all."

"Yes, but now I wish that there were ten more of you."

"You should have wished that sooner General," Cliff said.

"Yes it is too late, master Gnome."

"Call me Cliff."

"Very well Cliff. Glad to have you on our side."

Cliff bowed and the General did likewise, then they both laughed.

He then turned to Jocko and Sir Hamard.

"You must be the archer."

"Jocko's my name, but I was merely a humble woodsman and hunter before you destroyed my village and murdered most of those in it."

"I'm very sorry about that, but if I didn't do it the sorcerer would have just found someone else to, then we wouldn't be here today planning to destroy him and his evil empire."

Jocko still wasn't happy about the explanation and it was very clear that Sir Hamard was not at all pleased.

"You must be Sir Hamard. I respect you as an enemy sir, you turned what I thought would be a simple campaign into a war. But let us forget our past grievances and join forces to destroy a greater enemy."

The General offered him his hand. Sir Hamard looked at it and said, "I have come to hate you over the years. Your armies have killed my King, destroyed my home, and murdered my family. I will join with you in killing your master but will not take your hand."

"Very well, I am not asking you to like me. I did what I had to do to get to this point today, but if you help me this day, that is all that can be asked. But know this. Never in my heart have I let Malux become my master."

The General and Sir Hamard nodded heads in acknowledgment of a workable agreement.

I hadn't put much thought to what might happen when these two met, but it turned out okay after all.

The General continued, "While you were on your way, I had Bree and Anu bring up all the armor that we have in my home. Please feel free to take any of it or any of the weapons from my walls. They are all in excellent condition. I insist that you at least take a shield. There are strange creatures that guard Malux' tower."

Goryl and Dux put on their armor then each took a shield and a sword and mace from the wall.

Bartu took his time but he found a chain shirt to put over his leather shirt and took a small shield. Sir Hamard didn't add anything to his armor except a large shield. Jocko didn't want a shield, he said he was going to stand back anyway. He took out his bow and strung it and inspected all of his arrows. Cliff took nothing. He was always ready for a fight, having a shortsword always by his side. There were no small weapons here that he could use anyway.

Brun just picked up a mace and shield and carried a large knife in his belt.

The General looked at me and said, "Aren't you going to take anything Einu?"

I had my uncle's sword and felt somehow that was all that was needed, but picked up a hand ax for my left hand just to make the General happy. I didn't want any armor or a shield ... for speed in the upcoming fight was more necessary than any other protection.

"Is everyone ready?" General Harauld asked.

Everyone either nodded or said yes.

"Then let's do it. And may God be with us."

There were a few amens.

The General then addressed all of those that were unfamiliar with the fortress, "We leave in groups of three and make our way to the tower. Just follow our lead. We have a plan of what to do when we get there. All we need is for you to add your swords to our own when the fighting starts. I will go with Janus and Einu. Einu will carry Cliff in a sack."

Cliff scowled. He didn't want to have anything to do with sacks any more, but he accepted one from Brun reluctantly.

"Brun will go with Sir Hamard and Jocko. Krue will go with Bartu and Dux. Goryl will go with Bree and Anu. If anyone stops you, just say that you are under orders of the General to go to Master Malux' tower. That should be easy enough. I will go first and wait for you just outside the antechamber to his tower.

Everyone got that?"

We all nodded.

"Leave one hundred heart beats after the group in front of you has left. Take your time and do not draw any attention to yourselves. It should not be that unusual for anyone to be seen in armor today. I called upon a good portion of the fortress guard to go with us to the fleet and have replaced them with other more loyal soldiers. So there should be many new faces arriving at the fortress today and many in armor leaving. That should be sufficiently confusing to any guard that you encounter. Brun, maybe you should put your shield and mace into a sack. Seeing you with them might make someone who knows you suspicious.

"Very well. We're off."

I followed the General down the stairs with Cliff on my back. My breathing started to be a little heavier as I tried my best to give Cliff an easy ride, and tried at the same time to make it look like the load was light.

No one dared to stop the General or even question him as to what we were doing or where we were going. Fortunately, we didn't run into any apprentices.

We could only hope that the rest would have just as easy a journey through the fortress. The General had taken a direct route to the tower. The others would take a route more befitting their status and it would be safer for them. It would be less likely to find the apprentices in the kitchen than in the dining area.

We came to a set of ornate double doors. There was a guard standing in front of each. They were wearing the armor of the fortress guard. A silver breast plate covered their chest with a chain shirt underneath. The chain covered their arms and went down to their waist. They had ornate gauntlets over their hands and they carried a spear and shield. What made them appear comical however was the fact that they had no armor, or clothes for that matter, from the waist down, except for their boots. On the rare occasion when one of the guards did leave the fortress, they were allowed to wear a short skirt.

The General stopped us in front of the guards. They crossed their spears together and said, "Where would you go, General?"

"I wish to see our Master. There is some important last minute business to be attended to."

"Forgive me General. But our Master has said that none may disturb him today."

"I will take full responsibility for disturbing the Master."

The two guards looked at each other and one of them said, "I'm sorry but it will mean our lives if he is angered."

The General just stared at the guards but did not say anything. They shifted nervously under his stare.

After a while Brun, Sir Hamard, Jocko, Captain Krue, Bartu and Dux showed up almost at the same time. Krue must have taken a more direct route and Brun a more indirect one.

The General finally said, "Very well. Have it your way … Captain?"

"Yes General?"

"Have we enough fops to service the army yet?"

Krue smiled then said, "No General. We need two more."

The General walked over to the guards and said, "Do you think that these two would do?"

"Yes General. I think that these two would serve wonderfully."

"Then go to the Captain of the guard and request that two new guards be sent to our Master's door and inform him that these two will now go with the army."

The two guards shifted uneasily and almost shouted as Krue turned to leave, "Wait! I'm sure that the General knows what he his doing, and will explain his presence to our Master."

"Certainly."

The General did nothing.

The guards shifted nervously again and the other said, "It is okay if you go in General."

"Yes I know. We are merely waiting for my advisor and two of my servants."

The guards relaxed somewhat, but I was beginning to wish that they would hurry. Cliff was getting very heavy now. I shifted his weight on my back and must have jostled Cliff too hard, because he jabbed me. I gave a muffled grunt, which drew the guards' attention.

Janus and Bartu helped me by each lifting the load with one arm each. It was just enough to make it tolerable. The guards eased their watchfulness and eventually Goryl, Bree and Anu showed up.

The General motioned the guards to open the door and we all passed in. When the doors had closed behind us. The General motioned Bree and Anu to go to the door to the tower. Brun and

Goryl listened at the door we had just come through.

With help, I let Cliff down and he crawled out of the sack somewhat flustered. He pulled his short sword and was ready for battle.

Bree nodded his head to the General after he and Anu had finished examining the door. The General nodded back and Bree slowly and silently opened it. Inside was a small room with three other doors leading from it. The General quickly went in with the rest of us following as quietly as we could ... all except Brun and Goryl ... they shut the door behind us.

The General must have planned all of this ahead of time with his servants in the time between when I became myself again and now. They were the worst fighters among us, yet their strength lay in their use of words. They could use their tongues to delay any that might respond to a call of help from Malux.

The General whispered, "Wedge the doors."

Bree, Anu and Dux each went to a door and shoved wedges under them, then forced them in as tightly as they could. Then they placed chairs that were in the room in front of them. They were large heavy chairs, yet they looked very comfortable. They were probably used for those waiting to see Malux.

Bree gave extra attention to the door that we had just come through.

Bree and Anu then went to the last door and listened at it. They quickly nodded and again opened it silently. On the other side was a spiral stone staircase leading up.

A small gust of wind blew down the stairs. It was cold and ominous. Everyone except Cliff and Bartu gave a shudder.

The General signaled to Dux and he examined each step carefully. He held up three fingers and then very slowly started up the stairs, but did not step on the third step.

The General whispered, "Watch closely what Dux does," to Bree and Anu.

He then whispered to everyone else, "Watch what the one in front of you does very closely. Do not step on those steps that Dux does not step on."

Cliff went after Anu, and I followed him. Bartu came behind me.

I stopped and looked at the third step to see what Dux had seen and noticed that there was the slightest difference in the sheen of the step. It was as if it had not been stepped on as often as the others.

"Come on lad, we are not here to see the sights," Bartu whispered in my ear.

Hopping over the third step, I followed Cliff.

There were three steps in all that we did not step on. The third, the seventh, and the eleventh.

We came to a door at the top of the stairs. Bree went ahead of Dux and examined it. When he tried to open it, he gave out a hushed curse. The door was locked.

Anu and the General came up. Bree said something but, "barred," was all I heard.

The General eventually came down two steps then Bree and Anu went into quick action. Anu took out a bar from his under his tunic. He wedged it into the door and pulled it back with all his might and held it there. This opened a small crack between the door and the frame. Bree then took out two small tools. One was dull thin shears. He shoved this one in first then opened the shears up and rotated them up until they hit the door. He then used the other tool, which resembled a fork missing the center tine, by wedging this one and keeping pressure on it as he took out the other tool. He then put the shears back in and rotated them upward again, removing the other tool as he did this.

He did these maneuvers a few times until he was satisfied. He then used the shears tool, first holding them tight while he shoved in the forked tool and now jerked his hand to the side away from the door. He began to remove the shear tool, holding with the forked tool before reinserting the shear tool. This process went on for several minutes. I could see that both Bree and Anu were straining. Anu was tiring of holding the bar so tight. His fingers were white. It looked like all the blood had drained from them. Bree was going as fast as he could and his fingers too showed sign of strain.

Eventually there was a slight tap on the door. Bree smiled and Anu pulled the bar out from the door. Bree silently opened the door. After going through I saw that the door had been bolted and somehow Bree had raised the bolt and slid it open.

We quickly entered the room. There were two voices inside. Two boys were relaxing in a large round room. There were cushions everywhere. I had never seen so many cushions in my life. Large ones, small ones. A wild mix of colors, fabric and embroidery hit my eyes.

The boys had been lying on cushions stacked high and deep.

Bree and Anu went immediately to the boys, grabbed them and put their hands over the boys' mouths.

We saw that there was no one else in the room.

As Dux entered, he froze instantly. He grabbed the General and pointed at the door at the far side of the room. There was a large statue in front of the door. The statue was extremely large but none of us except Dux had noticed it when we entered. It was at least seven feet tall and extremely ugly. Stranger still was the fact that it was right in front of the door making it impossible to open unless the statue was much lighter than it looked.

Dux looked frightened, something I'd never seen. Then the statue snorted.

I half jumped out of my skin. It was obviously watching us. It was a creature that had skin the same color and texture as stone.

Cliff had been one of the last to enter the room. When he saw the creature he went up to the General and said, "I'll go and see what's ahead."

Cliff walked right up to the creature and it moved out of the way for him. Cliff and the creature totally ignored each other. Cliff opened the door and went up the stairs on the other side. He left the door open behind him.

I gathered up my courage and walked cautiously up to the door, never taking my eyes from the creature. It watched me approach and moved quickly in front of me, blocking my passage. It moved much too fast for my liking.

"Where you think you go?" it demanded in a harsh voice.

"Just following the gnome," I said innocently.

It didn't move. I tried to go around it. It reacted by swatting me like a fly. The blow of his hand on my chest sent me flying back into the room. Fortunately, a pile of cushions softened my landing. My chest hurt though as I struggled back up to my feet.

At that moment Janus reacted. He ran up to the creature, sword and shield in hand. He swung a blow that would have killed any human. He hit the creature across the chest, but he barely made a mark. The creature did not stand there and let Janus hit him again. He tried to do to Janus what he had done to me, but Janus reacted in time to avoid being hit. He fell down backwards. He used his momentum to twirl around and brought his sword onto the creature's leg. It made a more noticeable indent, but the wound produced no blood. The creature winced then tried to grab Janus.

Janus rolled away and got to his feet fast and then lunged back at the creature. His sword went into the creature, but not deep. The creature reacted by grabbing Janus' sword and Janus had to let go or risk being grabbed as well.

It pulled the sword out of its body and broke it with one hand.

It now went after Janus. I ran forward, but everyone else came out of their stupors and charged the creature at the same time and they arrived there before me. Bartu was first. He stabbed it in the arm. It responded by striking at Bartu. Its other arm came down on Bartu's shield, sending Bartu down under the force of the blow. It did seem to have troubling moving the arm that Bartu stabbed, however, when the General, Sir Hamard and Dux attacked. They attacked in unison, all driving their swords into the creature at the same time.

It reared its head back and gave off a high piercing scream. Bartu then got up, leaving his shield behind and leapt up, holding his sword with both hands, and swung a mighty blow at the creature's neck, severing its head from its body. The body fell backward and quivered when it hit the ground. The head however, went on screaming.

At that moment Cliff came back down the stairs. He yelled to me, "Come on Einu, quickly, up the stairs."

I had still been trying to get back to the fight but at Cliff's words changed my direction and rushed through the door, past Cliff and up the stairs.

There was the sound of hacking behind me and eventually the screaming stopped.

I ran quickly up the stairs with Cliff, surprisingly, keeping up behind me.

"Einu you'd better stop time," Cliff said.

I did but we were not in stopped time. Instead we were bathed in a blue light. The whole tower must have been under a spell that prevented time from stopping within its confines. But it was still worthwhile to stop time because it would probably prevent any help from getting to Malux from outside his tower.

Our companions followed behind us. We passed many doors off the staircase as we went up. I was wondering whether we should be going through any of these doors, and was about to stop and suggest we wait for the General. In fact I was just taking a look back when Cliff shouted, "Einu, look out!"

I followed Cliff's hand up to where he was pointing.

I saw Malux staring down at us from the top of the stairs. His hand was glowing with a green fire. He spoke some words and a green sphere appeared in the air before him. It looked like it was made of glass and it had swirling mist within it.

The sphere started to turn then it hurtled towards us.

I dodged to one side and the ball exploded as it hit the wall beside me. The mist escaped and a horrible smell filled the stairway. It caused me to choke and it burned my eyes. I ran up to get away from the mist. Cliff merely sneezed then continued up, ignoring it.

There were shouts then coughing from below, the mist was traveling downward.

Cliff marched ahead of me. Malux was nowhere to be seen.

"Come Einu, it is time for you to meet your destiny," Cliff said as he approached a door.

Cliff waited for me at the top of the stairs. We looked at each other, nodded then we opened the door together and rushed in.

26

Battle

We burst into a circular room, full of strange smells and sights. It was dark. The room was lit only by a few candles, when combined with the blue light of Malux' spell, cast an eerie glow. There were many strange metal contraptions that defied description, but they appeared to be based on some sort of weird geometry. Malux was beside one of these devices, standing absolutely motionless. His hands were on a sphere that was set in the middle of the protrusions coming from the device. Cliff placed his hand in front of me and stopped me in my tracks. He was much stronger than he looked.

Right in front of us was another gnome, shortsword in hand. I would have run into him on my way to Malux, as I hadn't seen him upon entering the room.

"Cliff," the gnome said.

"Precipice," Cliff answered.

"Your way has been *rocky*, Cliff."

"I see that you fight for Malux. You are one *living on the edge*."

"You think you're so *high and mighty*."

"You've been drinking too much again Precipice, you're *hung over*."

Precipice scowled then said, "I'm tired of this inane banter."

Cliff shrugged his shoulders then said, "Why, as far as I'm concerned, it's the best part of being a gnome."

"Some may be content with the way that they are, but not I. I'm changing my very nature."

"You really don't understand your true nature and you are lost and *overhanging*."

"Stop it," Precipice yelled.

"Sorry, I couldn't help myself. But we have a conflict of interest here."

"Yes we do Cliff. You want to change the balance of power on this planet. That is an unwise course of action. It will mean that there will be less space for the likes of us."

"It is what the majority wants."

"And you will help these humans do this?"

"It comes with the territory. Besides I always liked taking the *high ground*."

Precipice just stood there and fumed. He obviously wasn't comfortable with the normal way gnomes communicated with one another.

My eye caught movement where Malux was standing. Swirls of mist appeared in mid air. They started to rotate in a circular pattern.

At that moment Cliff and Precipice leapt at each other and there was a sharp clash of metal.

Also there were the sounds of people coming up the stairs, coughing heavily as they came. As Cliff was fighting Precipice, he yelled, "Get Malux."

I leapt into action at his words as the call to battle rang through the air. I ran at him, but before I reached him, the mist hung in the air and transformed into a black circle. Out jumped one of those strange creatures that had guarded the staircase. It blinked, then ran to intercept me. I stopped, then leapt sideways to avoid the creature's charge. It couldn't stop, and ran right into one of the many devices in the room, totally destroying it.

I continued running toward Malux, but another creature jumped right out in front of me.

It was impossible to avoid it. It swung at me and missed. I tried to use my momentum to push it out of my way.

That was a miserable failure. It obviously weighed much more than me, because all that happened was I moved it back a few feet. Just far enough that it barely missed me with another swing of its fist. The blow from the last creature was still fresh in my chest as I was ducking and dodging a series of blows from this creature. Low grunts accompanied its swings. The other creature recovered, then came towards me as well.

Taking my hand ax from my belt I swung it firmly at the hand of the creature when it made its next grunt. The ax passed between two of its fingers and cut straight through its flesh. It yelped in pain and stopped its attack. Just in time too, because the first creature tried to grab me.

I was ducking and dodging again when another creature came out of the black circle.

But there was coughing at the door. Sir Hamard was the first one through, followed by Bartu.

Sir Hamard yelled to Bartu, "Someone must stop the sorcerer from letting more of those demons loose or else we are lost."

Cliff yelled in between sword strokes, "Break the device that Malux is holding."

The same thought had occurred to me but I was unable to get there.

Two demons were trying to catch me. In my attempt to dodge them I jumped up onto a long bench with many bottles, jars, flasks and bowls and kicked one of the large bowls at them. The liquid caught one right in the face. The demon screamed as smoke surrounded it. The screaming demon backed into the other demon, knocking it over and then fell on top of him. This gave me a moment to see what was happening.

Cliff and Precipice were fighting each other like two dogs, back and forth with lightning-like speed. Precipice had a nasty gash on his forehead and his face was slick with blood. Cliff had a cut on his hand, almost as if he had grabbed his opponent's sword. Neither of these wounds slowed either of them.

Bartu and Sir Hamard were fighting three demons between them. They were having greater success. With their heavier swords they could actually do some damage and the demons were more cautious in attacking them.

But the greatest boost to my heart was seeing the General, Janus and Dux coming through the door. Janus had a scimitar in his hands. It must have been one of Bree's.

I yelled, "General, stop Malux."

I was now on the farthest side of the tower away from him. Malux had not moved much from the time the battle began. At my yell, he opened his eyes. The black circle wavered just as another demon came out. This one seemed to have trouble coming through. Malux' face turn to rage, but instead of reacting, he closed his eyes again and the circle grew blacker and larger than ever.

The demon that had struggled through was smaller in size than the first five, but after Malux closed his eyes, two much larger demons came through the black gateway.

The General yelled to Janus, "Help Einu," then yelled to Dux, "Dux, with me."

Janus came running in my direction, while the General and Dux went to help Bartu and Sir Hamard. They had six demons to fight between the four of them.

The two demons in front of me were now up. I furiously kicked more bottles and jars at them to slow them, but had to jump off of the bench when they kept coming.

Janus came in time and he definitely made them notice when he chopped off the hand of the demon that was still smoking from the liquid.

Janus had that demon backing away with a series of circular swings of his scimitar, but the other still came for me. I tried to hit it with my sword. The demon just barely missed me with a wicked swing of its enormous hands. I felt the wind of its fist as it passed narrowly by my face. I had to leap backwards to avoid him.

I hit the wall and found myself in a corner formed where an enormous cabinet met the wall. I had no other choice but to lunge with my sword at the oncoming demon. As I leapt, the point of an arrow came out through the front of the demon's throat. The force of the arrow forced its head slightly forward and the demon put both of its hands over the arrowhead while it made a choking sound.

I took advantage of the moment by changing my weapon of attack. I brought my hand ax down hard on the top of its head. The ax clove the demon's skull in two, and it fell.

Janus had removed more of his demon's arm and then with one mighty swing of his scimitar removed the demon's head from its body.

I turned back to the rest of the battle.

Jocko was in the room. His arrow had saved me, but he was now aiming at the sorcerer. Krue, Bree and Anu had also come into the room. They had joined the fight at the General's side, but they were now facing eight demons. Two more huge ones were fighting for Malux.

At this moment Bartu and the General were fighting on either side of Sir Hamard. They both, as if given a signal, attacked Sir Hamard's demon. This left them open for attack, but they managed to chop the arms off of his demon. It screamed in pain, but not for long, because Sir Hamard stabbed his sword straight into its head. It fell like a rock, taking Sir Hamard's sword with it. Sir Hamard didn't waste any time. He leapt over the body of the fallen demon and ran through the gap in the defense straight toward Malux. He grabbed an iron rod from a table on the way and brought it smashing down in a long high arc on the device that Malux was holding.

The device bent out of shape and the circle disappeared instantly. Malux reacted, opening his eyes wide and holding his hands in front of him. He said some quick words and a brilliant flash of light came from them, accompanied by a booming, thunder-like sound. The flash blinded me as to what happened, but I did see the result.

Sir Hamard hit the wall by the door with great speed and a sickening sound. He fell to the ground and didn't move. There was a hole in the front of his armor, square in the middle of his chest. It was scorched and smoke rose from the hole.

After the flash, Jocko fired an arrow at Malux, but it burst into flame and was totally consumed before it got to him.

The two demons that were fighting the General and Bartu had swung at them when they attacked Sir Hamard's demon. Somehow Bartu managed to avoid the blow from his demon but the General did not. He took the full force of the blow on the side of his head. He was lifted off the ground and twirled in the air. He dropped his sword and shield, and his helmet was bent out of shape before he hit the ground heavily.

Janus and I both yelled, "No!" simultaneously.

We ran towards the Sorcerer. I had a clear path, but Janus had the two gnomes in front of him.

Janus leapt at Precipice as he came up to them. The gnome saw him coming and leapt away, but Cliff did an amazing lunge, jumping sideways in unison with Precipice all the while twisting his body in mid air and reaching out with his sword.

This had the effect of Cliff riding up Precipice's sword arm and stabbing him straight in the heart.

It only took a momentary distraction for Cliff to win his hard fought battle.

Krue, Bartu, Dux, Bree and Anu were hard put defending against seven demons. There was quickly only five as Jocko placed an arrow into one of the large demon's eyes and Bartu chopped the head off the small demon as the large one fell. As soon as Janus got to the fight he hacked the leg off a demon that was stepping on the General, lowering the number of fighting demons in the room to four.

I had now come within ten feet of Malux. He had watched everything transpire and was quite aware of what was happening. He looked at me and smiled.

We were winning but Malux didn't seem to be worried. Suddenly the blue light shrank until it was just a small circle around where Malux stood. Somehow, Malux had changed his anti-timestop spell so that it covered only himself. The rest of the room was stopped in time instantly.

Cliff was still running towards Malux. He shouted, "Restart time."

Of course, what would it matter now? Help could not get here in time before we would win.

I restarted time. For an instant time flowed normally, but then it stopped again.

From out of the cabinet beside Malux popped Caines.

He was holding a new sword, smiled at me then said, "I told you that you would live to regret humiliating me."

The blue sphere around Malux again changed shape. A large tentacle reached out and grabbed one of the huge demons and brought it back to the blue sphere. Then the sphere grew and covered the half of the room that we were in, but leaving the others still stopped in time.

Cliff ran right by the demon, who ignored him, straight at Malux. Malux had grabbed a long staff that was leaning on the wall and used it to keep Cliff at bay. The old sorcerer moved remarkably well.

The demon and Caines, in the meantime, moved between me and the barrier which marked stopped time. Had I moved into that area immediately, it would have meant that I would have only had Caines to fight, but my reactions were too slow. Now they approached me. I moved back, trying to decide what to do and quickly realized that if Caines were dead then time would restart again, and the others in the room could help me.

I made my mind up to stop moving back and prepared for one desperate lunge at Caines.

When he was close enough I acted and tried to move to one side and then lunge at Caines. But Caines must have sensed what was about to happen, because he stopped moving forward. The demon however, moved quicker. So my lunge towards Caines was too far away. The demon loomed over me. Caines easily stepped back and two huge hands grabbed me, one on each of my forearms. They held me in a vice-like grip. The demon drew me in and stretched my arms apart. I was lifted off the ground.

Caines now walked slowly up to me with his sword aiming at my throat.

"I told your uncle this ... no one makes a fool of me and lives. Do you have anything to say before you die, boy?"

I looked at Caines with detachment, I knew now how my uncle felt before he died. There was only pity in my heart for Caines.

There was a loud whack and Cliff gave a loud grunt. Turning my eyes slightly, I saw Cliff lying on the ground holding his head, with Malux standing over him. Cliff's sword was nowhere to be seen.

Malux was gloating over Cliff, the same way that Caines was gloating over me.

"Nothing boy? You have nothing to say? Very well then, I'll just have to say something for you ..."

At that moment, unexpectedly, the demon let go of me and its head fell in front of me.

Caines looked behind me and Bartu said, "What did you want to say?"

I half turned and was as in as much shock as Caines. How did Bartu pass through stopped time?

"How ... ?"

"I'm a fast learner, lad."

Caines began to move. I reacted by bringing my sword up and heard the clash of metal. I swiped my ax by and felt it connect. A gash appeared on Caines' side. Again Caines swung and I parried perfectly with my sword and again brought my hand ax across. This time aiming higher and hitting Caines in the jaw. It tore through his face and he turned with the force of my blow. He was now defenseless.

I kept turning in the direction of my swing and came about completely in a three hundred and sixty degree turn and swung again. This time using my sword.

Caines' head severed neatly from his neck before he hit the ground. Time resumed instantly.

Bartu had run in defense of Cliff when I started my fight with Caines. Before he reached him Caines was dead and time had resumed. Bartu could not help Cliff however. Malux raised his hand and said a word in a strange language. It sank deep into my skull. It was a booming sound and stopped Bartu in his tracks. He merely stood swaying back and forth.

The others in the room took it harder. They were hit by the word as if hit by a blow and were knocked off of their feet. The remaining demons dissolved into smoke and a strong wind just blew them away.

Cliff wasn't affected by the word, but he remained on the floor, holding his head.

Malux looked older after he finished speaking. He stood there for a moment with his eyes closed, breathing heavily.

All at once my mind blurred. I was still conscious yet I felt even more detached than when Caines was about to kill me.

The world turned foggy. I was viewing it down a tunnel. It no longer seemed real to me.

I turned and saw my wife, and this time truly knew who she was. The strangest thing was that I was not Einu. I was Claude.

There before me was an ordinary house, with a computer, telephone and television.

I remembered it. I lived on the planet Earth and didn't live where Einu lived.

"What are you doing back here?" my wife said.

"I don't know ... what are you talking about," I said, confused.

"Look there."

She pointed back down the tunnel. It was like looking at a dream through a pool of water that floated perpendicular to the floor.

I was totally confused. While looking at my house there was very little recollection of Einu's world. But when I looked back into the tunnel, I remembered everything.

Malux recovered and looked about the room. He saw Cliff on the floor and raised his staff.

Everything was moving in slow motion. Time was slowing down as I watched.

My wife said, "Go and finish what you have started."

I focused on the tunnel and headed down it. The image started to recede. I ran faster. My legs were pumping as hard as they could, yet the image at the end of the tunnel kept receding farther.

Suddenly a familiar feline voice said, "Rrrun not with yourrr legs, but with yourrr mind."

Something inside of me understood and I saw myself running in my mind and catching the image. The image came at me and flashed by. I was totally immersed in the image and it resolved back in Malux' tower. However I was no longer Einu. I was still Claude. My perspective was not of that of the five-foot-six Einu. It was that of my full height. That of the six-foot-six Claude.

A panic rose within me and I knew that this was not right. I should be Einu in this world. Just as Einu had become Janus. Claude had become Einu.

But now my body had replaced Einu's. I should be Claude in Einu's body not Claude in his own body.

Malux looked at me. He stood still. Staff in the air. Ready to come down on Cliff. He was puzzled and didn't know what was wrong, only that something had changed.

I had Einu's sword and hand ax in my hands and didn't waste another second. I wound up and threw the hand ax at Malux.

It traveled in a perfect arc but before it hit him it stopped in mid air then fell to the ground, narrowly missing Cliff.

I ran to Malux. He slowly lowered his staff. He did nothing to stop me.

I swung my sword at him. He did nothing to defend himself. My sword arrived at his body but slowed as if passing through molasses, and stopped before it hit him.

Malux laughed at me. A cold laugh. A laugh that chilled my blood.

He put down his staff and made clutching motions with his fingers. Invisible hands clutched at my throat and no air was getting into my lungs.

I stood paralyzed with fear and dropped my sword. I reached with my hands to feel where the attack was coming from.

There was nothing there. The attack must have been coming from one of Malux' spells.

Looking at him, I realized he was a short man, maybe four-foot-ten. I was six-foot-six.

I lost my fear and went for his throat. As I approached him something slowed me down. I remembered the tunnel and how I couldn't get to the end of it until I pictured myself reaching the end in my mind, I did the same thing here. So I pictured myself in my mind reaching Malux' throat, then suddenly surged forward and grabbed it. Malux gasped in surprise as my large hands squeezed tightly around his small throat.

It was my turn to smile at Malux. There was something that he didn't know. In my youth I did a lot of skin diving, in ponds and lakes north of my home and was quite good at holding my breath. I could easily hold it for two minutes and on one occasion had held it for three. I had kept in good shape as I grew older and still had a good lung capacity.

I was cutting off his air quite effectively with my fingers, but it was only a matter of time before one of us passed out. Malux still clutched one hand, but with his other he started to hit at me feebly, then tried to gouge at my eyes. I moved my head and bit his hand. But quite suddenly he stopped moving.

I could breathe again. I took in a large gasp of air and let Malux fall to the ground.

My breathing quickly returned to normal and everyone in the room groaned then started to move.

Janus, Krue, Dux, Jocko, Bree and Anu all got up off of the floor. Bartu opened his eyes and went over to Cliff and helped him up. But there was something strange in appearance about the two of them. Their images were blurry for some reason. I could not focus on them clearly. There were two images of each in the same place at the same time. One slightly larger and slightly different from the other.

Before I could figure out what was wrong with them, there was a movement and with a shimmer Drux suddenly appeared from thin air. He landed right where the General was lying. He looked quickly about then muttered some words and his hands burst into flame. The flames were forming into two balls. One on each hand.

The General moved and grasped for his sword. When he found it he plunged it straight into Drux' belly up and out through his upper back. Drux curled forward and the balls of flame he held shot straight down and exploded right at his feet. The heat caused me to turn away.

When it had passed, almost everyone ran to where the General was rolling on fire. Janus, Krue, Dux, Bree and Anu were there first, beat at the flames and put them out with their bare hands.

When I got there, the General was holding onto Krue and Janus. His face was burned almost beyond recognition. His charred lips parted and he said, "You two … must lead … now. Kill the rest … of the apprentices."

His voice was coming in hard gasps. He must have breathed in the fire.

He looked up at Janus. All the pain left his face and his eyes rolled back into his head. His gasping stopped and he fell, limp, in Janus' and Krue's arms.

Janus started to cry in sobs. The others either bowed their heads or cried softly.

My eyes were wet too and my throat constricted from an inner pain. I looked at the still burning body of Drux and knew that the General would die happy knowing that we had won the battle and he himself had ended Drux' life.

But it was little consolation to me. I would miss him but then realized that I shouldn't be here at all.

At that moment Cliff said, "Krue, you should go to the apprentice's tower and complete the task that the General has given you."

Krue rose with a face that was as hard as steel. He had a purpose to fulfill. Mourning had to wait. Indeed, having a purpose allowed him to remove himself from his feelings. He was now a cold, ruthless killing machine. Nothing could stop him.

He looked over at Malux.

"Is the sorcerer dead?"

"Not yet. Leave that to Einu. It is his destiny. His name means 'the one' in the tongue of your ancestors. Bartu and I will remain here to see that it is done. Take the others and go quickly," Cliff replied.

"Okay, you heard the gnome, let's go."

Everyone got up and ran to the stairs, all but Janus. Krue had to grab him and drag him to the stairs. Once Janus was at the stairs, he began to run.

Cliff looked at me and said, "Now Claude, you should finish doing what you came here to do."

When Cliff said my proper name, suddenly he and Bartu came into perfect focus. I knew who they were.

27

Spider

Spider began to bounce around as only Spider could.

"Spider, you owe me an explanation."

"No, you owe the people who are reading this book an explanation first," he replied.

"What book?"

"The book you're going to write in the future," Spider said with a grin.

"I've written a book?"

"More than one."

"You're kidding?" I asked.

"Have I ever lied to you before?"

Spider grinned an unearthly grin before continuing, "But as I said. In this point in your story, it is unfair to just pop us in and not give an explanation."

I shook my head not fully comprehending what Spider was trying to tell me. The present was my concern.

"But wait a minute. How come no one here noticed that I am different? And for that matter how come no one can see you two either?"

Spider sighed then said, "This world has altered its collective reality agreement to accommodate us being here. The majority just wanted change bad enough. So to them all is as it should be. The individuals in the collective would have to be more aware than they are to have noticed any changes. To his credit Malux knew that something was different when you came back to this world as you are, even though he wasn't too sure what had exactly happened.

"But we digress. You still owe your readers an explanation."

It was impossible to avoid thinking about what Spider wanted me to think about. So I tried, but was still very unclear about it. Whenever I am unclear about something, the best way for me to get answers is to ask questions. The simpler the better when it comes to Spider.

"Spider, I don't understand. How do I do that?"

Spider grabbed me by the ears, pulled our faces close together and said, "Alter your point of view."

28

Explanation

Hi.

I'm the author, Claude, and you're owed an explanation.

This violates all the rules of writing a book, but so many strange and unusual events have happened to me that this transgression is justified.

So for those of you who have not read my first book, *Afterworld - When Ghosts Disappear*, a brief explanation will follow of who Spider, Bill and Cat (that familiar feline voice) are, and for that matter who I am, before you return to Spider and myself in conversation.

This story occurred before I started writing. Now when I say occurred, I mean occurred. I'll risk the wrath of skeptics and the threat of the men in the white jackets with the rubber rooms and say that I was Einu and have traveled to his world.

Yes, there is a possibility that I am delusional, and I am one of the first to admit it, because it is impossible to eliminate any reasonable explanation for what has happened to me, and to this day is still happening to me. But we will proceed from here as if everything that I have written is reality.

So who is Spider?

I know little about him at this moment in time and you can judge for yourself what he is.

Spider 'lives' in a cave. Now that is not to say that he is a well defined person for whom a good physical description exists. It's a little more complicated than that.

Let's just say Spider's first appearance to me was a little frightening.

I met him on a vision quest. Spider describes himself as an Earth Spirit. So when I first 'saw' him, he was a frightening apparition to my mind.

Of course he never introduced himself to me, and I moved away from that cave at a good pace, but over time we became familiar to each other.

At the time of my first book, I did not know him well and still saw him as that frightening apparition.

But now I see him as a totally naked, little old wiry 'man' with a floor-length beard. 'Man' is used loosely here because he shows no sign of ever having had genitals.

So for the past years I have been drawn back to the place where Spider lives and now feel quite at home in his cave.

Unfortunately, civilization has encroached on Spider's cave and it has become difficult to visit him there for any length of time. His cave is on private property, so during my last visit there, Spider said that he will visit me from now on in.

I can only imagine at this point what that might mean.

The one thing that makes my belief in Spider firm, is what he has told me. However much I would like to claim some of the ideas in my books as my own, credit must be given where it belongs. Spider, as well as the others, have said some amazing things, only a small portion of which has been written down.

I'll try to write as much of it down as possible.

But as to what Spider really is, remains a mystery to me. What is a spirit anyway? Hints were given to me as to what a spirit is, and I will try to clarify that in later books as I am able to decipher all the clues that have been given to me.

Right now Spider is more of an enigma.

As is his apprentice Bill. Bill claims to be a human spirit in between bodies who is trying to learn how to ascend. He has attached himself to Spider and now me in his quest for knowledge.

I do not know what Bill could learn from me, except

maybe how not to do things. He certainly has taught me more than I have taught him.

Where there is Spider, you'll find Bill. A double enigma.

Speaking of enigmas, an even bigger one is Cat. I named him that because he has never given me a name.

We met on my very first venture into shamanism. During my first ceremony, he suddenly appeared to me, two inches from my face. He almost gave me a heart attack, but I survived our first encounter and have had literally hours of frustrating conversations with him. He takes the unclearness of my thoughts and throws them back at me. As long as I am perfectly clear and precise in my words then we get along just fine.

He describes himself as my animal spirit guide, which is quite confusing sometimes, because sometimes he is in a humanoid form. A puzzle for sure.

But the biggest puzzle for me is another important spirit that I have encountered. Now this spirit is quite special to me, but poses no ends of problems.

It is the spirit of my wife. Now the confusing part is that my wife is still alive. This spirit claims to be my wife's spirit from the future.

My wife, of course, claims no connection to this spirit and these encounters with her future dead self have led me to actually have arguments with my flesh and blood wife.

Arrgh! You think you have trouble with your spouse.

That leaves only myself. I am an ordinary person (even though most of my friends would laugh at that statement), to whom some extraordinary things have happened.

If I started to tell you all the things that have happened, this book would more than triple in size. So that will be saved for future books.

We will simply leave it with, I am the guy writing this book.

But getting back to some sort of an explanation.

If you missed the first book, I had adventures with these characters in the future after dying.

In the end they told me that my consciousness should not be limited by time and that if I so desired, I could go to any part of my existence in time and place my consciousness there. That was what I did and have been changing my future ever since.

Now some people might argue that all I had was an elaborate dream. But I know that this world was subtly different from the one that I left, after I came back.

I noticed minor changes in this world that if noticed by anyone else would have had them screaming 'I just entered the twilight zone.'

I believe that all of my experiences have been real, and that is why I have written them down.

So, let's leave Spider to explain the details, and return you now to the story as it has progressed so far.

29

Spider Continued

"I understand. I just closed my eyes and saw myself typing something about you on my computer. It was like actually being there."

Spider turned to Bill and said, "I think Claude is finally getting the hang of reality, or should we still call him Einu?"

Bill started to laugh then Spider joined him.

When Bill stopped laughing, he said, "Claude sure has a lot of names. When I first met him we called him Nexus. Now he has Einu."

"Don't forget his other names, the one that the shaman gave him and the one he gives his inner self," Spider added.

I looked at these two impatiently. We had more pressing business to attend to, than to discuss what my name was. Malux moved his leg, or at least it twitched. The last thing we needed now was for Malux to wake up. What concerned me more was how to get back to my wife and kids.

Spider looked at me deeply as if reading my mind and said, "Well, all that is left for you to do is to kill Malux."

"Kill him?" I asked with doubt.

"Yes kill him, what else do you think you are here for?"

"But ..."

"But what?"

"But I've *never* killed anyone before," I said weakly.

Spider and Bill burst out in laughter. Spider's knees gave out on him and he started to roll on the floor.

Bill recovered before Spider and said, "What about those soldiers you killed outside of Cliff's cave?"

"Or Heru? Or those soldiers you killed when you were Janus? Don't you remember them?" Spider added after recovering from his laughing fit.

"But that wasn't really me. This is me right now. This is my body," I protested.

"Oh, so you're not responsible for what you do when you are not in your own body? Killing someone while you're not in your own body doesn't really count then. I understand," Spider said with a big smile on his face.

Spider and Bill resumed laughing.

I had to admit to being quite annoyed and didn't find what they were saying the slightest bit funny.

"But that wasn't really me, was it? I was just 'along for the ride' so to say. It was like watching television except through someone else's eyes, wasn't it?" I said hopefully.

When Spider stopped laughing again, he spoke to me in a most serious tone, "That, Claude is the most pathetic explanation for consciousness transference I have ever heard."

"What was that?"

"I said consciousness transference."

"I heard what you said. What does that mean?"

"Do you remember everything that Einu and Janus did while you were in their bodies?"

"Yes."

"And who made all the decisions for you while you were in their bodies?"

"Well ... no one."

"So you made your own decisions?"

"I guess so."

"So tell me what the difference would be if you made the decision to kill someone while you were in someone else's body, or decided to kill someone in this body?"

He emphasized his point by jabbing his finger into my belly.

222

"Well ... I guess logically there is none ... but it just doesn't feel the same."

"Just because you're used to residing in the body you are residing in now doesn't mean that the experiences that you had as Einu and Janus are any less real than the experiences that you had while in your current body."

"So the sooner you do what you have come here to do the sooner you can go home," Bill added.

"Wait a minute. I don't remember agreeing to do to any of this. So how come I have to kill someone?"

Spider whacked me on the back of my head. This took me by surprise. I thought that he was a spirit without a body and I was flesh and blood.

I staggered a bit and said, "What did you do that for?"

"Well, I always heard that if you give a person with amnesia a good whack to the head that they get their memory back. But you can't always believe what you hear about humans."

Bill laughed and Spider gave one of his inhuman smiles.

"But going back to your question. You did agree to all of this. Remember during one of your visits to me you asked me to show you some of the things that I know about time and consciousness."

"Oh yeah."

"Well, you got the works."

Bill was laughing again. He was holding his belly very tightly. He stopped laughing only long enough to hear what Spider was saying before resuming his laughter.

I could only assume that he too had experienced 'the works' from Spider.

"Okay, but what does this have to do with killing someone?"

"Don't you remember me saying that you will have to do what I say if I show you."

"Vaguely."

"Don't give me vaguely. I was quite specific in saying that you may have to do something that you would not like. You were so anxious to learn what I knew, that you readily agreed. Well, everything has its price. So here is yours."

Spider pointed to Malux then to my sword and made a cutting motion across his own neck.

"There, I told you in sign language. You always seemed to understand that better than words."

"But why me and why does Malux have to die?"

"It's you because you chose yourself by getting involved with me. Malux has to die because the humans that inhabit this world want it that way. During the last time stoppage they even allowed us to come here in full to make sure that the job got done.

"You see they want a world more like your own. A more predictable world. Where more or less everyone is equal. They don't want any more magic giving a select few power over the rest. So over the last hundred years all of the sorcerers have been killed off, their exclusive club is gone.

"Malux is the last powerful one. With his death, magic will no longer be a part of the collective consciousness of the humans on this world. A similar thing happened on your world a long time ago."

I thought for a moment about what he said, then asked, "When you say that we have come here in full, that means we are here totally. This really is my body?"

"Yes."

"So I ask you again, how come no one notices me that I am totally different?"

Spider put his hands on his almost non-existent hips and said. "If you ask anyone here they would say that you were always that way. The humans here changed their collective reality agreement. Don't you understand?"

I shook my head.

"When a group of humans living on a world that they are connected to change as a whole how they are to perceive reality, then whatever they agree upon goes. So any human in that collective will perceive reality as the agreement calls for them to perceive it. So when they agreed to let you here everyone agreed that Einu was six-foot-six instead of five-foot-six.

"And to keep everyone informed of their reality, they keep in communication with each other in between the moments."

Communication? I thought about what he was saying and something clicked inside of me.

"The voices ..."

Spider looked deep into my eyes and said, "Yes, the voices. You have heard them. They repeat constantly the rules of reality for the collective. Some rules more strongly than others, depending on how much energy the majority puts towards whatever aspect of reality they want the collective to adhere to."

"You mean that these rules are not fully agreed upon?"

"No. Only a majority of energy expenditure towards whatever aspect of reality that the majority spends counts. You do have individuals who opt out of the collective. They are usually called crazy or enlightened, depending on the circumstances.

"The majority of inhabitants of this world opted to let you come here in full from your world to complete your task free from the influence of anyone from this world. So you can not be influenced by the minority of humans who still want magic on this world.

"So you have free will to do what ever you want. You can base your actions solely on the information that you have and not be influenced by the desires of anyone on this world. In essence, you have been brought in as an independent judge to determine if this world is better off with or without magic."

I looked at Malux and wondered what to do. He moved his head slightly, again it could have just been a twitch. I wasn't sure. Whatever had to be done, there was little time to do it in.

One thing that was undeniable, Malux was not a nice person. I realized that that had nothing to do with it.

The question was whether or not to eliminate magic? All I had to do was kill one man and that would be accomplished.

I remembered how as a child I wanted magic to be real and part of my world. Well, now, here in this world there was magic.

I was here for the entire life of one child and grew to be a man here. I knew what a world with magic was like.

So what to do now?

"Why can't you do it?" I asked Spider.

"I am not human remember? These people want one of their own to judge them."

I tried to remember all that Spider ever told me about himself, which wasn't much, but wasn't closer to an answer.

"Just what are you? Back home you told me you were an earth spirit but here you are a gnome named Cliff."

Spider smiled then said, "I thought you would appreciate that little joke."

"What joke?"

"Why my name of course ... Cliff."

I stared at him blankly.

"Cliff ... where did we first meet?" he asked.

Then it dawned on me. I first met Spider during a vision quest, on the edge of a cliff over a cave that I didn't know existed.

When the spark of realization shot through my head and translated through to my eyes and face, that was the cue for Bill to continue laughing. I looked at Bill and remembered that he was human, a dead one, but still a human.

"Why can't Bill do it?"

Spider looked towards Bill.

When Bill finished laughing he said, "Claude, I told you once before that the reason I am following you about was for the purposes of learning."

"So you're telling me again that it is up to me, right?"

"Right," he said before he continued to laugh.

I looked at them both, frustrated again.

"Are there no other options?"

"Sure, there are Claude. Thousands. You're just limiting yourself by your lack of imagination again," Spider said.

"Well, just assume I'm an idiot and tell me one."

Spider gave me one of his unusual grins again then said, "You could join up with the higher consciousness of this world and change the way in which magic is done here."

"How can I do that?"

"Just take the time to find out."

At that moment Malux groaned. Time was short.

"I don't have any more time and just want to go home."

"Then your choice is clear. Kill Malux and go home, or just go home," Spider said.

I was a little anxious and had to ask a question, "Just exactly how do I get back home?"

"Well, if you had come to this world before you met me, you might have experienced your entire existence here as a dream, and you would have simply just woken up to return to your world, but you have become more aware than that.

"Now you have to realize that you have actively placed your consciousness here and to get back you have to let go of all your connections here. In effect, you have to let go of your conscious placement of your consciousness in this world and go back to the world where you are to write all this down."

I thought about what he said then looked at the bodies of Sir Hamard and General Harauld. A tear rolled down my cheek while looking at the General. He died because he believed that killing Malux was the right thing to do.

Now I was forced to look at all the things that had happened to me in a different light.

Malux groaned again. He was stirring, but his eyes were still closed. I walked over to him and placed my sword at his throat. All the memories of what happened to me as Einu and as Janus flooded back. I then thought of what Spider said.

I had the choice to mold a world and stood at the crux of deciding many peoples' fates. Do I leave this world with magic or remove it and let magic become only a memory to be passed down in old wives' tales and myths?"

Malux stirred and awoke. I had to make a choice now.

Malux' eyes opened fully and he stared at me with bright eyes that burned into me.

But that was the last thing that I remembered.

30

Mate

I found myself in my basement and was sitting naked on the floor with the lights out. I had my drum in my hand and beads of sweat dripped down my body.

The haunting vision of Malux' eyes still stared at me. What had happened at the end? I couldn't remember.

It was well past midnight. I had had something on my mind and had trouble sleeping. I remembered deciding to come downstairs to drum to ease my mind and hadn't expected an adventure.

Going back upstairs to my bedroom, I put my drum away then got back into my bed.

My wife woke up and asked, "Is everything okay?"

What was there to say? My heart was still beating fast and I must have had a look of distress on my face.

"I'm okay, I'll tell you about it later."

I lay down and turned off the light then listened to the breathing of my wife after she snuggled up to my warm body.

My heart eventually slowed after a couple of hours and I fell asleep.

The next morning came and my wife never asked me again about what had happened to me that night. I had assumed that she knew something but was merely waiting for me to tell her.

Time passed. I never said anything.

Another adventure 'happened' to me that really made me begin to wonder what was going on.

I thought long about what Spider had told me and him telling me about writing 'more than one book' then wondered indeed if it was possible to write any of this down. One day I just started and found it almost like magic how the words appeared on my computer screen. It was as if I was watching my television while remembering all my adventures.

The first book was finished in what felt like no time at all.

This book took a little longer to write, but that was only because of all the many tasks that I had set myself. I began to live my life with more gusto and didn't waste time any more and loved living my life.

When I got to this point you are reading right now, I stopped writing and gave the story to my wife to read.

When she had finished reading it I asked, "Well, what do you think?"

"About what?" she replied.

She always did that to me.

"The story?"

She looked deeply at me and said, "You keep referring to me as just 'wife'."

"Well, if you would let me. I would use your real name."

"No. We've been over this before."

I didn't want to argue with her so didn't say anything else.

"There wasn't enough sex in the story," she said with a large grin on her face.

"But ..."

"No buts. If you want we could add some in right now."

I mildly protested, "We're here to discuss my book ..."

She grumbled something then continued, "The ending is a little weak."

"But that's what happened."

"That may be, but you have to tell your readers what happened to Malux."

"But I don't know what happened to him."

"Then go and ask Spider."

I felt like hitting myself. Why didn't that come to me earlier? Was I deliberately avoiding asking Spider that question, or did I have selective amnesia as Spider said?

There was nothing else to do but go and see him.

31

Cave

"Where are you going dad?" my daughter asked me.

Have you ever been asked a question by one of your children, and not known exactly how to respond? Telling her the entire truth at the moment seemed hard to do.

"I'm going to sit in a cave."

"Are you going to be long?"

"I don't know. Probably just a couple of days."

She paused a moment then asked, "Can I sleep in your bed while you're gone?"

I laughed. Everyone always has an ulterior motive.

"You'll have to ask your mom. I think she might have something to say about that."

"Okay," she said.

I hugged her, my wife and son good-bye, and drove away.

It only takes about an hour to get to the village and find a place to park my vehicle on my journey to Spider's cave. It takes about another hour to walk the rest of the way. The walk is a difficult one. The path goes over many hills.

Near the cave I have to cut off the path through a forest with a marshy floor and at the end have to climb a very steep slope that is part of the Niagara Escarpment.

Every time up until now, the journey had been exhausting. Usually the biting insects are so bad that just stopping for an instant gets you swarmed. So I usually try to keep ahead of them by moving very fast along the path, not stopping until reaching the cave. For some reason there are no insects anywhere near Spider's cave, so it was okay to rest there.

I usually arrive exhausted and perspiring profusely.

And when there, I usually experience some hardship then feel fear before going into Spider's cave and then find it hard staying inside once there.

On this occasion, my visit to Spider was very pleasant. This year was extremely dry. The insects were very tolerable. So it was an easy walk.

My stay outside his cave was extremely enjoyable. The weather was beautiful.

Going into his cave was easy for some reason. I felt no fear and eased through the crack in the earth to his cave quite easily.

My stay inside was comfortable. The temperature which is normally at the freezing mark no matter what time of the year, was not that cold, even though my breath could still be seen. The rocks inside were almost comfortable.

After a while my eyes got used to the dark. I felt absolutely no fear. During other visits I would feel like the stones were closing in on me. This time I felt welcome instead. The Earth comforted me and I didn't want to ever leave that place.

Spider's cave is on the inside of a deep crack in the ground on the edge of a cliff. Following the crack leads to a point about one third of the way down the cliff. His cave lies on one of the turns in the zig zagging crack about thirty feet down from the top. Very little sound trickles down to the cave. Silence and darkness prevails.

Now something amazing happened. Towards the back of the cave, a beam of light suddenly appeared. The sun's rays came down through a small crack in the earth. I had been there many times before when it was sunny but this had never happened.

The sun must have been in the right position at that time of the year in order for the light of the sun to penetrate so deeply.

I moved so as to look up the crack and see the sun.

I marveled for a moment then noticed a small glistening where the light was landing in the cave.

Moving closer I saw a perfect spider web, but no spider.

"Is that you Spider?"

There was a clear voice, "Yes."

I smiled and watched as the light slowly disappeared.

It took an act of will to bring myself to focus on the purpose of my visit. Being in this place made all desires feel less important.

"So, tell me Spider. What happened at the end?"

"At the end of what? I don't think that we have the same meaning for that word."

"Which word?"

"End. There really are no ends."

"Surely a string has an end," I protested.

"Not really, the string has an influence beyond what you perceive to be its border of string and what is not string. It has an energetic presence that resonates throughout the universe. Everything has its own song, all it takes is for the trained ear to hear it."

"Okay, okay, we have different meanings for end, but I still want to know what happened."

"You do have to be careful with words. They are excellent tools for your kind. They can resonate with your entire being. You have learned how to do it. People feel the spirit that vibrates with your words as they read them. Not all understand what is happening when they do read them, but many know that something is different afterwards.

"You're not the best writer in the world, but you have learned to pay attention to the sounds of spirit while you write. Which is a plus, but you should learn to play some more. Now take the word borange ..."

"Wait a minute. There's no such word," I complained.

"See that's one of your problems, you're too stiff, not as open to new concepts as you think you are. Borange is a sort of a yellow-orange color. Besides, poets on your planet have been looking for a rhyme for orange for centuries. Now we have given them one. You could become famous just for that one concept alone."

I frowned and felt that this conversation was going nowhere. My curiosity was coming back in full force. Malux. What happened to him?

"Spider, I know how much you like to talk nonsense ..."

"It's not nonsense. Creation is an important process. Your kind uses words for concepts and depending on how much energy your kind devotes to the creation of a concept means how much a force that idea will have in the future. Everything touches everything else and concept creation fuels the joining and separating of all things all at the same time."

I struggled with that one for a while then said, "Spider. Okay, I'll think about that later, but right now you must tell me about Malux. Is he dead or alive? What did I do in the end?"

"You can't remember can you Claude? I just don't know what to do with you. I can take you to another world, but I can't make you remember what happened while you were there."

"I'm not asking you to make me remember. I'm asking you to tell me what I did there."

"So you are. So you are. But you could do it yourself if you really tried."

"I've tried many times," I whined, "I don't seem to be able to remember anything except Malux' eyes looking at me. Anything after that is a blank."

"Look, Claude. You can go back there any time you want. All you have to do is place your consciousness there. You already learned that you can place your consciousness at any point of your existence."

"How can I go back there? The first time I did it there was a lot of help. I have no idea how to start."

He shook his head and rolled his eyes then said "It's really quite simple. Just totally immerse yourself in the moment and see yourself there."

Spider's words came to me. Then my world expanded. It felt as if time had longer to go in order to get from one minute to another. I remembered Malux' eyes and slowly saw the entire scene with total clarity.

My feelings and thoughts of the moment were experienced with total awareness. Time moved extremely slowly. I examined my feelings towards Malux and realized my deep hatred of him. No, I hated the pain he caused others. Or did I really hate him? Or was it that I feared that if presented with the same circumstances I would have made the same choices for myself that created a Malux in the first place, and hated myself for seeing that in me?

My feelings were all over the place. If I had to act on my feelings alone then death would have come to him immediately.

Then I saw my reasoning as well. It was like a separate entity from my feelings.

The thought came to me that I was to be a judge for a world's course. It was a simple task. To determine if magic was to be abolished. There were those who wanted it to remain the same and there were those who wanted it to change.

Change was the best teacher for us humans, and that since a majority of the people in this world wanted the change anyway, then who was I to deny them that?

My reasoning and feelings came together. They were in agreement.

Malux' eyes widened as my sword plunged into his throat. He grabbed the sword with his hands. I could not move my sword out or in. The handle of the sword grew hot. Malux was trying to cast one last spell.

I leaned heavily on my sword.

Beads of sweat poured off Malux' forehead. He had a terrible time trying to breathe. He blew blood out of his mouth as he tried to clear his breathing passage of liquid.

Eventually his grip lessened on the sword and it went in deeper. I twisted it and Malux convulsed and in a one last horrible gurgling of breath, he stopped all movement and his eyes rolled into the top of his head.

I felt an overall feeling of completion and I felt the presence of Heru, Sir Hamard, the General and many others all smiling at me. I looked at the figures that were Bartu and Cliff, and their solemn faces nodded in approval.

Then my focus of that place was lost and I found myself at home, then back in Spider's cave.

"See, it wasn't that hard after all," Spider said.

Suddenly a wave of doubt washed over me.

"Yeah, but was it real?" I asked.

Spider started to laugh. He had been very serious up until now. But hearing his laugh in the cave gave him a wild presence, and I shifted nervously.

"What's so funny?"

"Just look at what you are doing. You're sitting in a dark cave asking me to judge about reality when over half of your kind wouldn't even acknowledge my existence."

I saw the humor in his statement and laughed with him. There was a release with that laughter and all my cares of what others would think of me left.

When Spider finished laughing he continued, "Well under those circumstances ... of course it was real. Reality is what you experience, is it not? Let's just say that you are a little better at experiencing things than others of your kind."

We both laughed a little longer.

"But how is it possible to do such things?"

Spider became serious again then said, "You experienced the entire adventure between moments. You were Einu while time was stopped here. Many people choose to do this but not all of them are aware that they are doing it, thus they can not remember anything that they did."

I sat in thought for a while, thinking about what Spider had said and wondering if there were other adventures that I went on without knowing it, then came back to thinking about the last one. There were many questions that begged for answers.

"Could you tell me why when we have an adventure we always end up fighting someone?"

"It's not me that has to fight. It's you. I'm just there for the fun of it."

"Okay, *why do I have to fight*?"

"You enjoy male energy. You really don't have to fight. There are other ways to do things, but I think fighting keeps you awake and alert enough so that you can learn what you want to learn."

Two questions sprang to my mind from that explanation. I was torn as to which to ask first.

I eventually asked, "How could I have resolved the situation with Malux differently without fighting?"

"There are many answers to that question, but one would have been to befriend Malux and invite him to your world."

"What?"

Spider nodded his head.

The problem with talking to Spider was that with every statement he made, more and more questions arose in my mind. I wanted to pursue how Malux could come here but wanted to know also what Spider was trying to teach. This question sprang to my mind from the previous question. I made a mental note to come back to the Malux question and decided to ask more about him.

Spider just sat and grinned at me. It was as if he saw that my mind started to spin while I was talking to him and he was just waiting to see how many times it went around before asking him something again.

"Why do I have to go on these adventures to learn, why can't you just tell me what I need to know? Can't you just tell me everything now?"

"Sure I can."

Spider started talking. He talked in the most serious tone that I had ever heard him use. He talked and talked without a pause for what seemed like hours.

I remember being astounded at the things he said, but the astonishment lasted only as long as he was talking. The moment he stopped all memory of what he said left me.

I was perplexed.

"What did you just say?"

"All that you want to learn from me."

"But ... how come I don't seem to remember any of it?"

"Learning is dependent on whether you are ready to really hear what is said. It was a waste of time for me to tell you what you were not ready to hear. But I thought that if we went through the exercise you would understand why you have to go through those uncomfortable adventures with me. Besides I love a good laugh now and then. Seriously though, if you could go to a state of higher consciousness and stay there, you would know all that I just told you with very little effort on your part, but since you are not yet capable, I guess that you are stuck with me."

I sat and tried to join with a higher level of consciousness. And for a moment, I understood, but that moment was fleeting. I was stuck with Spider and doing things his way.

"Claude, it's really quite simple. Remember when as Einu you met with Janus after splitting from him? You remembered all that happened while you were Janus, but Janus had trouble remembering. Well, you are now Janus, trying to remember. As Claude right now your consciousness is not able to make that leap to a higher level that would enable you to remember."

I nodded my head and understood what he was trying to say to me.

"So that is why you are in my life then? To help me get to that higher level?"

He grinned unnaturally at me. His mouth opened from the tip of each ear, and the teeth that showed just went on forever.

"Everyone has their own agenda," was all he said.

"What's yours?" I asked suspiciously.

"Well, one of the things that I am to do with you is to help you stay at a higher level of consciousness while at the same time you remain at a lower consciousness so you can still communicate with your fellow humans."

"How is that done?"

"Tricky," was all he said.

I knew that was the only answer that he was going to give to that question.

"So what else are you here for?"

"To tell you of coming changes to your world. To tell you of upcoming events, like the time when all but a few of your kind will fall asleep and I will teach you how to stay awake, so that you will be one of many who will reawaken your kind so that you can teach them how to join to a higher consciousness.

"But you will have to get more serious about this if indeed you want to stay awake. You've only been at this part-time so far since you came back to this time line. You have to go to the collective consciousness of your kind more often with your messages. Those messages will resonate within the collective consciousness as others join into your vibration and others will begin to say what you are saying even though you will not seem to be saying it."

A heaviness came upon me as Spider said this. As much as I wanted to hear it, I had to change the subject before something pulled me down into the earth and put me to sleep.

I went back to my question about Malux and felt lighter.

"So tell me Spider, just how could I have brought Malux to this world?"

"How did you go to his?"

"I'm still not sure about that."

Spider very quickly gave me a swat to my head.

"Ow!"

I paused to rub my head then quickly continued, "You are a spirit aren't you? So how did you do that?"

"I'm connected to you."

Again more questions came to me but I decided to keep to my original line of questioning.

"Okay I'm not sure as to how to get there …"

Spider raised his hand again and I quickly continued, " … but I originally placed my consciousness there while drumming … and while concentrating on a focal point just a few minutes ago. At least that is what I've gathered from what you told me."

"Well, if you could do this, why couldn't you teach Malux how to do that?"

"Because I'm not sure how I do it."

Spider laughed then said, "Sometimes I get the impression that you want me to think you are hopeless."

He continued to laugh. What he said and his howling laugh made me chuckle a bit.

"If you are unsure, then practise it until you are more sure, then we can discuss it again sometime, like maybe in another book."

This statement I found so funny that it was now my turn to laugh uncontrollably. Spider joined right in. He could laugh at the slightest change in the world, and someone else laughing always set him off.

When we finished he said, "But don't worry, you did a good job with the Malux adventure. The sorcerers no longer talk to each other because on Einu's world they are no more, and the collective human consciousness there is content with that situation."

"Then tell me Spider, just why was there magic in Einu's world?"

"The humans there wanted it that way."

"You keep saying that, but I really don't understand all that well. How can they choose to have magic then not have magic?"

"They all agreed to it."

I was a little skeptical and said, "What … the population of the entire world sat around and had a vote?"

"Not quite. But from where you are coming from I see how you might think that. What really happens is that in between the moments the entire population of a planet communicates with each other and defines what their reality is going to be. That was what you heard when you heard the voices repeating endlessly, phrases that defined their reality. The stronger or more frequent a phrase is 'spoken' the stronger that that aspect of reality is adhered to.

"Some people hear the voices as either a ringing in their ears or a sound that is like music. The voices are most powerful when major changes occur and a lot of people then complain of hearing something but they do not know quite what. Listening closely can be quite enlightening. Because once you hear the voices, you have the option of opting out at will and no longer being tied to your species consciousness, thus being freer to join to a higher consciousness."

"I'm still confused, just how does an issue of reality get decided?"

"Basically it comes down to whoever has the most energy wins. If a majority of people want it then it is part of your reality, then it is acted upon energetically to shape your perception of reality. For instance, a majority of people on your planet believe in spirits. Even though in the western world it is a minority belief, overall planet-wide people want to believe in spirits. So that is why you are able to communicate with me. But take the case of alien beings. The majority of people on the planet do not want to have aliens in their world, even though in the western world most believe that aliens exist, overall planet-wide the majority do not want them."

"So you're telling me that aliens won't be a part of our world until a majority of people want it?"

"Precisely."

"But what about the current sightings of UFO's?"

"Ah, now that's where things get interesting. What I just said to you wasn't one hundred percent correct. There are divisions in your collective human reality agreement. There are, let's say 'clan' divisions that were agreed upon by the whole. So minor variations can exist between the clans as to what each of the clans want. This has led to most of the conflicts among your species. So sometimes reality is slightly different across your planet because it was agreed to that way. So some clans on your planet want to communicate with aliens but the majority still do not.

"Then there are the aliens themselves, some of them have a desire to talk to humans, but are dismayed that most humans still don't want to talk to them."

"So there really are aliens?"

"Ask yourself that question Claude. You already believe, so why do you need absolute proof when you have faith?" Spider replied.

I sat in silence trying to digest that. But today was a learning day for me, so I had little time to do that.

"So the combination of some clans on your planet combined with the desires of the aliens themselves, has poked holes in your current collective reality agreement. So, sometimes, there is communication between individuals on your planet with individuals from other planets. But if the reality agreement was firmly in place then a whole herd of aliens could stand in a crowd of humans and the humans would never be able to even see them, let alone communicate with them."

"Would the aliens see us?"

"It depends on the aliens. Some have reality agreements that allow it and others don't. It also depends on the level of their consciousness. So the answer to your question is, maybe."

Thinking about aliens for some reason brought me back to thinking about Spider. He has an alien feel to him, but if he is a spirit, then again I wondered how he was able to hit me.

"You told me earlier that you were connected to me, what does that mean?"

"Well, everything has spirit within it. Your body has spirit within, but spirits tend to travel in groups and they retain a close connection to each other.

"They do not necessarily have to join into the same species consciousness or even choose living matter to enter for that matter, while they remain together, but they always retain a connection that is not subject to the rules of time or space, or in other words what the local reality agreement is," Spider said, then looked behind him.

"Can anyone join this session or is it a closed meeting?" Bill asked.

"Certainly you may join us, unless you have an objection Claude?"

"It's okay by me."

"So what is the lesson for today?" Bill asked.

"We're just discussing how spirits tend to stay together in groups as we pass through God's domain."

Bill laughed then said, "I am here right on schedule then."

We all laughed then Spider continued, "But those spirits that choose to enter bodies are using those bodies as tools to expand their spirits. Entering the life game can have its hazards. Life can be very distracting and many forget why they entered the body in the first place. That's why there are those like Cat and myself around. We just love to kick you sillies who start to fall asleep, as we helpers like to say.

"You forget that the best way to handle being human is to pretend that you are spirit actors taking on the role of the human host. Make being human part of you, yes, but keep a small part separate so that you can keep a higher perspective when the role becomes very heavy on the spirit.

"Just like Maru. I think she did an excellent job, don't you think Bill?"

"Oh yes, a marvelous performance, I agree."

I looked at these two and knew when they were hiding something that I would want to know, and always kicked myself when I found out what it was.

"Okay, what am I missing?"

Bill took my hand and gently patted it then said, "Maru was your wife."

I looked at them with mixed reaction. Of course they both started to laugh uncontrollably. Maru was my wife? I had to ask her about that after getting home.

When Spider's laughter came under control he said, "Of course, the funniest part was not the fact that you didn't realize who your wife was again, like in your first adventure. The funniest thing was that on Einu's world the name Maru means … Friend!"

Bill and Spider laughed for about half and hour. It was getting close to sunset in the outside world, because what little light there was down here was almost gone.

For those of you who do not understand what the joke's about, it's fully explained in my first book.

While I was waiting for these two to stop laughing at me, something brushed up against me in the darkness. It was fur. There was an animal in this cave with me.

Just before I could properly panic, a familiar purring voice said, "So how come you forrrgot to send me an invitation to this adventurrre?"

"Cat?"

"Who else?" he replied.

"Cat, welcome to my cave," Spider said while still chuckling.

"Thank you Spiderrr, but Claude has not answerrred me yet."

"I didn't know that was possible. But I'll be sure to remember that the next time an adventure falls in my lap, you'll be the first one that I'll call. So what brings you here?"

"You do, we arrre connected, orrr can you not feel that?"

"Oh," was all I could say.

Somehow the thought about being connected to Cat somewhat unnerved me, so I asked Spider the first thing that came to my mind.

"Spider, tell me what you think of my first book?"

Spider and Bill broke out laughing, so I prepared myself for their criticisms.

"Well, Claude, or should I call you Nexus? I think that you bent the truth somewhat."

"What do you mean?" I said defensively, "I wrote down everything that happened to me."

"Of course you did write it to cast yourself in the best possible light, did you not?"

"Well, maybe."

Suddenly claws dug deeply into my right knee.

"Okay, okay, I did!!"

"Why do you ask?" I said when Cat removed his claws.

"Well, unlike your present state, you have to admit that you were much more frightened of my presence while you were alive than you let on, now, weren't you?"

"Yeah, I suppose so."

"You suppose so? You wet yourself when you first saw Spider," Bill added.

The usual laughter at my expense echoed throughout the cave. I was at first upset at being reminded about that ... then giggled inside ... and eventually laughed along with them. Even Cat was purring loudly.

"The other thing that bothered me was that you said that I said 'should.' I don't use that word. Maybe the meaning of my words translates to should in your head, but I never use that word.

"Other than that, the book is fine. You put your spirit in there for all to read. You learned that lesson well.

"Unfortunately it is getting close to the time for you to go, though before you leave I want to remind you to keep on practising to stop time."

"I can stop time in this body?"

"Surrre you can, you have done it twice beforrre. Once in yourrr washrrroom and once in the forrrest, don't you rrrememberrr?" Cat purred.

"Oh, that's what happened to me? Time stopped? But it felt so different than when I was Einu."

"Claude, do you forget that every body has its own abilities? Some are more aware than others, and most experience events in different ways. Instead of thinking of the differences between the perception of the two bodies you were in, think of the similarities."

Even though I remembered that the perception of objects

was much different when I was Einu, as to what I experienced, the 'feel' or the energy was the same.

There was no better explanation than that.

"And Claude, keep on using your crystal bowls, tuning forks and drum, their sounds will help you understand the voices of the collective human consciousness better," Spider added.

Suddenly there was the sound of a drum, then the singing of a crystal bowl followed by many others. The music that they made was so beautiful that tears started to roll out of my eyes.

Spider said, "You no longer have to come here if you want to talk to me. Just take some cedar leaves from the forest floor near my cave and burn them, then play your drum and I will come."

Spider and Bill left. With the passing of their presences, the music slowly died away.

I left the cave, and in the faint light saw Cat come out behind me. I assumed that he had left with Spider and Bill and was surprised to see him out of the cave.

He said to me, "Spiderrr forrrgot to tell you one thing. The rrreason for killing Malux was not to liberrrate a worrrld as you would like to think, but it was to make you pull away frrrom the human collective consciousness so that you could underrrstand wherrre you arrre coming frrrom."

Having said that Cat jumped to the top of the crack in the earth in three hops, bouncing off the walls, confirming in my mind that he was no natural animal. His eyes stared down at me then he quickly moved away from the edge and was gone.

I climbed out slowly and saw no sign of Cat. I thanked Spider, Bill and Cat, for taking time to teach me and left an offering of fruit and nuts for the animals there.

I then stuffed my pockets full of cedar leaves, took one last look at this magnificent place of nature. Tears came to my eyes because this may have been the last time I would see it, then forced my feet to start the journey home.

Epilogue

Since the last time in the cave I have talked to Spider, Bill and Cat many times. They have told me enough to write another book, but there were three things that they told me that I must pass on now. Three little pieces of advice that I now keep in my heart.

You must always start with faith. Because without faith, what answer do you give when you ask yourself, 'Why am I doing this?' With no faith, there really is no answer.

Find truth by being true to your endeavors. Whether it is in the realm of science, religion or wherever your heart takes you, be true to yourself and avoid the politics of the endeavor.

And lastly, don't infect your future with your past.

Thank you for letting me share this story with you, and may God be with you.

"*Timestopperrr* takes you beyond imagination. You crrross over the boundarrries of time and glimpse what is waiting therrre ... *Timestopperrr* is exciting, insightful and illuminating ..."
Cat - Animal Spirit

"I never imagined that the nature of our reality could be taught in such an exhilarating style ..."
Bill - Dead Accountant

"*Timestopper* tells you more than you ever wanted to know about time."
Spider - Earth Spirit